Dear Reader,

Arabesque is pleased to publish the **Sizzling Sands** summer series: four romance novels set against the backdrop of beach resorts frequented by African Americans, including Martha's Vineyard, Massachusetts; Highland Beach, Maryland; Idlewild Lake in Michigan; and Sag Harbor, New York. The heroines in each novel are all Howard University alumnae who belonged to the same Alpha Delta X sorority in college.

Each Sizzling Sands novel introduces you to one of the Alpha Delta X sorority sisters. In the first novel, **Lady in Red**, Scarlet "Carly" Thompson is a cosmetics company CEO who finds adventure and romance on Martha's Vineyard. Next, in **Southern Comfort**, we meet Rachel Givens, a jewelry designer drawn to Highland Beach, where romance and mystery unfold. In the third novel, **Last Chance at Love**, journalist Allison Wakefield finds love and passion while visiting Idlewild Lake. And in **Dare to Dream**, painter Desiree Armstrong looks to recuperate in Sag Harbor after a fire destroys her gallery and her spirit, but instead finds an old flame.

With marquee romance authors **Deirdre Savoy**, **Sandra Kitt**, **Gwynne Forster** and **Donna Hill** contributing, we know you'll enjoy the passion and sizzle of this hot summer series, one of the best in Arabesque's decade of publishing romances.

We welcome your comments and feedback, and invite you to send us an e-mail at www.bet.com/books/betbooks.

Enjoy,
Evette Potter
Editor, Arabesque Books

Deirdre Savoy

Lady In Red

ARABESQUE
BET BOOKS

BET Publications, LLC
http://www.bet.com
http://www.arabesquebooks.com

Lady in Red is a work of fiction and is not intended to provide an exact representation of life or any known persons on the fabled island of Martha's Vineyard, Massachusetts. The author has taken creative license in development of the characters and plot of the story, although historical facts and sites referenced may be actual. The cover photography is meant to evoke beach life in Martha's Vineyard and may not be an exact representation of the shore or environs. The sorority, Alpha Delta X, is fictitious and does not represent as fact any known women's service organization. BET Books/Arabesque develops contemporary works of romance fiction for entertainment purposes only.

ARABESQUE BOOKS are published by

BET Publications, LLC
c/o BET BOOKS
One BET Plaza
1900 W Place NE
Washington, DC 20018-1211

All Kensington Titles, Imprints, and Distributed Lines are available at special quantity discounts for bulk purchases for sales promotions, premiums, fund-raising, and educational or institutional use. Special book excerpts or customized printings can also be created to fit specific needs. For details, write or phone the office of the Kensington special sales manager: Kensington Publishing Corp., 850 Third Avenue, New York, NY 10022, attn: Special Sales Department, Phone: 1-800-221-2647.

First printing: June 2004
10 9 8 7 6 5 4 3 2 1

Printed in the United States of America

For my former agent James Finn, a true gentleman, and my first real friend in the publishing industry. They say nothing good's going to last forever and I guess they're right. But I thank you for your kindness, your wisdom and your guidance.

ACKNOWLEDGMENTS

Thanks to my fellow authors in this series—Sandra Kitt, Gwynne Forster and Donna Hill. Knowing I was in a series with you guys inspired me to great literary heights.

Thanks to my readers who have stuck by me since my first book *Spellbound*. I hope you don't mind taking this third trip with me to Martha's Vineyard. I hadn't intended on writing this book until BET asked me to participate in the 2004 Summer Series, but I truly enjoyed revisiting old haunts, if only on the page.

And special thanks to Joyce Peña for her help in making the beach scene memorable.

Chapter 1

Jackson Trent leaned back in his chair, folded his arms behind his head, and propped his feet on the credenza behind his desk. For the first time in a long time he was looking forward to doing nothing.

He'd joined the NYPD as soon as he'd finished putting himself through college, going from patrol to narcotics in just two years. Most cops didn't last long as narcs and he hadn't been the exception. After three years he'd called it quits, leaving not only the division but the force as well.

He'd worked his ass off for the last four years, building his P.I. business into something worthwhile. He'd started this agency by buying the skip tracing business of another. He'd given up most of that, too, as many folks who skipped town rather than deal with the law usually did so for a reason, and weren't usually too amenable to being brought back. He'd eventually sold that aspect of the company for more than he'd paid for it. Now he concentrated on what he did best, finding missing people, lost children, deadbeat dads who wouldn't pay their child support. For the first time his agency netted him a six-figure income and he had six other investigators working under him.

Life was sweet, except for one thing. The one man he'd spent half his life trying to find still eluded him.

Or he had until two days ago. Surprise of surprises, Duke Anderson called him, wanting to arrange a meeting. For almost twenty years the man seemed to have fallen off the earth. While Jackson wondered what had caused the man to resurface, he refused to question his good fortune.

Maybe finally he could make sense of a long-ago murder that had cost his father his job, his reputation, and almost his freedom. Maybe finally he could find out who was responsible for Sharon Glenn's death, though if he found out he'd be the only one looking.

But for today, he planned on getting out of the office, smelling some rosebuds while they were still in bloom. Maybe he'd go to Central Park and watch some people go by whom he didn't have under surveillance. Something, anything that didn't involve clients or zoom lenses or computer databases of missing children.

He dropped his feet to the floor, just as his intercom sounded. His secretary's voice blared at him. "Jack, there's someone here to see you."

"Damn!" He'd been minutes away from a clean getaway, ruined by his own procrastination. "Who is it?"

"She says her name is Charlotte Hicks."

The name didn't ring a bell, but there was no reason why it should. "Have Danny take it. I'm on my way out."

"She says she'll only talk to y—" Peggy's voice died out on the phone, but he could hear her say plainly, "You can't go in there."

A second later, a woman—tall, voluptuous, and dressed completely in red—burst through his office door. She clutched some little rat dog so tightly to her ample bosom that he wondered if the poor thing could breathe. "I'm so sorry to intrude," the woman began. "But I really must speak to you."

He looked past the woman to where Peggy stood,

"That's her stage name. Her maiden name, I guess. Her married name is Charlotte Thompson."

Luckily, Peggy had already turned to leave, so she didn't notice how the mention of that name and its implications momentarily poleaxed him. It didn't just rain, it poured, and he was s.o.l. for an umbrella. Was it coincidence that she had come to him, or had she sought him out on purpose? And if she had, why hadn't she made it plain who she was?

Oh, damn. He was going to have to help her after all.

Chapter 2

Carly Thompson looked around the crowded conference room with dissatisfaction. The meeting to finalize plans for the upcoming press junket to Martha's Vineyard to celebrate the tenth anniversary of Scarlet Woman Cosmetics had gone well. In those few short years, Scarlet Woman had gone from a tiny mom-and-pop operation to a multimillion-dollar corporation. Yet as everyone packed up preparing to get back to their own desks and their own work, it reminded Carly that one chair had remained unfilled during the entire meeting—the one belonging to her mother.

Usually Charlotte opted for the late and dramatic entrance with the emphasis on dramatic, but rarely did she skip meetings altogether. Carly had wanted her mother here so that she couldn't later claim that no one had given her the details of the trip or that she didn't know what was expected of her. As the "front woman" for the company, it was imperative that she knew exactly what to say when the press came calling. Carly preferred to run things from behind the scenes, out of the limelight.

Realizing she'd been drumming her fingers on the surface of the glass conference table, Carly folded her hands in her lap. Where the hell could her mother be? Unlike some people, Carly actually did more for the company than shmooze celebrities and take interviews. Carly didn't have time to sit around contemplating her fingernails.

Just as she stood to return to her own office, the double doors to the conference room burst open. Johnny, her mother's chauffeur, stood to one side, allowing Charlotte to breeze into the room. The scent of roses reached Carly clear at the other end of the long table. As usual, Charlotte was dressed head to toe in red, this time a Valentino with high-heeled stiletto pumps. She clutched Mr. Jingles, her bison frize, tightly against her bosom as she paused at the foot of the conference table.

"Darling, I'm so sorry to be late." She fanned herself with her free hand. "Bruce and I are off our schedule."

Before Carly could ask who the devil Bruce was, a man strode into the room. He was tall, maybe a foot taller than her own height of five feet four, dark, and definitely handsome with high cheekbones, a square jaw, and deep brown eyes.

Charlotte continued, "Meet my new personal assistant."

Personal assistant, my eye. Every one of her mother's personal assistants, and there had been many, were in reality the men who shared her bed. For once she couldn't fault her mother's taste, even if the selection surprised her. Usually, her mother stuck with the sort of fey and sycophantic man that danced at her beck and call. This man was so far from being a "Bruce" that whoever named him ought to be hauled in for child abuse.

Focusing her gaze on her mother, Carly gritted her teeth. Charlotte beamed at her as if she'd just executed the coup of the century. Why her mother felt she had to buy the affection of men with some made-up position she didn't know. Nor could she understand why

Charlotte thought Carly would put this man on her payroll. After the last one, six months ago, Carly had balked and told her mother that she could pay her men out of her own pocket. There hadn't been any "personal assistants" since then. Her mother must really want this man, to open that can of worms again.

Carly's gaze slid to "Bruce." She wondered how quickly he'd make it out the door when he discovered she had no intention of paying him one red cent. His gaze met hers, strong and steady. She'd admit there was something commanding about him, something magnetic. She could understand her mother's attraction to him, but she couldn't let her mother's desire rule what was in Carly's mind best for the company. She raised her own eyebrows and crossed her arms in silent challenge. "Bruce, is it? Well, Bruce, would you mind waiting outside while I speak with my mother?" She'd formed it as a question, but she meant for him to leave.

Charlotte patted his arm in a possessive way. "Yes, dear. Why don't you wait for me in my office? You know which one that is."

Thankfully he nodded and left without any fuss. As he did so, Charlotte slid into a seat with a dramatic sigh. "What did you want to talk about, dear?"

Carly folded her arms. "How about you missing the meeting, for starters?"

Charlotte adjusted the red bow around Mr. Jingles's neck. "Oh, that. I'm sure you can fill me in."

"That's just the point. I don't want to have to fill you in. I wanted you to hear it all firsthand, perhaps offer a little input."

"Oh, please, you treat every suggestion from me as if it were the bastard child in the attic—to be hidden and avoided at all costs. You didn't need me here."

Carly pursed her lips, realized what she was doing,

and stopped. "That is not true. I have followed through on many of your ideas."

"Only after someone else made you see the wisdom of them." Charlotte crossed her legs and sat back as if she hadn't a care in the world. "Go on."

Annoyed by her mother's nonchalance, Carly gritted her teeth. Charlotte knew she hated it when she took a cavalier attitude toward the business and was deliberately baiting her. But why? Did it really matter? Carly could give as good as she got.

Canting her hip to one side, she said, "I don't care how good that man is in bed, I am not putting him on the payroll of this company."

"You don't have to, dear. I already did. I spoke to Carrie in human resources this morning."

Blast! Leave it to her mother to put the staff in the middle of this. Carrie wouldn't have questioned her mother's request or brought it to Carly's attention before completing the paperwork. Charlotte had hired employees for legitimate purposes before, and the true purpose of her former personal assistants had been kept between mother and daughter.

"So you went behind my back."

"I did nothing of the kind. I do need a personal assistant for this trip. Johnny refuses to come. He hates the ocean. Besides, he's on vacation next week. I'll need a driver at least. Who knows? With all the press, I might need a bodyguard as well."

Carly gave her mother a droll look. "Are you trying to tell me you are not sleeping with that man?"

Charlotte petted Mr. Jingles's head. "I didn't say that. But he does perform legitimate services. I didn't think you'd mind."

Right. More likely Charlotte had expected to talk her into letting him stay, which in fact she'd done, more because Carly lacked the will to fight with her mother with the trip coming up than anything else. Carly sank back into her seat. "What exactly do you plan to do with this man while he's here?"

"You don't really want me to answer that question, do you?"

Carly cast her mother a narrow-eyed glare. "I didn't mean sexually, Mother, which you know. I meant, what are his duties? Do you need somewhere for him to work?" Like she'd actually make him work in the first place.

"Oh, that. I gave him my old office."

For months Carly had been trying to persuade her mother to move her things from that office considering she rarely set foot in the building. That office provided great views of Manhattan in both southern and easterly directions, views Carly coveted. "That office is bigger than mine."

Charlotte shrugged. "The man has to sit somewhere."

Carly resisted the urge to tell her mother exactly where and on what the man could rest his behind. But "Bruce" wasn't really the problem; Charlotte was. "Absolutely not. That man is not using that office."

To Carly's surprise, her mother stood, letting Mr. Jingles scamper onto the floor, and a look of steel came into her eyes. "Yes, he is."

"No, he's not," she said, equally determined. "I am president and chief executive officer of this company. I make the decisions here. How would it look to have some glorified errand boy occupying the largest office in the company?"

"And maybe you are forgetting who *owns* this company. Fifty-one percent of it is mine. I have allowed you to run it however you saw fit for the last ten years, but it is still my company. And he will be staying in my office."

Carly bit her lip, a habit left over from childhood. Maybe she had been running this company so long that she forgot who held the purse strings, but her mother had never pulled rank on her before. That she did so now over some man smarted. It more than smarted. Carly had always wondered where her mother's greater allegiance lay, with her men or her daughter. She supposed she had her answer.

Momentarily nonplussed by her mother's betrayal, she stood. "Fine, Mother. Do whatever you want. You always have. Just keep him out of my way." She stalked out of the conference room as Mr. Jingles scampered to get out of the way. She went to her own office and slammed the door. She flung herself into the leather swivel chair behind her desk, but stopped, seeing her father's picture on her desk.

She touched her fingers to the glass covering the image of his face. Although she had only been seven years old when he'd suffered a heart attack while driving, she remembered him as a kind, gentle man. He had been twenty years older than her mother and, in some people's minds, the wrong race, but the three of them had been happy.

Carly swallowed with a throat suddenly clogged by emotion. The last words he'd spoken to her had been "take care of your mother." Then he'd slipped off into nothing or whatever awaited one after the grave. After he was gone, her mother had closed in on herself in a way that Carly thought she would never come out of. In a way, she'd lost both parents that day, because even when her mother did snap out of it, she'd never come back to being herself. She'd always been a little flaky, but never the woman she was now—spoiled, demanding, vain. At eight years old, Carly had morphed into the adult in the family and Charlotte had regressed to be the child. Even this company had been Carly's idea, a means of supporting themselves while capitalizing on her mother's former fame as an actress. It had even resulted in a few cameo parts for her mother, which had served to promote the company as well.

She had always tried to keep her promise to her father, but sometimes it was hard, it was damn hard. "I miss you, Daddy," she whispered, wiped the dampness from her cheeks, and got to work.

Jackson Trent stared out the window at the view of Midtown Manhattan, but he paid little attention to the scenery. Instead he wished his father, Donovan, had never laid eyes on Alexander Thompson. The two men had met when the elder Trent was accused of murder in a case that made headlines, and Thompson had agreed to defend him for free. Thompson had gotten the case dismissed when it was revealed that the only witness, and therefore the only evidence against his father, was a drunk who recanted his testimony under Thompson's examination.

Donovan had considered Thompson a miracle worker. Jackson remembered that long-ago day when his father had looked him in the eye and said, "If you ever find a way to repay that man, you do it." Jackson promised he would, but the next day Alex Thompson was dead. Everyone had speculated that the stress of the trial had contributed to the heart attack that took his life.

Jackson assumed the debt had been voided at that moment. But when his widow, Charlotte, came to him, asking for his help, he figured the debt had simply been transferred.

But Charlotte Thompson was nothing like his fourteen-year-old recollection of her. Nor was she the screen persona he'd come to know from the few films she'd made. The Charlotte that had come to see him was more of a caricature of her screen self, a cross between Diahann Carroll and Eva Gabor.

And the story she'd told him. Too bizarre to be believed. In the ten years he'd been a P.I., he'd heard some whoppers, but hers took the cake. He figured there had to be some truth in it, but which part and how much was anybody's guess.

Oddly, there was something maternal about her as well. Or maybe that was merely that boy still in him, the one who had lost his mother before he was old enough to retain her memory, seeking what wasn't there.

And the girl. He'd met her once while her father was defending his: a tiny thing with dark, inquisitive eyes and a cloud of orange hair. He'd called her carrot-top and she'd kicked him in the leg for his troubles. Then she'd dragged him up to her tree house and showed him all the treasures she secreted up there.

He held that memory fondly, though he saw nothing of that little girl in the woman he'd seen today. He hadn't intended to start that mini staring contest in the conference room, but her appearance had surprised him. He hadn't expected to find the same little girl, nor had he expected the severe woman who'd stood before him with a pinched expression on her face, her hair, dark, not the flaming red he remembered, pulled back into some awful bun, dressed in a shapeless suit that was as revealing as a burlap sack. He smiled to himself. At least she was still short.

Yet he didn't understand her mother's need for subterfuge. If Charlotte was receiving threatening notes as she claimed, wouldn't she want her daughter to know about it, to be on her guard if nothing else? Why she insisted on insinuating him into the company in such a manner he had no idea, and it didn't sit well with him.

No, he'd probably be better off if Donovan Trent had never heard of Alex Thompson.

Hearing a dramatic female sigh, he turned to see Charlotte striding into the room. She took a seat in one of the visitors' chairs and arranged the dog on her lap. "Everything's settled," she said, as if she'd just secured a dinner reservation.

"Your daughter didn't seem pleased to have me here."

"She isn't, but she'll get over it." She hadn't really been looking at him before, but she focused on him now with a wide-eyed, innocent expression that didn't fool him. "What?"

"When exactly did my name become Bruce?"

She gave a short tittering laugh. "On my way into the conference room it occurred to me that if I told my daughter your real name, she'd ferret out who you were in two seconds. My daughter is no slouch in the brains department."

"But Bruce?"

She shrugged. "It was all I could come up with on short notice."

She shouldn't have had to come up with anything. She should have leveled with her daughter. But since his pleas to do so had so far gone unheeded, he didn't bother. "I heard back from the lab. The only fingerprints on the letters belonged to us. They were printed on paper you can buy at any office supply store using ink you can purchase anywhere."

"So they weren't helpful."

"Not in narrowing down any suspects, no."

She lifted her shoulders and let them fall in a defeated way, dramatic even for her. "You see why I need your help. Who knows who could be sending those letters?"

Indeed. She could be mailing herself poisoned pen

letters for all he knew, but he suspected the fear he sensed in her was real. "Why do you want me to hang around the office then, if you are in danger?"

"You read the notes. 'I'll take away every Scarlet thing you own.' It's not my business I'm worried about, it's my daughter. She calls herself Carly, she always has, but her real name is Scarlet. She needs your protection, not me."

"I'm a P.I., Mrs. Thompson, not a bodyguard."

She looked at him with a hint of challenge in her eyes. "Would you let anything happen to my daughter?"

"No."

"Then that's close enough." She sat forward, clearing her throat. "There's one more thing. I don't think you're going to like it."

Why was he not surprised? "What's that?"

"I have, in the tiniest way, led my daughter to believe that we are sleeping together."

Not for the first time since he'd met Charlotte Thompson, his temper threatened to overflow. "How does one, in the tiniest way, lead someone to believe that you are sleeping with someone else?"

"She assumed and I didn't exactly deny it. It wouldn't have done me any good to deny it. She never would have believed me."

"Why is that?"

She shot him a droll look. "Have you looked at yourself in the mirror lately? And, unfortunately, my daughter thinks of me as some nymphomaniac dowager gobbling up young men like a Hoover snaps up dust bunnies."

She pressed her lips together and looked away from him. For the first time, he sensed real pain in her. "It's a harmless ruse," she said in a quiet voice.

He wanted to protest. He wanted to get the hell out of there, for as sure as he stood there he knew she lied to him. He didn't need to stick his neck out for a woman that couldn't even be straight with her own daughter. But he'd made two promises to his father. One would have to wait while he took care of the other.

"What do you want me to do?"

"Stay with her. Tell her you want to go over my itinerary. Whatever." She stood, grasping Mr. Jingles in one arm and smoothing her skirt with the other.

"Where are you going?"

"Friday is facial day. I'll see you at home later." With a swish of her hips she was gone.

Once outside in the car, Charlotte relaxed against the Mercedes's leather upholstery and let some of the tension she'd felt all day seep out of her. It was all arranged. She'd seen to it. Alex should be proud of her. She looked heavenward as she always did when she thought of her husband. "Finally, Alex, I've done something right."

She hadn't been a good parent to Carly. She knew that. While Carly's friends had thought she had the coolest mother imaginable because she didn't nag Carly about her grades or impose curfews like their mothers, Carly herself had needed something different. She'd needed stability and structure and order. Since Charlotte had been incapable of providing it, Carly had created it for herself.

Charlotte had always admired that about her daughter, but lately she had come to realize that Carly had gone too far. She'd structured her life to include nothing but work: no friends, no men, no dates, no fun. Charlotte had tried to get her daughter to lighten up, but Carly saw every attempt as another example of her mother's frivolity. Now they were like the two opposing poles of a magnet, but rather than attracting, they repelled. Frankly, Charlotte didn't know what to do about it anymore.

Even so, Charlotte had bigger worries than Carly's opinion of her. What she did now could make the difference between life and death for all of them. If only Jackson hadn't gone snooping around, digging in the past. He'd left it alone for all this time. Why now, when the risk was so much greater?

Her sweet Alex had already paid with his life for the answers Jackson sought. One of the last things Alex had said to her was to watch out for that boy. Alex had known what Jackson didn't: that his father had been diagnosed with cancer and wasn't expected to survive. Donovan Trent had lasted only a few months longer than Alex had. Newly orphaned, the boy had gone to live with an aunt in upstate New York.

Charlotte had lost track of him, until the phone calls started, the ones warning her what would happen if he persisted. She knew the voice and the man it belonged to, though she doubted he knew she knew. This time, rather than threatening her husband, he targeted her daughter. And Jackson. She'd had to divert Jackson, make him stop looking somehow. All she'd come up with was a crazy plot about someone trying to sabotage her business, some competitor threatening to expose her for stealing their ideas.

She was certain he didn't believe her. What sane person would? But he'd agreed to help her, which was all that mattered. He would keep Carly safe until she could figure out what to do—even if that meant telling him the truth. If he would even believe her when she told him. She'd gone to the police twenty years ago and they had practically laughed in her face. She was on her own now, and that thought terrified her most of all.

Chapter 3

Standing in the doorway to Carly's office, Jackson watched her without her noticing. In the background a radio played Rod Stewart's "If You Think I'm Sexy." Over the low volume of the music he heard her humming as she typed something furiously on her keyboard. The first thought that assailed him was, maybe she ought to try another song. From what he could tell, her mother had kept all the feminine attributes in the family to herself.

In a way he was glad Charlotte had put him on her daughter's trail. The number-one rule of detective work was start with the obvious. Apparently, Charlotte and her daughter didn't get along. Whether the animosity stemmed from personal or business reasons, he didn't know, but he intended to find out. But Carly's devotion to the company was equally apparent. Would she sabotage her own firm just to spite her mother? Unlikely, but it wouldn't be the first time it had happened. Or did she resent her mother enough to try to frighten her out of any involvement in the company?

He didn't have the answer to those questions either, but he knew he didn't want to believe her capable of such duplicity. He'd sensed an openness and a basic honesty in her as a young girl that, despite her outwardly sharp demeanor, he hoped life hadn't wiped out of her. But if Carly wasn't responsible, that left him with two possibilities: either Charlotte had made the story up herself, or someone outside, unseen intended to harm her.

Abruptly, she lifted her head and glared at him. "Did you want something or are you planning to grow there, like grass?"

So much for his assumption that she hadn't noticed him. He stepped into the room as she watched him with a disdainful gaze. He wondered what that was about, but he'd get to that later. He stopped between the two visitors' chairs. "Your mother asked me to get a copy of her itinerary from you."

Her eyebrows lifted. "She actually has you doing work? There's a first time for everything."

Despite his intentions, curiosity got the better of him. "What is that supposed to mean?"

She sat back in her chair, crossed her legs, and folded her hands in her lap, a sardonic expression on her face. "Usually her assistants only show up on Fridays to collect their paychecks, if at all."

Now he thought he understood. Charlotte had led her daughter to believe that he was her lover and Carly didn't approve. Just to be sure he asked, "What exactly have you got against me?"

"My mother pays for your . . . um . . . services, does she not?"

He didn't know why the prim way she said that amused him, or why he felt the urge to bait her. Maybe because the only service he'd provided was listening to the most outlandish story since Ruth Wonderly walked into Sam Spade's office and the only one paying him anything was her.

Before he thought about it, he gave in to that urge.

"Which bothers you more, that your mother avails herself of my services or that she pays for them?"

She shot him a narrow-eyed glare and stood. "Let me get you that itinerary." She crossed to a credenza that ran perpendicular to her glass-topped desk and plucked several pages from the printer. Turning back, she tossed the papers onto the desk near him. "Here you go. I also included detailed notes of the meeting she missed this morning." She arranged herself in her seat. "Don't let the door hit you on the way out."

"Does that mean you're not going to answer my question?"

"I have work to do." She turned back to her keyboard and resumed her typing, ignoring him.

Shaking his head, he left the office. Which one qualified as the nuttier of the pair: the brusque, abrasive daughter or her flamboyant, cloying mother? Like two opposite faces on a coin. No wonder they didn't get along.

He walked back to the office Charlotte had given him and dropped the papers on the desk without looking at them. Despite what Charlotte said, he had no intention of hanging around the office all afternoon. He'd already found out from Carly's secretary that she rarely left before seven on a Friday night. What he needed to do would only take a few minutes. He'd be back long before she left.

Charlotte told him there were only two people she'd confided her story to besides him: her driver and the security guard on duty by the elevators. They were also the only two who knew he wasn't Bruce. Before leaving, he asked the guard to keep an eye on Carly until he got back.

He had to walk crosstown three blocks and downtown two to the parking spot he'd found. He climbed into the car, a silver Lexus, and started the motor. He knew he risked not finding another parking spot on his way back uptown, but he'd prefer not to go where he was going without a means of quick escape. Over the last few years, gentrification had come to the meatpacking district, but there were places where hard men who had fallen on hard times still gathered.

He found the particular man he was looking for at one of the stools that lined the bar in the aptly named Hole-in-the-Wall Pub. He slid in beside the man who sat hunched over as if protecting his drink from intruders, and ordered a beer for himself. He'd barely taken a sip when the man said, "You Cappy's kid?"

To his knowledge, no one had ever referred to his father by that name, but Jackson nodded. "What have you got for me?"

"I really liked your old man. I never had no grudge against him, like they said. I only said I'd meetcha a-cause a' him."

"I appreciate that." Jackson surveyed the man who sat beside him, Duke Anderson, the man who had testified against his father. He was probably in his late sixties now, his skin almost blue black in the dim barroom light. Combined with his yellowed eyes, the pattern of missing teeth gave him the look more of a decomposing jack-o'-lantern than a human being.

Jackson had learned from newspaper accounts that Anderson had been a c.o. under his father's command as a captain at the Bronx House of Detention. He'd been the one to claim that Donovan Trent had been seeing the woman who was killed. Jackson had spent years hating this man for his role in what had transpired, but all he felt now was pity.

"What have you got for me?" he repeated.

Anderson shifted on his stool, darting a glance at

him. "Just a bit of advice. Don't go looking for trouble and you won't find none."

"What kind of trouble?"

"The kind where you wake up with six feet a' dirt over your head."

"I can handle it."

Anderson cast him a scoffing glance. "Look, kid, maybe nobody ever told you that some stones are better left unturned. Nobody needs to go pokin' under 'em to see what's underneath. That's all I got to say. You watch your back, kid, and stay outta trouble." Grabbing his drink, he ambled, crablike, to a table at the corner of the room. With his back to the bar, he huddled over his glass again.

Jackson turned back to his beer. That had gone amazingly well. He'd gotten all he would ever get out of Duke, which was precisely nothing, save the certainty that if Anderson hadn't really held a grudge against his father, someone had put him up to testifying. The question was the same as always. Who?

As he got back to his car, he noticed a familiar vehicle parked at the opposite curb. Shaking his head, he got in and drove away.

At six-fifteen, Carly stood, stretched, and began to pack her briefcase to get ready to go home. She was tired, famished since she'd skipped lunch, and there wasn't anything she could accomplish in the office she couldn't do just as well at home.

Unfortunately, before all this mess started, she'd promised to have dinner with her mother. Charlotte had found some new Italian place she wanted to check out. Carly wanted a plate of fettucine like she wanted another hole in the head. She'd stop by her mother's apartment long enough to beg off and go home, open that bottle of wine she'd been saving, and tune out in front of the television for a while.

"Leaving us so early?"

Carly looked up from the task of shoving one more file in her bag to find her assistant Nora leaning against the door frame. Nora had been scarce all afternoon, which suited Carly just fine seeing as she actually got some work done. "It's only forty-five minutes."

"Hey, I'm not complaining. That means I get to go home, too."

Finding Nora's good humor infectious, Carly smiled. "Why don't you treat yourself to some of the new seafoam bath crystals in the sample room?"

"Oh, I plan to. I'm looking forward to a nice hot bath and a nice hot man to go with it. Speaking of which, who's the hunk in the corner office?"

Carly hadn't bothered to explain "Bruce's" presence next door, figuring the office grapevine would take care of that for her. But if Nora was questioning his being there, either the gossips had swallowed their tongues or the man was up to something. "Why?"

Nora held up both hands. "Don't get me wrong, I don't mind the eye candy, but this one's been snooping around all afternoon. He asked me a zillion questions, mostly about you."

Carly's eyebrows lifted and the smile fell away from her face. Bad enough that the man was here at all, but to find herself the target of his curiosity unsettled her. For all she knew he could be some reporter hoping to sniff out some dirt to print to ruin their anniversary celebration. And knowing Nora she'd spilled everything she knew just to go on enjoying said eye candy a little longer.

"What did you tell him?"

"Nothing really. Mostly he wanted to know what kind of products we made, who our competition was, what you did for the company." Nora lifted one shoulder the way a child does when caught doing something wrong. "I didn't see the harm in telling him."

Carly sighed. She supposed if he'd confined himself to those subjects, she didn't really object. She couldn't do anything about it anyway. Maybe her mother really did intend for him to do some sort of work while he was there, but what sort she couldn't fathom. Too tired to puzzle it out, she lifted her bag from the desk and forced a smile for Nora's sake. "No harm done. Have a great weekend."

"You do the same, boss."

Considering the mound of paperwork and the number of disks she'd crowded into her bag, she doubted it, but she waved as she passed Nora in the doorway. No use ruining everyone's weekend with thoughts of work. Carly was almost to the elevators when she noticed *him* lounging against the wall, his arms and ankles crossed, as if he owned the place. Apparently, he'd been waiting for her, because he straightened and pressed the button to summon the elevator.

Annoyed, she stamped to a stop a couple of feet in front of him. "Can I help you with something?"

"I heard you tell your secretary you were leaving for the day. Your mother asked me to see you to her apartment."

Carly pressed her lips into a thin line. She almost asked him if he did everything her mother told him to do, but managed to keep that thought from exiting her mouth. "That isn't necessary. I'm perfectly capable of getting on a bus by myself."

"I insist. My car's right downstairs."

The elevator came, leaving her two choices. She could either stand there arguing with the man or she could go with him and ride, hopefully in comfort, to her mother's house. Truthfully, she had only one real option. Refusing a ride from him was juvenile and churlish, and she questioned her own motives for wanting to.

Still, she couldn't seem to let go of her pique. With a huff, she said, "Fine," and stepped onto the elevator as he made sure the doors didn't close on her. She stationed herself in the front corner and stared up at the light panel as he got on. He stood to the left of and slightly behind her, where she could cheerfully ignore him. Or so she thought until his fingers brushed hers to slide her briefcase from her grasp.

For a moment, she simply stared at him. Not one man she knew would have considered relieving her of her bag as he had. They were all too busy wondering what was politically correct these days to risk it. Did they open the door for a woman? Did they hold out her chair? Did they give up their seat on the subway? That's the excuse they claimed for putting chivalry to death. Yet they had no problem deciding if it was p.c. to step right over you in their climb up the corporate ladder or stab you in the back when you weren't looking. That was definitely okay.

But she suspected "Bruce" had taken her bag as a matter of course, without thinking—a retrograde gentlemanly impulse. Maybe there was more in him for her mother to see than broad shoulders and bulging pectorals. "Thank you."

He offered her a hint of a smile before turning his gaze toward the opening elevator doors.

He wasn't kidding, his car was right outside, parked in a no-parking zone. A neon orange ticket had been secured under one windshield wiper. Carly pressed her lips together, waiting to gauge his reaction. Most New Yorkers finding a ticket for a hundred dollars and change on their car exhibited some sort of negative behavior, if only a few invectives hailed at the traffic cops, the city, the mayor, and anyone else they could throw in. His only response was to pluck it from the windshield and crumple it in his palm as he opened the door for her. He threw it and her bag in the back-seat before rounding the car to get in on the driver's side.

He fastened his seat belt and turned to her. "Ready?"

She nodded. She focused on the view outside the window as he pulled from the curb. Thankfully, traffic this time of night was manageable and the distance to her mother's place was short. Then she could be rid of him. A few minutes after that she'd be rid of her mother and on her way home to her own place. Her nice quiet sanctuary where she could enjoy her solitude.

Carly swallowed. Who the hell was she kidding? Most of the time she agreed to her mother's outings to keep from going home to that same lonely house. No matter what other complaints Carly might have about her mother, Charlotte knew how to have a good time. She knew how to get others to have a good time. Carly wondered how much of her desire to go home stemmed from wanting to punish Charlotte, who would be disappointed by her absence. She decided not to think about it too much, figuring she might not like the answer she came up with. She hoped she wasn't petty enough to try to pay her mother back in that way.

The car drew to a halt at a red light. "Dollar for your thoughts." When she looked at him, uncertain she'd heard him say what she thought she'd heard, he shrugged. "Inflation."

She stared out the window, not knowing what to say, which surprised her. She didn't usually have any trouble handling the men her mother brought around. There had been some who were nice to her, others whom she managed to be civil to but hadn't really liked, and some whom she'd actively disliked and hadn't bothered to hide it.

But this one was different somehow. She should just tell him to mind his own business. She'd been doing that all afternoon in one form or another. She'd been flat-out rude, and he'd seemed unfazed by her treatment. She could excuse her earlier behavior as the aftereffects of dealing with her mother. She'd been angry and she'd taken it out on him. Besides, she'd suspected he'd been amused by her situation. But he'd been nothing but pleasant since then. There really wasn't any sense picking a fight with him when she knew whose side her mother would come down on.

"I was thinking of all the things I have to get done before we leave for Martha's Vineyard."

"That's on Wednesday."

"I'll be driving up Monday afternoon to make sure everything is ready."

"Don't you have staff to do that for you?"

"Yes, but it's my company. If things aren't right it's my name that will be mud."

"Then why did you let me stay on?"

She knew what he was asking. If she was so in charge, why had she allowed her mother to hire him when she'd made it plain she didn't want him around? She was not about to tell this perfect stranger her mother had one-upped her on his behalf. "What difference does it make?"

He shrugged again. "Just curious. You two don't seem to get along."

"Really? The last man of my mother's who seemed *so* curious about how my mother and I got along was really trying to arrange a ménage à trois with the three of us. Do I need to give you the same answer I gave him?"

"I'll skip it if you don't mind. Really, I was just curious. You're not much like your mother."

And that was supposed to be a bad thing? "Not many people are like my mother."

He chuckled. "True."

Something in his voice made her turn to look at him. His eyes were focused straight ahead, but he smiled in a way that made her wonder what dirty thoughts were rolling around in his mind. Disgusted, she turned back to the view outside her window, wishing the light would hurry up and change.

"Darlings, you're early. I'm not even dressed yet," Charlotte said, opening the door to them. She wore a patterned silk robe, a pair of high-heeled slippers, with boa poofs on the front.

Carly snorted. She could have shown up half an hour late and Charlotte would still be in her underwear. Dutifully, she turned her cheek for Charlotte's air kisses. "It doesn't matter. I'm not in the mood to go out anyway."

"But I promised Brucie I would take him to La Pequena Ragazza. Isn't that right, dear?"

Carly didn't know why it hadn't occurred to her that "Brucie" would be joining them. She turned to look at "Brucie" to gauge his reaction to her mother's latest appellation, just as Charlotte leaned up to kiss him on the mouth. Carly turned away and blinked, hoping the action would clear that image from her vision. She definitely had not needed to see that. She didn't know why it bothered her, except her mother was usually a bit more circumspect when she was around.

But since this afternoon's run-in, Charlotte felt the

need to reinforce her position, or perhaps she herself smarted more than she wanted to admit. It was one thing to believe your mother was more interested in her own pleasures than she was in you. It was another thing to have her smack you in the face with it.

Biting her lip, Carly walked into the apartment, away from whatever the lovebirds were doing by the door. Charlotte had redone everything in the apartment, from the kitchen cabinets to the carpet on the floor, when she moved in. Her mother's taste, in décor anyway, was understated and expensive, as if it only existed to showcase its owner. Delicate lacquered pieces and handmade appointments dotted the room, giving it an airy feel.

Normally, she enjoyed being in her mother's apartment, but tonight she just wanted to get out of there.

"I had Johnny make some appletinis," Charlotte called, still by the doorway. "They're in the dining room. Would you get them, darling?"

"Sure," she called back. Why not? It was probably just an excuse to get her out of the room anyway. Fine. Nobody had to ask her twice. While she was at it, she'd hunt down Johnny, who had to be around here somewhere. Johnny, who, unlike some people, actually liked being around her.

"Get a grip," she warned herself as she made her way toward the back of the apartment to keep from slipping into a pity party for one. She got to the dining room to find it empty of any alcoholic presence.

"Where the heck are you, Johnny?" she said aloud. "'Cause I really could use that drink."

"Is she gone?"

Jackson looked past Charlotte to see Carly rounding the corner at the edge of the room. "Yes."

Sighing, Charlotte stepped away from him, fluffing her hair. "Thank goodness that's over with."

Yes, whatever that had been. Obviously a performance for her daughter's sake, but to what end? He pulled his handkerchief from his back pocket and blotted a spot of dampness that lingered on his cheek. "What was that about?"

"It's called a cheat, darling. You learn that in the movie business. You know and I know that I kissed you on the cheek, but from where Carly stood . . ."

It had looked like something more. "Was that truly necessary?"

Charlotte canted her head to one side. "Darling," she began in a patient tone, "I told you my daughter is not stupid. How long do you think it would take her to get suspicious if she never saw any display of affection between us?"

He had no idea, but he hadn't imagined the look of distaste he'd seen on Carly's face when Charlotte kissed him. He'd admit he had found Carly's immediate reaction to the idea that he was sleeping with her mother amusing, but he wasn't laughing anymore. Just now, he'd seen something else in her eyes, something that disturbed him though he didn't understand it.

"Don't do it again."

She patted his arm, as if consoling him. "There's no need to. We just made a true believer out of her." Charlotte sighed, taking a step away from him. "Make yourself at home. I'll be back as soon as I can."

"Where are you going?"

"To get dressed. About now, Carly's feeling sorry for herself. I intend to cheer her up."

Charlotte breezed away, apparently oblivious to his annoyance or the fact that she had engineered whatever mood her daughter might be in. Could any woman really be that self-absorbed, or did she know and seek to make amends with her daughter? He sighed. It wasn't any of his business anyway, but since Charlotte insisted on keeping up this charade, he intended to set some ground rules for its performance. Charlotte would either go along with them or, the promise to his father be damned, he was out of there. The sooner she understood that, the better.

Chapter 4

"I'm in here."

Carly followed the sound of Johnny's voice. She found him in the kitchen downing one of the drinks himself. Carly took a position at the counter across from him and lifted one of the drinks from the tray. "Hey, Johnny."

A jovial man with a wicked sense of humor, Johnny raised his nearly empty glass to salute her. "Evenin', Miss Scarlet."

Carly shot him a wry look before sipping her drink. The warm liquid heated her insides, and since she hadn't eaten, provided a light buzz as well.

She rested her elbows on the counter. "Don't start with me, John." Johnny was the only person—man, woman, or child—Carly allowed to call her by her given name. Johnny only resorted to it when he thought she was being high-handed, or at times like now when he thought she needed a dose of humor. "I'm fine, really. Long day."

"I bet. How is Bruce getting along?"

She studied Johnny for a moment. She'd always thought that he might have harbored a bit of a crush on her mother. Not that he was obvious about it. He'd never made a single comment, made a single advance, that she knew of, but whatever his feelings, Carly was sure he didn't approve of her mother's latest conquest. As for Charlotte, she treated poor Johnny with total indifference, the invisible man in the uniform. The only reason Charlotte had him living here was that she hated to live alone.

"About as well as a blueberry at a pie-eating contest." She set her glass on the counter. "You don't happen to have any of those little tart things you made last time?"

Johnny brightened. "I've got something better." He went to the refrigerator and came back with a tray full of hors d'ouvres and set it on the counter. He pointed to one at the center. "Try that one."

She popped it into her mouth. "What is that?"

"Cucumber with crab mousse."

"Delicious. You've outdone yourself." She took another and devoured it as quickly as the first. When she reached for another, he snatched the tray out of her reach.

"That's enough for now." He rounded the counter, headed toward the living room. "Make yourself useful. Bring the drinks."

Laughing for the first time that day, Carly did as she was told.

After Charlotte left, Jackson surveyed the expansive living room. The delicate pieces suited her. The artwork that hung on her walls was worth more than he ever hoped to make in his lifetime. A curio at the corner of the room caught his eye. At its center was a statuette with a white base and a globe on top. The 1974 Best Actress Golden Globe she'd won for her role in the movie *Scarlet Woman,* a remake of Carmen Jones, which had itself been a remake of the opera *Carmen.* Using her most famous and acclaimed role to segue into another business had proved profitable for her.

But knowing what little he did about Charlotte and Carly, he wondered which of the two had been the mastermind of that maneuver.

Speaking of maneuvers, he needed to make sure a few things were in place before the women got back. He pulled his cell phone from his belt and called his cousin Drew. Being a P.I., it paid to have friends in low places, and having a relative on the police force sure didn't hurt. Drew had gotten Charlotte's letters dusted for prints without tipping anyone off that they had come from him.

Drew answered the phone on the third ring. "It's your dime."

"Hello to you too. I need to ask you a favor."

"Don't you always? What is it this time?"

"I need you to watch my client's place for me until I get there. She doesn't live too far from you."

"You planning on telling me why I should give up a Friday night to stare at some broad's apartment?"

"It's not an apartment, it's a house."

"Whatever. What's the deal?"

Jackson rehashed the story he'd already told Drew twice.

"Oh, yeah. The actress's daughter. Is she at least something to look at?"

"She has a lovely personality."

"Aw, man."

"Look, it's not all night, just for a couple of hours so I can get some sleep."

"All right, but you owe me."

"Put it on my tab. He gave Drew the address for Carly that Charlotte had given him. "I'll let you know when she's on her way home."

Jackson clicked off the phone, just as Johnny came into the room to deposit a silver tray on the coffee table. The older man cast him a look that among lesser primates was an invitation to fight. Carly came in a second later, giving him the feminine equivalent of the same look. She carried a martini glass half-full of a lime-green liquid in one hand and a crystal pitcher full of the same in the other. The appletinis, no doubt, though he wouldn't know one if someone threw one in his face, which, with any luck, she wouldn't.

She set the pitcher on the table. "Where did my mother disappear to?" she asked.

"She's changing."

"That ought to take a good hour." She downed the remains of her glass. "Have fun at dinner." She adjusted the strap of her purse on her shoulder and started toward the door.

"You're not staying?"

"No."

She paused in her escape to pick up her bag from where he'd left it, giving him a chance to catch up with her. "Why?"

"Look, it's obvious the dew is still fresh on the leaf with you and my mother. I'm not interested in being a fifth wheel."

"That's not a problem."

She canted her head to one side, a gesture reminiscent of her mother. "You don't have to be nice to me for my mother's sake. First of all, she doesn't care. Second, if you're worried I'll make things difficult for you, I won't. I know I didn't treat you very nicely today, but I have nothing against you, really, except you would probably be better served in another line of . . . um . . . work, shall we say? Especially, if you're expecting to ride the Scarlet Woman gravy train for any length of time, you're going to be disappointed. She's way too fickle for that."

She shook her head and lifted her hands in a gesture

of exasperation. "It's been a very long day to end a very long week."

She offered the last of it as an explanation for her behavior and a warning about what she thought he could expect from her mother. He understood that and figured, despite what Charlotte believed, he owed her a bit of honesty himself. He grasped her arm as she moved to turn away from her, but she shrugged him off before he could say a word. "Just tell my mother I went home, okay?" She yanked open the door and slipped out.

Jackson let her go, partly because he'd probably have had to sit on her to keep her there and partly because he didn't trust his own impulse to level with her. Honesty might be in his nature, but it wasn't always the wisest course. For now he'd have to trust Charlotte's judgment about what was best for her daughter.

By the time Charlotte returned to the living room, Jackson had downed half the martinis and three-quarters of the hors d'ouvres. He sat on one of her too-small chairs feeling testy and out of sorts, resentful of being in the center of a feud between mother and daughter.

"Where's Carly?"

"She left."

Alarm flashed in Charlotte's eyes. "How could you let her walk out? If anything happens to her—"

"Relax. It's taken care of. But we need to get a few things straight. Sit down."

Her eyebrows lifted and she huffed at his high-handedness, but she perched herself on the end of one of her chairs. "What things?"

"First, never, under any circumstances, refer to me as Brucie again."

"Is that what you're worried about?" With a wave of

her hand, she sat back. "Believe me, neither I nor my daughter has any doubt about your masculinity."

He didn't know how she could possibly know what her daughter believed, considering that they hadn't spent two moments alone with her since their showdown in the conference room. "Second, why was your driver following me this afternoon?"

"You knew?"

"Just a hint for future reference. If you're going to tail somebody and you don't want them to know it's you, it helps if your plates don't read SCRLTWMN."

She shrugged. "I hadn't thought of that. But I shouldn't have had to. You told me you were going to stay with her, not go traipsing off to God knows where. What were you doing, anyway?"

"Carly was perfectly safe. Do you honestly think someone would burst into the offices of Scarlet Woman to harm her?"

"I guess not." Sighing, she shifted in her seat. "Is that all?"

"No. I think you should reconsider going to the police."

"Absolutely not."

"Why not? If you are afraid for your daughter's safety, they have the manpower to find out who is behind this and protect her better than I can."

"Don't you see, if I do that, it goes public? Everyone will know someone is blackmailing me. There will be a scandal no matter what I do."

She looked at him, a plaintive expression in her eyes as if she was asking him to understand. Unfortunately, he thought he did. When it came down to it, her reputation, not her daughter, mattered most of all. He didn't ask her if there was any truth to what the notes claimed, figuring he probably knew the answer to that, too.

Tired, irritated, hungry despite the hors d'ouvres he'd eaten, and just about fed up, Jackson stood. "Good night, Charlotte." He started toward the door.

She was on her feet and after him in a second. "Where are you going?"

"To do what you asked me to do."

Charlotte frowned as Jackson slipped out her front door. She hoped he meant he was going to look after Carly. Maybe he was right. Maybe she should go to the police, but she couldn't chance it. What if they had the same reaction the policemen twenty years ago had? She'd be putting her daughter at greater risk for nothing. And if anything happened to Carly she didn't know how she would survive that.

Charlotte jumped and her breath caught as she felt a pair of masculine arms close around her waist. "Shh, baby," Johnny said against her ear. "I didn't mean to startle you."

She leaned back against him, absorbing his warmth, inhaling his scent, willing herself to relax. "This whole thing has me jumpy."

"I know."

She'd fed him the same nonsense story she'd given Jackson. She'd had to. If Johnny knew the truth he'd drive her to the police station himself. She suspected he didn't believe her any more than Jackson did, but in the absence of any other truth he hadn't called her on it.

He scrubbed one hand up and down her arm, while his other arm tightened around her waist. "Come. Let me make you feel better."

She turned in his arms and burrowed her nose against his neck. He did that just by being with her. If anyone had told her five years ago when she'd hired

Johnny that she would fall in love with him she'd have told them they'd been eating too much of his exhaust. While she'd always found him attractive, she'd kept that knowledge to herself. At work he'd exuded a competent, no-nonsense, professional manner that didn't brook any flirtations with the boss.

It hadn't occurred to her that he was even attracted to her, until one night when she'd bemoaned the loss of one of her lovers and Johnny had told her the man was a fool on so many levels he couldn't begin to describe them. A familiar sentiment spoken to raise the spirits of the loser in love's game, but she'd seen in his eyes and the quiet way he'd spoken that he meant those words. And she'd seen something else—desire.

That surprised her so much she'd gone to his room that night to make certain she hadn't imagined it. As she stood on the threshold to his room she hesitated. Maybe she ought to leave a good thing alone. Johnny was a good employee, he took care of her. When the last cook quit, he'd taken over the responsibility, claiming he'd always had a secret desire to be a chef. What if she was mistaken? What if she offended him with her advance? She'd end up without transportation and starving since she'd never learned to cook anything that didn't come out of a can.

Screwing up her courage, she decided to chance it. What did she have to lose but a little dignity? Maybe he'd just slam the door in her face. But she'd never been one to be shy about going after what she wanted. She wasn't even sure why she suddenly felt so strongly about him. Maybe the breakup had affected her more strongly than she'd supposed. Or maybe she sensed that with Johnny she had the chance to reach for something more.

She took a deep breath and rapped on the door. A few moments later, he opened it, wearing a robe and a pair of pajama bottoms that matched the pattern of his collar. His eyebrows lifted in surprise. She knew her presence alone could not have caused that reaction, as they were the only two people in the apartment and Johnny had never had any guests that she was aware of. It had to be the peignoir set she wore, both items scarlet red and almost completely see-through.

She couldn't back down now. She'd already blown her cover with her skimpy covering. But now that she stood before him, she couldn't think of a coherent word to say. "Um, Johnny, I need to talk to you about something."

"My name is John."

She blinked, not understanding the reason for his declaration. Her throat worked until she finally forced out one word. "Okay."

"When I'm driving your car or cooking your food you can call me anything you like. When you come to my room, my name is John."

She understood then. If she wanted to be with him, it would be as equals or not at all. "Yes, John."

He stood aside to let her enter the room. She'd never been in here before, not since he'd moved in. In this small space he'd fit a bed, a dresser, a desk, and two side chairs in a way that didn't look cramped. "I like what you've done."

"Have a seat."

She chose to sit on the bed. She woke up there, though he hadn't touched her. They'd talked for long hours until she'd fallen asleep. When her eyes opened she found him sitting in the same chair he'd occupied the night before, his feet propped up on the bed. He was awake and staring at her in a way that actually made her blush. She had her answer then—he did want her. So why hadn't he taken advantage of the situation? Was he afraid for his job? Another man might be, but she doubted he was. Then what?

"Why didn't you . . ." She trailed off, not knowing how to end that particular sentence. Not with him, anyway. Anything that might have come out of her mouth with another man seemed crude and unworthy.

"Take you to my bed?"

That was close enough. She nodded.

"I'm not going to be the rebound guy you turn to every time some young buck disappoints you."

"I don't want you to be."

His skeptical expression told her he didn't quite believe her. "I care for you, Charlotte, I'm not ashamed to admit that, but I will never let you walk all over me like you do your other men. Can you live with that?"

She nodded. "As long as you're not with me just because of my money."

He grinned. "Fair enough. But I don't want to rush into anything with you. I want us to take it slow. I want us to get to know each other."

She rose to her knees and extended her hand toward him. "It's a deal."

But rather than shake her hand, he pulled her forward until his mouth claimed hers for a kiss. Just one. One long, wet, erotic kiss that put to shame every twenty-something male she'd ever known.

When he set her away from him, he stood. "Time for me to see how well the cold-water pipes work in this place."

She'd laughed and sat back on the bed, drawing her knees up to her chest as he disappeared into the adjoining bathroom. In all the while he'd been driving her, she'd never suspected he had a sense of humor hidden beneath the professional exterior. She remarked on that to Carly one day when she couldn't control the giddiness she felt from falling in love. Carly had responded, "Duh, Mom, he's only that stiff around you."

Carly didn't suspect a thing, and by mutual consent they had decided not to tell her until they were sure about their feelings for one another. No matter how much Carly liked John and despite her father's long absence, Charlotte suspected Carly's allegiance still lay with her father.

And now that they were certain, the right time to tell her seemed to elude them. First the preparation for the anniversary and now this. John was wise enough to know that she couldn't tell Carly about them now, but she didn't suspect he'd wait much longer. Truthfully, she didn't want to wait. She loved him and wanted to do so openly, not through a veil of secrecy.

She squeezed him more tightly, burrowing closer. This was what she wanted for her daughter. Oh, God, how she wanted Carly to know what it was like to be loved by a good man, a man who cared for her and allowed her to care back. A man who accepted her warts, affectations, frailties, and all, and could still love her despite them. John was the only person in twenty years who had seen her without her makeup. Even Alex, as much as she'd loved him, had wanted the illusion of being married to a star. She'd been his second wife, a trophy to keep pristine clean and on a pedestal. With John she could be herself, even though some days she wasn't quite sure who that self was.

He pulled away from her enough to see her face. "What's the matter, baby?"

"I was just thinking about Carly, wondering if she's all right."

"I'm sure she's fine, but I wish you hadn't told her I wouldn't be going to the Vineyard."

"I know, but I need you here. What if that fool tries to contact me again and no one's here?"

"I understand, but that doesn't mean I have to like it."

"As soon as all this is over, I'll make everything right, I promise."

"I know you will, but remember one more thing. If you ever put your hands on that boy again, I'll give you the spanking you deserve."

She didn't know how he knew about the kiss she'd given Jackson, but she wasn't about to argue with him. She smiled a siren's smile as she tightened her arms around his neck.

"Oh, John!" she said. "Promise?"

Chapter 5

Carly peered out her front window through the thin slats of her Venetian blinds. He was still out there. Or someone was. Around midnight she'd noticed the men switch places. One tree trunk of a man had gotten out of the car and walked away, while another man had gotten in. She'd gone to bed shortly after the exchange, but as far as she could tell, the same car with the same man in it sat across the street from her house.

What had spooked her mother this time? The hole in the ozone layer? Alien invaders from Mars? The Loch Ness monster? She let the curtains fall back in place. If she had a dime for every time her mother had set some man on her to watch her, she could forget about her company and retire to a condo in outer space. She'd been the only child to show up in kindergarten with a notebook and a bodyguard, who sat in one of the baby chairs at the back of the classroom.

Years later, when Carly had asked her mother why she had embarrassed her in such a fashion, Charlotte told her that there had been a string of child abductions in the city around that time and she hadn't wanted to leave her unprotected. Like a band of child molesters was going to break into the Forster Academy and snatch kids. Carly wouldn't have been surprised if her tree house had been bugged too.

The worst time had been while she attended Howard University as an undergrad. She'd thought this cute guy she kept seeing everywhere was actually interested in her. She'd known she wasn't pretty, too skinny and about as sexy as a piece of bread, but here was this gorgeous hunk following her around. It had devastated her to find out that her mother had hired this man to watch her because there had been a string of rapes on another school's campus.

Carly had finally put her foot down about her mother's constant surveillance. That had been years ago, so why had Charlotte fallen back to her old ways now?

It really didn't matter anyway, since Carly had no intention of putting up with it. Hearing the whistle of the teakettle blow, she was seized by an idea. She wasn't about to risk losing one of her matching coffee mugs. Instead she found a cup she wouldn't miss and filled it with orange juice. The morning paper hadn't come yet, so she grabbed the magazine at the top of the rack she kept in a corner of the living room, tucked it in her pocket, and headed out the front door. If Charlotte wanted to make a nuisance of herself, Carly could prove herself just as annoying.

She marched up to the driver's-side window and rapped on it. The car's windows were tinted black as night, making it impossible to see the driver. Slowly the window rolled down, revealing the last person Carly would have expected to find. "Bruce!"

He nodded toward the cup she held. "Is that for me?"

Surprised at his presence and angered by his flippant comment, she did the first thing that popped into her head. She threw the drink in his face. Juice sluiced down his face and tiny bits of pulp stuck to his forehead.

He wiped one hand across his eyes and flicked away the excess. "Should I take that as a yes?"

She didn't give a damn how he took it. She whirled around and hurried toward her open front door. For all she knew he was some psycho voyeur whom Charlotte picked up God only knew where. If that was the case, she'd be better off finding out from the safety of her own house with the police on the way.

The only thing that bothered her about their little encounter was her own behavior. Throwing drinks in people's faces was definitely not her style. Well, he'd gotten what he deserved as far as she was concerned. She glanced back toward the car. At least he had enough sense not to try to follow her.

Watching Carly retreat, Jackson pulled his handkerchief from his back pocket and mopped the remaining juice from his face. He knew what she must be thinking right now, who was this whack-job stalker who was sleeping with her mother? Damn! He hadn't intended to frighten her. He hadn't intended for her to know he was there at all, but in this quiet suburban neighborhood where every house came with a two-car garage, any stray car on the street was bound to be noticed.

He'd been half dozing, figuring she must still be asleep at five in the morning, when he'd noticed her watching him from the window. He'd been debating whether to drive off or not when the front door opened and she marched out. The only way he could have driven off then was to run her over. Besides, he'd figured he'd already blown his cover, or else why would she have come out of the house at all? But she'd been shocked to find him behind the wheel.

Damn! If he had his druthers, he'd let her be, go back to Charlotte's place, and tell her that she had to find some other way of protecting her daughter, like perhaps telling her the truth so that she would cooperate. But he also knew that if Carly made it back to the house, she'd be on the phone to the police in two seconds flat. That he didn't need.

He rolled up the window and got out of the car. He overtook her as she got to the walk in front of her house. With a hand on her arm, he spun her around to face him. "I need to talk to you."

She snatched her arm from his grasp. "No. No, you don't. What you need to do is get back in your car and go away."

"If I wanted to hurt you, I wouldn't have spent the night in my car. I'd have come in through your back door, which is unlocked, by the way."

Her eyes widened and she pivoted away from him, toward her door. Abruptly, before she'd even taken a step she turned back. Anger replaced the fear in her eyes. She crossed her arms in front of her. "Okay, you want to talk, go ahead and talk. Start by telling me who you are. If the name Bruce gets anywhere near your mouth . . ."

Her words trailed off, as if she couldn't find a dire enough threat to attach at the end. Considering he topped her height by a good twelve inches and outweighed her by a hundred pounds, none would be believable anyway. "My name is Jackson, Jackson Trent. I'm a private investigator. Your mother hired me."

He threw the last of that on there in hopes of distracting her from who he was. Apparently it hadn't done him any good, as her gaze narrowed on his face and he saw recognition in her eyes.

"You're Donovan Trent's son?"

He nodded. "Your father defended mine on a murder charge."

Her eyebrows lifted and she bit her lip as her gaze traveled over him in a desultory way. "And this is how you repay him? By sleeping with his widow?" She shook her head and dropped her hands to her sides. "I really have to hand it to Charlotte. She's found a way to combine her two favorite hobbies: younger men and butting into my life. Please congratulate her for me when you see her."

She turned away from him, starting toward the house, but for a second he detected a different emotion in her eyes, not surprise or fear or even anger. Something close to defeat, which unsettled him. "That's not what's going on. First off, I wasn't spying on you."

"No? Then give me one legitimate reason my mother has for hiring a private investigator."

"She told me a competitor is trying to blackmail her because they believe she stole some company secret."

She laughed, and he realized just how ludicrous that story sounded now that it had come out of his own mouth. But Carly's laugh contained no humor and was directed at him.

"My mother told you that? And you believed her?"

"No, not entirely."

"Let me tell you something, Jackson. The only ideas my mother might have stolen from some other cosmetic company would be whether to place the toilet paper in the ladies' room with the flap over or under. I run Scarlet Woman. Any product ideas have been generated by me or my staff. My mother confines her interest to what looks good and what other people think of her. Neither concern is conducive to running a business. Except when it comes to packaging. My mother is great at packaging."

She said that in a way that made him wonder if Carly was talking about her mother packaging cosmetics or packaging herself. "That may be true, but I am not imagining her worrying about you."

She rolled her eyes in a way that suggested she'd been through this before. "Did you ever see the movie *Terms of Endearment?*"

"No."

"It figures. Anyway, in the first scene, the mother wakes the sleeping baby up just to check that she's all right. That's Charlotte to a tee. I shouldn't call her my mother; she's more like my smother. Only she doesn't do it herself. She hires people to spy on me."

She let out a put-up sigh. "Why would anyone want to harm me? I mind my own business, I don't sleep with anyone's husband, I don't take out loans from the neighborhood shark. And I have never stolen anyone's trade secrets. Why would I? Scarlet Woman is the third-leading black-owned cosmetics firm in the country. I'm ambitious, but I wouldn't resort to deceit to get on top."

Jackson pondered this. Carly might be right that Charlotte was overprotective, but he suspected there was more to Charlotte's story that neither he nor Carly knew about. If she'd simply wanted him to tail her daughter, why wouldn't she have come out and hired him directly?

"Despite what you think, I believe your mother is in some sort of trouble or she wouldn't have gone to such lengths to invent an elaborate ruse."

She was silent for a long moment, biting her lip with her eyes averted. When she looked at him again, she said, quietly, "Do you really think so?"

"Yes, I do. As melodramatic as Charlotte is, it could turn out to be nothing serious, but she is worried about something connected to you."

She didn't say anything, but this time when she started to walk back to the house he didn't try to stop her. He figured she had enough to digest for the moment, and he wasn't going anywhere. But she surprised him by leaving the front door open instead of slamming it in his face.

He gazed up at the house a moment, a two-story, Spanish-style house with an Italian tile roof. When Charlotte told him that Carly owned a home in Westchester, he'd been surprised. Didn't driven career women prefer the city? Or maybe a town house in downtown Brooklyn or Jackson Heights where gentrification had sent property values skyrocketing? This house didn't exactly have a white picket fence around it, but it was a comfortable-looking home in a quiet neighborhood, the opposite of what he would have expected from her.

The house appealed to him on a different level as well. Though he'd lived in an apartment all his adult life and passed his adolescence in his aunt's house in upstate New York, he'd always wanted a house like this one, a house like the one that he'd shared with his father after his mother died and before his father passed away. The house on Bruner Avenue hadn't been as large, nor did it possess as much land around it, but it had exuded the same homey ambiance. He wondered if the welcome on the inside was quite as warm.

He crossed the threshold and closed the door behind him. The small foyer opened onto a staircase directly in front of him. To the right was a large dining room with heavy Spanish-style furniture. To the left was a living room complete with a fireplace and a window seat. All that he could see was decorated in soft shades of cream, white, and pink. Indeed a very inviting and feminine space, one that seemed at odds with what he knew of the woman who lived there.

He moved into the living room where she was already pacing with her head down and her arms crossed. She looked up at him as he entered but didn't motion for him to sit.

"We can't tell her I know who you are. She knows me

well enough to know I'd never put up with someone following me around willingly. Then we'll never find out what she's up to."

He admired her in that moment. She'd decided to trust him, and having made the decision she was willing to act on it. And he also realized the reason she'd come outside in the first place was not that she'd known who he was, but what he was. It was her way of letting whoever her mother had hired know she was on to them and embarrassing them with that knowledge at the same time.

"I was afraid you'd say that."

She tilted her head to one side. "Why?"

"Otherwise we could let 'Bruce' die the slow torturous death he deserves."

He saw that his attempt to lighten the mood had worked when Carly smiled. Not much of a smile, but the first he'd seen from her. "You know, if you two were trying to fool me, you should have picked a better name than Bruce. It tipped me off immediately."

"I don't strike you as a *Bruce*?"

"Uh, no. Not even Bruce Wayne." She inhaled and let it out in one huff. She was back to being all business again. "What do we do now?"

"For starters, you point me toward your bathroom so that I can wash up. Then you tell me about this anniversary celebration you're planning."

She looked at him as if she hadn't been staring at him for the past half hour. "Oh, of course. This way." She walked past him. "You think that's what this has to do with?"

"It seems logical. Is there anything else new going on?"

"Not that I can think of." She led him to a small bathroom back past the staircase. "There are fresh towels in here, whatever you need. If you like, I have a shirt I think will fit you."

"I'd appreciate that," he said, though he had another in the car. He might as well take advantage of her accommodating mood while it lasted.

He watched her walk off toward the stairs before shutting the door and turning on the faucet. The fixtures were in the shape of small birds, almost too tiny for his big hands to operate without breaking. Shaking his head, he thought of Carly. What a contradictory woman!

He didn't understand her, her animosity toward him or her relationship with her mother. Then again, it wasn't his job to understand her, just to make sure nothing happened to her. But even that didn't seem like the easy task Charlotte had assured him it would be. She was too independent and too headstrong to make his life any easier. But she did trust him, at least a little bit. That had to count for something. If Charlotte was right about her daughter being in danger, he hoped it would be enough.

Chapter 6

The first thing Carly did when she got to her bedroom was to examine her face in the mirror above her dresser. She sighed, relieved that the heat she felt in her face didn't show in her complexion. "I hate that man, I really hate him," she told her reflection, but without any conviction or feeling.

It really wasn't his fault that she'd finally gone and done the unthinkable after all these years. She was attracted to one of her mother's lovers. God, what a laugh Charlotte would have if she knew.

Now she realized what had bothered her about Jackson from the beginning. The moment he'd walked into the conference room, she'd started salivating as if she were one of Pavlov's dogs and someone had rung the dinner bell.

Okay, she could deal with that. She had dealt with that. She'd put that initial attraction out of her mind. He was her mother's man and therefore a nonman to her. That's how it had always been. But then she'd never found herself attracted to any other man her mother had brought home. They'd simply existed, like a harem full of eunuchs.

Why did this one have to be different? Especially when it seemed required of her to spend time with him to figure out what craziness her mother had gotten herself into? She wasn't the sort of frivolous woman developing a new crush every other week. And that's all it could be. What man in his right mind, given the choice between her and her mother, would actually pick her? He'd have to be a blind paraplegic with no sense of smell. Maybe then, but there really wasn't any competition. Charlotte had already won.

She reminded herself that she didn't know him, wasn't sure she wanted to know him. She had a vague memory of him from her childhood. He'd made fun of her hair that thanks to Ms. Clairol she now wore in a more suitable shade of dark brown. She'd gotten into trouble with her father for doing what came naturally: kicking the stuffings out of him. Her father told her she had to be nice to him because he and his father were going through a rough time. She'd obeyed, but thankfully she'd never seen him again.

No, she didn't want to know him. She just wanted to make sure her mother hadn't gotten into any trouble she couldn't get out of. In all likelihood, one of her mother's boy toys had finally wised up enough to sue for sexual harassment. And while such a prospect wasn't life-threatening, Carly wanted to save her mother from public embarrassment if she could.

She looked her reflection square in the eye. "I will not be attracted to my mother's boyfriends. I will not be attracted to my mother's boyfriends."

She sighed. Like that was really going to help any. But she should have learned her lesson, shouldn't she? *The attractive guy following you around is not interested in you. He may take what you offer, but he still works for your mother, and in this case he is sleeping with her, too.*

She brushed her fingertips across her eyes. What a mess! Massaging her temples with her forefingers, she made a vow to herself. If it killed her, she wouldn't let him know how he affected her. She could do that.

She'd done as much so far. She threw off her robe and dressed in the most innocuous outfit she owned, a pair of white leggings and an oversized white T-shirt with a floral design on the front.

She put on her glasses, combed her hair into a pony-tail, and surveyed herself in the mirror. Now all she needed were some braces on her teeth for the real temptress in her to come out. She laughed both at her-self and the ridiculous situation in which she found herself. Then she found a shirt she knew would fit him, one of the ones she used as a nightshirt. Heading down the stairs, she reiterated her vow to keep her attraction to herself.

That promise lasted until the moment Jackson opened the bathroom door in answer to her knock. He stood there with a towel around his neck, but for the most part his chest and arms were bare. Involuntarily, her breath sucked in and her eyes went on a pleasure tour, roving over his exposed muscular flesh.

He plucked the shirt from her fingers, startling her. She blinked and looked up at him, mortified to find a knowing look in his eyes, a look of challenge. He pulled the shirt over his head. The damn shirt fell to her knees, but fit like a second skin on him.

Tucking the ends into his pants, he winked at her. "Thanks."

Carly gritted her teeth. So much for keeping her lit-tle crush a secret. He didn't have to look so smug about it though, did he? If having women fawn all over him was what his ego required, it was no wonder he was with Charlotte. She could dote on a man like no other woman Carly had ever seen.

Carly straightened her spine and looked at him as levelly as it was possible to look at a man a foot taller. "I'll be in the kitchen when you are ready to talk about my mother. Remember her? She's the one who pays for whatever it is you do."

Jackson laughed to himself as he watched her stalk off toward the kitchen. *Little Miss Incomprehensible strikes again.* First she showed up in that getup looking so young and innocent that only a pervert could manage to get turned on. Yet there was nothing innocent about the look she'd given him. He probably shouldn't have teased her, but until then he thought she found him as interesting as a piece of plywood. He didn't know why he cared one way or another, especially since she still believed he was her mother's lover. He didn't know why that bothered him either, except that he didn't like the idea of anyone believing he'd sleep with a woman for money. He'd love to disabuse her of that idea, but as stubborn as she was, he doubted she'd listen. He still doubted she believed either she or her mother was in any danger.

He followed his nose to the kitchen where she already had bacon frying in one pan.

She didn't look at him, but she said, "Do you prefer eggs, pancakes, or waffles?"

His stomach rumbled at the prospect of eating any of the proposed choices. "I didn't realize you were including me in your breakfast plans."

She shrugged. "I figured the orange juice you had this morning wasn't a sufficient meal."

She did dart a glance at him then and her eyes held a twinkle of mischief. His eyebrows lifted. Just when she had him convinced she possessed no sense of humor whatsoever. He also supposed that was the closest thing to an apology he'd ever get out of her. "Fair enough. What can I do to help?"

"You can stay out of my way. Have a seat." She motioned toward the kitchen table with the tongs she used to turn the bacon.

He did as she said, turning the nearest chair around so he could straddle it facing her. She moved around the kitchen briskly, with her back to him, ignoring him. That gave him time to glance around the kitchen. Tiled in a sunny yellow and white pattern, the kitchen was large by any standard and equipped with every imaginable appliance. Judging by what he'd seen of the downstairs, he'd guess that there had to be at least three bedrooms upstairs.

He focused on her again as she poured batter into a skillet. It occurred to him that he'd never given her an answer as to which he preferred and she'd stuck him with his least favorite choice.

"Do you live here alone?"

Blinking, she glanced at him. "I'm sorry?"

"I asked you if you lived here alone."

"Why?"

He shrugged. "Just curious. You have a lot of space for just one person."

Her gaze hardened and she frowned. "Last I remember we were talking about the anniversary celebration. The first phase of that takes place next Wednesday on the Vineyard."

He hid a smile. That was one way to tell him her personal life was out of bounds. "What does that entail?"

"Actually, it's in two parts. That morning we're taping a commercial for our fall color palette—Vineyard wines. We've invited some of the press up to cover the shoot. Later that night, we're holding a party, an old-fashioned clambake. We've made reservations for most of the guests to stay at one of the hotels off Circuit Avenue. A trolley will bring them back and forth between the party and where they are staying."

"What else?"

"That's it. Except we are providing a sightseeing tour around the island in the afternoon. The next day everyone either goes home or stays on their own dime. I was planning to stay a few extra days myself. Samantha Hathaway, the actress who models for us, and her husband have a house up there. They asked me to spend the week with their family."

He debated telling her he knew both Sam and Adam, probably better than she did. There would be time enough for that later. "And after that?"

"I'll be coming home. A month later, we'll have the official anniversary party at a hotel in the city, once the film from the shoot is ready."

As she spoke, he'd taken his notebook from his back pocket and written down most of what she said. "Who's invited?"

"Some of the press from the shoot. A lot of people from the cosmetic and fashion industry. I can get you a list if you like."

"That would be helpful." Hopefully someone with a real motive to threaten Charlotte would pop up on that list.

She came to the table and laid a heaping plate at the place where he should have been sitting. "Enjoy."

He rearranged himself to oblige her. He'd been watching her the entire time she'd been at the stove and hadn't realized she hadn't made the choice for him. She'd made all three, plus the bacon. "Thank you."

"I'll be right back."

He had no idea where she disappeared too, but his stomach growled too loudly for him to wonder about if for too long. He'd demolished half the food by the time she came back carrying a sheaf of papers. She dropped it on the table beside him and sat across from him.

"Here are the lists. One is for the shoot on the Vineyard, the other is for the formal event. I included everyone's contact information as well as their company affiliation. If there's any other information you need, please let me know."

He wiped his mouth with his napkin and picked up the stapled papers. All the information she mentioned was laid out in easy-to-understand grids. "Are you always this efficient?"

"I try to be."

He hid another smile by forking the last of the eggs into his mouth. One of these days someone was going to have to do some serious work on this woman's funny bone. "I appreciate it."

She checked her watch. "If there's nothing else, I'd like to get some work done today. Take your time. I trust you can let yourself out when you're finished."

She turned to walk away, presumably to head back to wherever she'd gotten the papers from.

He grasped her arm as she tried to pass him. "I thought we agreed not to tell your mother you know who I am."

She pulled away from his grasp, crossing her arms in front of her. "We did."

He stood and faced her. "What do you think she'll say when I show up at her apartment without you?"

"I don't know. I really don't care what you tell Charlotte. She's your problem, not mine. Why don't you go whisper a few sweet nothings in her ear or whatever it is you do that she finds so attractive and leave me out of it?"

"Maybe I'll just take my shirt off."

Carly bit her lip and glared at him, though she probably deserved that much or worse. "Look, what you and my mother do is none of my concern."

"No, it isn't. But for the record I am not sleeping with your mother."

She cast him a scoffing look. "Oh, really? How gullible do I look?"

"At the moment? Very. That little scene you witnessed was part of Charlotte's act to convince you I was one of her, what does she call them, assistants?"

Well, it had certainly been convincing. And now she didn't know what to think. She could believe he had better sense than to get mixed up with her mother. What she couldn't fathom was her mother, the woman who put the word *harlot* in Charlotte, not snapping him up like the last petit four on the platter. The old girl must finally be losing her charm.

"If you say so." She had meant to sound flippant, but instead she sounded unsure of herself and she hated that. "As I said, finish your breakfast. I'll be in my study."

He didn't bother to try to stop her as she moved off, even though he'd lost any appetite he'd had for food. He scraped his plate into the garbage pail he found inside one of her cabinets, washed the breakfast dishes, then went to check the lock on her back door. It wasn't unlocked as he'd first thought, but broken. It didn't appear to have been tampered with, but worn out from use. He called Drew to have him take over the watch again. Maybe he'd have better luck avoiding Carly's sharp tongue and breakfast beverages. He ought to call a locksmith, too. Even if Charlotte was wrong, an unlocked door was an invitation to trouble. He'd take care of it when he got back.

He debated whether he should tell her he was leaving but decided against it. He supposed they'd formed some tentative truce, and for the moment he didn't want to disturb that. When Drew showed up, Jackson got in his car and drove to Charlotte's.

The first thing she asked when she opened the door

to him was not the "what are you doing here?" or the "where's Carly?" he expected. Instead she arched one perfect eyebrow and said, "Why are you wearing my daughter's shirt?"

He walked past her into the apartment. "Long story."

"I have time."

She motioned for him to sit. Rather than choose the chair she indicated, he settled on the settee, the only item of furniture that seemed sturdy enough to hold his weight.

"If you must know, she dumped a cup of orange juice on me. Seems she has an aversion to having strange men sitting outside her house. Why didn't you tell me this isn't the first time you've hired a private investigator to watch over Carly?"

"I didn't think it was important." She sat in the chair across from him and crossed her legs. "Did she really throw her juice on you? That's so unlike her."

She seemed on the verge of laughter, which annoyed him. "Yes, and I don't find it particularly funny, either. She came out of the house to let me know she was on to me, which would have been a dangerous move if I had been someone else not hired by you."

Alarm flashed in her eyes. "I hadn't thought of that."

"I thought not. Look, Charlotte, I won't go against your wishes, but you should level with your daughter. She's a big girl. She can handle whatever trouble you've gotten yourself into. But how can she protect herself if she doesn't realize she's in any danger?"

Never mind that he'd already gone against her wishes and told Carly everything he knew, he'd just given her an opening to level with him too by implying that her troubles might not be exactly as described. He'd thrown in a little guilt on top of it, implying that she placed Carly in additional peril by leaving her exposed.

Charlotte didn't rise to any of the bait he'd left for her. "I can't do that, Jackson. I wouldn't presume to claim that I have been the perfect mother for Carly. I wouldn't even say I've been adequate. The only thing I've ever been able to guarantee is her safety. That's why I hired you."

She shook her head. "And if Carly ever objected to what I did so strongly, she would have complained about me to her father, which she never did, not even when she was very small."

Or maybe even as a young girl she'd been protective of her mother. As much as Carly might resent Charlotte's interference, she'd only been willing to talk to him once he'd mentioned that her mother might be in danger. He didn't understand Charlotte's adamant refusal to tell Carly the truth, but it didn't really matter. He had another, more urgent subject he needed to discuss with her.

Years ago, when he'd first started to investigate his father's case, he'd called her and asked her what she remembered from that time. She'd told him that her husband didn't share his work with her and that she'd liked his father and that it was a shame that he'd died so young. But that was all he'd gotten out of her. He'd honestly thought she didn't know anything, but given her penchant for keeping secrets, he'd changed his mind.

"What do you remember about my father?"

Clearly his question surprised her. She shifted in her seat, adjusting the red caftan she wore. "What do you mean?"

"I once asked you what you knew about my father's trial and you said you didn't know anything."

"I don't. I told you Alex never involved me in his work. He was old-fashioned in that way. He tried to shield me from the ugliness often associated with defending criminals."

"But you must have had your own impression of what was going on. You saw the news, you read the paper. The woman who was killed was a friend of yours."

"Yes, Sharon was my friend, a good friend. She was the type of person everyone loved. Black, white, young, old, it didn't matter. The entertainment industry produces so few genuine people, and Sharon was one of them. So, no, I can't imagine anyone wanting to kill her, not for any reason that makes sense. My guess would be that someone became obsessed with her. We didn't call it stalking back then, but more than one celebrity has met their end at the hands of a crazed fan."

He was aware of that. In fact, he'd recently seen an issue of *Unsolved Mysteries* about celebrity homicides and the Sharon Glenn case was mentioned. That's what had started him looking again. He'd contacted the producer who had put the piece together only to find out he hadn't done any real research into the case, he'd gotten all his information from old reports. Then Duke Anderson had called. Somehow Jackson didn't think those two incidents were unrelated.

"Do you have any of his old files? Case notes?"

"I got rid of all of Alex's records a long time ago. It seemed pointless to keep them, and once I moved out of the house I had nowhere to put them. I'm sorry, Jackson. I wish I could be of more help to you."

Somehow he doubted that. He didn't know why he suspected she lied to him or why she would want to, but he'd been around enough to know when someone spoke the truth and when they didn't. Besides, she was an actress; she lied for a living.

He stood, figuring he'd be wasting his time to question her further. "I better get going then."

She rose to her feet also. "Back to Carly?"

"Yes." Though the prospect of spending another night in his car held little appeal.

Charlotte gripped her fingers together, an uncharacteristically nervous action. "Tell her, tell her . . ."

The same thing every mother wanted to tell her daughter? "She knows, Charlotte."

She smiled. "You're a dear, Jackson." She kissed his cheek, then stepped back from him.

He snorted. If he was such a damn dear, why wouldn't she tell him the damn truth?

Chapter 7

When Jackson got back to Carly's, the first thing he noticed was that Drew's car was there but Drew wasn't. At six feet five and 225 pounds, there was only so much hunkering down the man could do. Jackson parked his car and checked anyway, just in case Drew had slumped over on the other side asleep.

"Damn!" Where the hell was Drew? And if he wasn't here, where was Carly? He pulled out his cell phone and called Drew's. Drew picked up on the third ring and issued his usual greeting.

There was laughter in Drew's voice, and in the background Jackson heard a woman giggle. If Drew was off somewhere partying, Jackson would wring his thick neck. Sometimes Drew could be as responsible as a two-year-old with a big box. "Where the hell are you?"

"I'm up in Carly's house."

That was Carly he'd heard laugh? Inconceivable! "Who else is with you?"

"We're here by ourselves. Where are you?"

"Outside. I'm coming in."

"You do that."

Jackson switched off the phone and clipped it to his belt as he walked up to the house. The door opened before he got a chance to knock. Drew stood there with one hand on the doorknob, the other holding what looked like a spare rib.

"Hey, cuz, how's it hanging?"

Jackson resisted the urge to give a flippant response. "Where's Carly?"

"She's in here, man. What's eating you?"

Jackson pushed past his cousin to find Carly on the sofa. A wealth of Chinese food was spread out on the coffee table before her. She had on the same outfit, but several wisps of her hair had come out of her ponytail to frame her face, lending her a softer look. She gazed up at him, her eyes twinkling, her mouth tilted in a smile. "Hi."

For a moment, he couldn't think of a comprehensible thing to say. Was this the same woman who'd thrown her damn juice in his face? Then he thought he understood the transformation. There were two empty beer bottles on the table.

"What exactly have you two been up to?"

"Just hanging out."

Drew's voice pulled his attention from Carly. "Really?" And how had Drew wangled his way into the house in the first place? From the looks of him, neither Drew nor his clothing had suffered a trial by liquid first.

He turned to Carly, intending to ask her what had happened to all the work she supposedly had to do that day. She was already on her feet, her smile of a moment ago replaced by a look of anger mixed with profound disappointment. For the life of him he couldn't fathom what caused her Jekyll-and-Hyde transformation.

"I'm sure you two have things to discuss. If you'll excuse me, I'll be in my study."

She marched off toward the opposite corner of the room without really looking at either him or Drew. He'd once wondered who was loonier, the mother or the daughter. He thought he'd finally found his answer.

"What is with that woman?" he asked more to himself than Drew.

Drew came up to stand beside him and pulled out his handkerchief and tossed it to him. "It might help, if you were trying to convince one woman that you weren't sleeping with another, if you didn't carry the first one's mark around with you." Drew flicked his index finger, indicating Jackson's left cheek, the same cheek Charlotte had kissed.

He wiped his face and the handkerchief came back streaked with the same bloodred color of Charlotte's lipstick. He said a few words he was glad Carly wasn't in the room to hear. He didn't care what Carly believed his relationship with Charlotte was, not much anyway. But he did care whether or not she thought he'd lied to her. The deeper he got into this mess, the more he was convinced Charlotte hid a secret that could be damaging to all of them.

If it ever came down to him really needing to protect her, Carly would never listen to him if she didn't trust him.

Jackson refolded the handkerchief so that the lipstick was on the inside and shoved it into his pocket. He focused on his cousin, who had already sat back down in front of a full plate. "How did you two manage to become so chummy?"

"Who? Me and Carly?"

"No, you and the pope. Of course you and Carly."

"She asked me if I wanted to come in. What was I going to say, no?"

"And I suppose she was the one downing the Tsingtaos?"

"Nah, those are mine."

"Drinking on the job—"

"Since you aren't paying me anything, I'm just doing you a favor. Drinking on a favor is allowed."

He couldn't argue with that kind of logic. He sat on the sofa opposite Drew. "So what did you two talk about?"

"You. Mostly." Drew shoveled a forkful of shrimp-fried rice into his mouth.

Almost dreading the answer, Jackson asked, "What did you tell her?"

"Only that you were the most decent guy I knew. That you wouldn't be taking advantage of her mom or anyone else's and that I'd trust you with my life if it came down to it."

Jackson leaned over and snagged one of the spare ribs from its container. He'd gone to live with his aunt, Drew's mom, after his father died. To this day Drew mostly treated him like a pesky younger brother cramping his style. So Drew's appraisal of him was surprising. "All that?"

"Yeah, then you breeze in here and blow it all to hell."

He bit into the spare rib. "Didn't I just?"

"What's the big deal? I thought you said you didn't think there was much to this. You changed your mind?"

"I don't know. Charlotte's hiding something. That much I do know."

Drew wiped his mouth with a paper napkin. "I'm out of here. If you need anything, you know where I am."

Jackson walked him to the door. "Thanks for everything."

Drew shook the hand he offered. "No problem. If you ask me, you'd be better off forgetting the mother and hooking up with the daughter." Drew poked him in the chest to emphasize his point. "See ya."

Drew sauntered off and Jackson closed the door behind him. Yeah, he'd make a play for Carly right after he had root canal surgery and a prostate exam. The last two would be more pleasant. He went back to the living room and cleaned up the remains of Carly and Drew's lunch. If this kept up, he'd end up charging her for maid service.

Afterward, he went to Carly's study and knocked on the open door. She sat on the sofa in her office surrounded by stacks of paper. "Got a minute?"

"Not really. Your cousin is very entertaining, but his visit put me off schedule."

Drew's *visit?* He ground his teeth together, wondering if she said that just to annoy him. He refused to rise to the bait.

"I know how it must have looked, but for the last time, there is nothing going on between your mother and me."

She lifted the paper from her lap that she'd been reading and focused on it. "If you say so, Jackson."

"I don't say so. It's true. And even if it weren't, why are you so bent out of shape over it?"

She tossed the papers onto the sofa beside her. "I'm not bent out of shape over anything. I don't care what you do. What I do object to is being lied to, to being made to feel like a fool because I believed what you told me."

He leaned against the door frame. "I didn't lie to you, Carly. Give me one good reason why I would?"

"Because you care about my opinion of you and you know I could never respect a man who was little more than a gigolo."

She had him pegged right. He did care. It did bother him that Drew made her laugh while he inspired nothing but her derision. Well, there was that one moment when she'd looked at him with a different emotion in her eyes. She probably held that against him, too, because what woman with any sense wants to be attracted to a man she holds in contempt? Either way, he was tired of trying to convince her she was wrong about him.

"Okay, fine. You win, Carly. Your mother and I are having wild animal sex, okay? Does that satisfy you? Or do you want the details, too? Or maybe there's a quiz you can administer. What side of the bed does she sleep on? How big is the mole on her left hip? Something like that."

"My mother doesn't have a mole on her left hip."

He pushed off the door frame. "I really wouldn't know one way or the other." He had already turned to leave when he heard her call his name. He didn't bother to stop.

"Jackson!"

This time he stopped and turned to face her. "What?"

"Don't go."

"Look, Carly," he began, not really knowing what he wanted to say.

"You can stay here. There's a guest bedroom next to the bathroom you used this morning."

He wondered if the reason for her about-face was that she finally believed him. This morning she couldn't wait to have him leave. "Why?"

"Between you and Drew, you're making my neighbors nervous." She sighed. "Let me ask you something. How would you feel if your mother brought home a string of men barely older than you were, treated them better than she treated you, cared for them more than she cared for you, even though they were disposable and virtually indistinguishable from one another?"

Still feeling testy, he said, "I'd be flat-out shocked considering she's been dead for thirty years."

"You know what I mean. Would you like those men?"

He sighed and his exasperation seemed to flow out with his breath. For the second time in two days, she sought to explain herself to him, which surprised him, and unaccountably pleased him. It meant that little girl he'd met was still in there somewhere. "No, I wouldn't."

"I can't change what my mother does, but I can control what I allow her to do to me, what she's willing to do to the company for her own pleasures."

Jackson shoved his hands in his pockets. He'd seen the same expression on Charlotte's face before he left her. She'd wanted him to tell Carly she loved her, and he didn't doubt that she did. But he also wondered if Charlotte had any idea how deeply she'd hurt her daughter.

But Carly's disapproval hurt Charlotte as well, a fact Carly seemed either not to notice or not care about. In fact, she seemed to revel in being as different from her mother as possible.

She canted her head to one side and crossed her arms. "What?"

He hadn't intended to voice his thoughts. How or whether Carly got along with her mother was none of his business, even if both women had a penchant for dragging him into the middle of things. But the challenge in her eyes changed his mind.

"I was just wondering. Is there anything you do or think or say that isn't designed to be in direct opposition to your mother?"

"You don't know anything about me or my mother."

He shrugged. "Maybe not. Maybe I don't know anything about anything. My mother is a photograph my father kept beside his bed. She died before I was old enough to remember her. It just seems to me you'd want to cut the mother you do have a little slack."

She looked at him as if he'd struck her. "Well, thank you, Jackson, for that bit of home truth. If you'll excuse me."

She slipped back into her office and shut the door with enough force to make the glass panes rattle. He

stood there for a long moment without moving. Part of
him wanted to go after her, to soothe whatever demons
caused the hurt expression in her eyes. Though she no
longer seemed to hold him in the same regard she did
before, at least not for the same reason. He knew she
wouldn't welcome any overtures from him, either.

Well, he couldn't stand there in the middle of the
floor forever. He went out to his car, got the bag he
kept there for just such emergencies, and went back to
the house. Time to do what he did best, wait. He'd
picked up the skill sitting at his father's bedside. In his
last days, Donovan Trent had lapsed into a coma from
which no one, not even Jackson, had expected him to
recover. For twenty-six days, Jackson had kept a vigil
until the line on his father's heart rate monitor had
gone flat and he had quietly slipped away.

That fall when Jackson started a new school in his
aunt's neighborhood to the ubiquitous "How I Spent
My Summer Vacation" essay, he'd written one line. *I
watched my father die.* He'd figured that summed up the
experience, but it earned him a trip to the school psy-
chologist's office for evaluation. Jackson could laugh
about it now, but no one had been amused when he
told the prissy, uptight woman that the ink blot hanging on her wall reminded him of female genitalia. At
fifteen, he'd had no basis for the comparison. It had
just been something to say sure to get on the woman's
nerves. That had gotten him several sessions with a private shrink until his aunt was convinced he wasn't some
sort of sexual deviant in the making.

Maybe that's what bothered him so much about
Carly's dislike of him. Here was another prissy, uptight
woman accusing him of wrongdoing without much
cause. If she knew how long it had been since he'd
been with a woman, she'd probably start calling him
Bruce again. It wasn't that he didn't like women or

hadn't had his share of them, but the type of woman that would jump into bed with you and expect little else tended to bore him and he tended to disappoint the type that wanted more before they'd jump into bed. He worked long hours unapologetically, he was never home, and when he was, all he wanted to do was sleep—alone. Not a profile conducive to building that long-term relationship.

He sighed. Rather than dwelling on his own inadequacies, he settled on the sofa with the list Carly had given him, Charlotte's phone records for the past month that a friend at the phone company faxed to him at his apartment, and his laptop. He started with the list Carly had given him. He didn't have too much interest in the media contacts that would be invited to the photo shoot. They were all a pack of vipers as far as he was concerned, and neither Charlotte nor Carly was likely to know any of them personally.

But Carly wasn't kidding when she said that the party a month later would be a major event. Of the three hundred names on the list, he knew about half from sports or entertainment industries, the society pages, or the political arena—including a former mayor of New York City. And judging from the number of checks in the confirmed column of her spreadsheet, this wasn't a wish list of folks who might show up. All these people were coming. He highlighted the names of the people whom he didn't know, to ask Carly about later.

He switched to Charlotte's phone records next, which didn't contain too many surprises: calls to friends, restaurants, and one particular health spa, which he sorted out using a reverse phone directory on his computer. The only name that appeared on both the guest list and Charlotte's phone bill was Paul Samuels, her husband's former law partner. At one time, Samuels had been a big deal in the legal and political arenas but had dropped out of sight. He wondered why Carly and her mother would still include him in their plans.

About six-thirty he rose from the sofa and stretched his back. His stomach rumbled, protesting the lack of sustenance. A lot of the time when he was working, he had no choice but to ignore his appetite, but thankfully he didn't have to now. That is, if the lady of the house didn't object to him nuking some of that leftover Chinese food in her microwave.

He hadn't heard a sound out of her since she closed the door to her study hours earlier. He knocked on the door. Rather than opening it, she called to him through the closed door. "Yes?"

"I was thinking of heating up some of the Chinese food."

"Help yourself."

"Can I get you anything?"

"No, I'm fine."

He thought he heard a sniffle, but he couldn't be sure. "Carly?" He tried the door, not completely surprised to find it locked. He contemplated going around to the side door to her office, but figured he'd find that locked, too.

"I'll have something later."

"Okay." He walked away, seeing there was nothing else for him to do save breaking down one of her doors. Maybe he shouldn't have been so adamant about proving to her that he wasn't having an affair with her mother. At least while she was busy thinking he was despicable she was speaking to him.

He supposed that fell under the heading of being careful what you wished for. Right now he wished he'd managed to keep his own mouth shut.

Chapter 8

Carly took off her glasses and swiped at the dampness on her cheeks. She hadn't gotten one iota of work done since she'd come back in here after closing the door in Jackson's face. His words kept circling around in her head. *Is there anything you do or think or say that isn't designed to be in direct opposition to your mother?*

Was that all she was, all that she had become? A reaction to whatever Charlotte did? She didn't have an answer for that. But she did know her worst fear on earth was ending up like her mother, a selfish, dependent woman whose chief goal was scratching whatever itch needed the most attention.

No, Carly was the good little girl without any vices. The selfless martyr who'd sacrificed her own desires to make sure her mother had enough money to squander. She'd given up her own dreams so long ago that she never even thought about them anymore, not even when she was alone. She'd kept her promise to her father to take care of her mother. But she couldn't remember the last time she'd felt contented with her life, let alone happy.

Despite everything, Carly loved her mother and knew that Charlotte reciprocated the best way she knew how. During one of their rare arguments, she'd accused Charlotte of being a spoiled, selfish older woman who had no clue how to be responsible. Charlotte had countered that it was better than being a bitter, frustrated younger one who took no joy in life. She had scoffed at Charlotte's words, but she saw now that her mother had been right.

In an odd way, what bothered her most was Jackson's easy appraisal of her. *Is there anything you do or think or say that isn't designed to be in direct opposition to your mother?* For him it was merely an offhand comment, tossed out because she'd demanded it of him. But how could this virtual stranger have such a clear vision into her soul when she hadn't seen it herself?

Especially considering how wrong she had been about him. She'd wanted to be wrong about him. Even though she was attracted to him, she'd wanted to believe that he was Charlotte's. That made him safer somehow, nonthreatening. When he'd walked in the door sporting Charlotte's lipstick, some part of her had been relieved, because she knew she could never really be tempted by one of Charlotte's men.

She'd invited him to stay, not because he'd finally convinced her that nothing was going on between him and her mother, but despite it. She knew if she hadn't, he would have spent another night staring at her house from a hot, stuffy car. She wasn't heartless enough to allow him to do that. But what was she going to do with him now?

Strike that thought. Even a dried-up almost-spinster like her knew what to do with a man like Jackson. Not that she would actually attempt to seduce him. Lord knew he had no interest in her and she had no need for rejection from a man she'd once thought was sleeping with her mother. But she knew something in her life had to give. Or rather she had to reclaim some of the life she'd given up. How to do that was the question.

Suddenly tired beyond belief, she pushed her papers onto the floor and stretched out on the couch. Like her fictional counterpart, she'd think about it tomorrow.

At eleven o'clock, Jackson decided to call it a night. Yawning, he stood and stretched his back. He hadn't heard a peep out of Carly since she'd closed her door that afternoon. He knocked on her door but got no answer at all this time. Maybe she'd fallen asleep on the sofa, but he showered and got into bed, gripped by a feeling of unease.

To top it off, he couldn't sleep. Too many things rolled around in his mind, not only Carly, but Charlotte's secret, Duke Anderson's warning, and the dull sense of dread that he'd never keep that promise he'd made at his father's grave site to clear his name.

He found the remote for the room's tiny television set and got back into bed. The drone of the local all-news station usually put him to sleep. Just as he was about to drift off to sleep, one news item caught his attention. Some bum had been found in an alleyway in Midtown Manhattan. The cause of death was unknown, but the name of that bum was Duke Anderson.

When Charlotte opened the door to Jackson the next morning, she knew her days of dissembling were over. Like his father, he was an even-tempered man, more prone to humor than to anger. She'd seen that in the little time she'd spent with him. But in his grim-set jaw and rigid posture she saw a certain brand of determination that would not be ignored. "We need to talk."

She'd seen the news report, and figured it would bring him here eventually. She gave it one last try, just to see if she could appease him without having to tell him anything or at least not everything. "Where's Carly?" He cast her such a chilling look as he walked past her to enter the apartment that she decided she'd be playing with fire to keep up the pretense any longer.

He stopped at the center of the room, hands in his trouser pockets. "Cut the crap, Charlotte. Either level with me or I walk out that door and you don't hear from me again."

She'd debated whether or not to go to tell him the truth once she heard about Duke Anderson's death, but now he wasn't giving her any choice. Life wasn't giving her any choice. If Alex's killer was willing to get rid of Anderson after all these years, he wouldn't stop there. They were all in danger. In an odd way she was relieved to give up part of the burden of it, even though she remained uncertain what Jackson would do with the information she gave him. "What do you want to know?"

"I spoke to Duke Anderson two days ago about my father's trial and now he's dead. Something tells me this is not a coincidence. You knew all along about my seeing him, didn't you? That's why you had Johnny follow me."

"Yes."

"Yet when I asked you yesterday what you remembered about my father's trial you told me you didn't know a thing. That was a lie, wasn't it?"

"Yes."

He didn't say anything for a long moment, and she wondered what ran through his mind because it didn't show on his face. Anger surely had to be a part of it. From his viewpoint, she had put them all in danger rather than trying to protect them. He was a private investigator and before that a policeman. To members of either profession, withholding information was tantamount to a mortal sin.

She could only rectify that by telling him what he wanted to know. All of it. Heaven help her, heaven help them all. "Sit down, Jackson, please."

Jackson did as she asked, though he noted she didn't follow her own suggestion. She paced the floor in front of the sofa, gripping her hands together. Finally she looked at him, and he saw such stark fear in her eyes that he wished for the first time that she had nothing to tell him.

"That man Duke Anderson didn't lie about your father. He was seeing Sharon Glenn. I know because she was one of my best friends. She was an up-and-coming starlet on one of the soap operas they used to film in New York. She'd just landed her first film role, a nice part, not the lead, but knowing Sharon, that wasn't far off, either."

She sighed, not in the dramatic way she usually did, but in a way that told him revisiting that time caused her pain. "She and your father met one night when he was moonlighting as a security guard for some cast party. She just struck up a conversation with him. Sharon was like that. She'd been raised in a little Bronx neighborhood and wasn't impressed with all the trappings stardom offered. She just wanted to act. Your father had no idea who she was, and she liked that. I think your father thought their relationship was some young girl's flirtation with jungle fever that would quickly fizzle, but Sharon had fallen in love with him."

Mentally, he shook his head. He didn't recall much of this time. Not about his father anyway. He only remembered his father hadn't been around as much as usual, which had suited Jackson fine. He'd been feeling his teenage oats, and not having an older authority around to cramp his style had held a lot of appeal. If he'd known how little time he had left with his father then, it would have changed things. But as they stood then, he was glad not to have his father on his back. "That's all very nice, but what has that got to do with anything?"

"Don't you see, Jackson? If I'd thought your father had been involved in Sharon's death, I would have done everything in my power to have him convicted. But I never believed that, not after the way she spoke about him. They did quarrel once in public that I know of, but that was because one of the men at some party they attended made a crude pass at her. Your father wanted to do the manly thing and punch his lights out. But Sharon convinced him it wasn't worth it. The man in question was powerful enough to make trouble for him."

"So you convinced your husband to defend my father?"

"Yes, and Alex was happy to do it. He loved Sharon like a daughter and wanted to make sure the right man went to jail for her murder. He didn't hold out much hope of winning though. Donovan's fingerprints were found all over her apartment. Sharon was strangled to death, and given that she was young, tall, and strong, it would have taken a powerful man, a man like your father, to accomplish that. Circumstantial evidence at best, but in the absence of any stray fingerprints the evidence seemed damning. Especially since Anderson, your father's supposed best friend, was ready to testify that he had picked Donovan up from her apartment on the way in to work. He said your father had seemed agitated that morning, not his usual demeanor."

No, his father had been one of the most even-tempered men he knew. "But your husband proved that Anderson was a drunk who had a grudge against my father."

"Not exactly. Alex was prepared to do that, hoping it would work. Donovan found Anderson drunk on the job and reported him. Anderson would have lost his job except he agreed to undergo treatment and counseling from the department of corrections. Anderson claimed he and your father remained friends, but Alex was trying to prove he had stayed near your father lying in wait for a time when he could pay Donovan back for nearly costing him his job.

"But Alex never had to do that. Anderson showed up in court visibly drunk. He recanted half his story and the other half he couldn't seem to keep straight. The prosecutor was furious, but there was nothing he could do. After that Anderson disappeared. No one knew where he went."

"To what did your husband attribute Anderson's about-face?"

"Alex thought someone had put him up to testifying but he couldn't go through with it. That's why he disappeared."

Jackson thought of the words Anderson had spoken to him. *I really liked your old man. I never had no grudge against him, like they said.* At the time, he'd thought Anderson had tried to intimate that someone had put him up to testifying against his friend, someone he feared, someone who had probably waited twenty years to kill him.

"How does any of this put Carly in danger?"

"Two things were going on back then that I thought were unrelated at the time. I had started receiving phone calls during the trial. A man's voice that promised harm would come to Alex if he persisted in defending Donovan. Vague threats, not like he would necessarily hurt Alex, but that someone would. For a defense attorney's wife, such calls aren't unusual. I told Alex about the calls, but he dismissed them like he dismissed all the others. I didn't know who that voice belonged to until that day in court when Anderson tes-

tified. I attended the trial every day and when I heard
his voice my blood ran cold, and when he disappeared . . ."

She'd assumed Anderson had tried to warn her and
gotten killed for his efforts.

She shuddered, seeming to draw in on herself. "Two
nights after Donovan was acquitted we were driving
home from his victory party. It was raining and the
roads were empty and very slick. Another car came out
of nowhere and rammed us from behind. They tried to
run us off the road. I was terrified, but Alex was a good
driver. If his heart hadn't failed him, we probably
would have gotten away."

She drew in a ragged breath and wiped at the dampness on her cheeks. In that moment, he wanted to
comfort her, but he also knew he needed to hear the
rest of her story. "What happened?"

"We crashed into a concrete barrier. I broke my leg
in two places and Alex was unconscious. I was pinned.
I couldn't even help him. Then I heard two voices, a
male and a female. I guess they were checking to see if
they had succeeded at their task. I pretended to be as
unconscious as Alex was, but I watched them through
half-closed eyes. I couldn't see the man, but I got a
good look at the woman."

"Why didn't you go to the police and tell them what
you saw?"

"I did, but they didn't believe me. They thought I was
having some sort of hallucination brought on by the
shock of the accident. You see, the woman I saw . . ."

"Yes?" he said, his anticipation boiling over.

"That woman was me."

Chapter 9

Jackson's brow furrowed. "What do you mean that woman was you?"

"It was like looking into a mirror. I was so shocked I almost gave myself away. Before either the man or woman could check us to see if we were still alive, the sound of sirens reached us. They ran back to their car and peeled out, I guess not wanting to be discovered."

"And you never saw this woman before or after?"

"Never, but that's the funny thing. A couple of weeks before Sharon died, she called me and told me she'd seen me the night before at some hole-in-the-wall Italian place up on Allerton Avenue in the Bronx. She'd been having dinner with her father and who should walk in to order takeout but me? She didn't think too much of my being there, because she knows how much I love pasta and this place had just been touted as the best in the city in one of the magazines. But my look-alike was there, dressed in red, with a man that wasn't my husband. She didn't approach me, because she didn't want to cause a scene in front of her father."

"But, boy, did she light into me the next day when she came over! She loved Alex, too. I had to get him to tell her that I was with him the whole time before she would believe me, that's how much this woman looked like me. I asked her who the man was she'd seen with

'me.' She said she didn't know, but I'm not sure I believed her. I think at that point she was embarrassed
enough just by accusing me of stepping out on Alex.
But you know what? Alex would never have believed
her if she'd come to him instead of me. When he'd get
on my nerves, I'd tell him that if I ever had to find myself a new man I'd get a younger man, not a crotchety
old coot like him, and I meant it, too."

Maybe she just realized what she'd said, how her
words to her husband had become a self-fulfilling
prophecy. She slumped into a chair facing him and put
her face in her hands.

He was tempted to ask her if she'd told him everything, but he figured that even if she hadn't, he heard
about as much as he could take for one day. Someone
had murdered Sharon Glenn and had been intent on
framing his father for the crime. Donovan would have
made a great fall guy if it weren't for Alex Thompson
and Duke Anderson going back on his story. So what
was this about? The lady who looked like Charlotte or
something else that none of them knew about? And
why now, after all these years, did someone seem intent
on silencing anyone connected to the crime?

He asked Charlotte as much. She lifted her head and
suddenly she looked every one of her fifty-seven years.
"They're reopening the case. The NYPD has this cold
case squad that looks into unsolved crimes and tries to
clear them. They're hoping to solve this one, a case
that might generate some interest to publicize the work
of the unit. A detective called me. I think his name was
Dutton. I have his number here if you'd like to have it."

"That would be helpful."

She pulled a slip of paper from the pocket of the red
caftan she wore. When he shot her a questioning look,
she shrugged. "I figured you'd want it sooner or later."

"What do you want me to do about Carly?"

"Oh, God, Jackson. I don't know." Her eyes brimmed with tears. "She's really in danger now."

"We don't know that. The last time I saw Anderson he looked like he could keel over at any moment. For all we know, his drinking finally caught up with him."

"Do you really think so?"

No, he didn't, but he doubted it was a wise idea to tell Charlotte that. "I don't know."

"You've got to get her away from here."

"How do you expect me to do that?"

"I don't know. I don't know. Tell her I asked you as my assistant to check on some things for me up on the Vineyard."

"She already knows I'm not your assistant, Charlotte." He motioned as if pouring juice over his own head.

"I forgot. I don't know what to tell you, Jackson. Just do it, please. I don't care how. As long as you don't tell her why you want her to go. I don't want to worry her in case it turns out to be nothing."

He groaned. She wanted results at the same time she tied his hands. "I'll see what I can do."

He left the apartment a few minutes later. He agreed with Charlotte that Carly would be better off away from here, at least until they knew the cause of Anderson's death. He couldn't fathom Charlotte's insistence on not telling Carly the truth, however. If worse came to worst, though, he knew he'd forget about what Charlotte wanted and do what was best for Carly.

Carly woke up with a start, disoriented and achy. It wasn't the first time she'd fallen asleep on that little sofa, but for a moment she didn't know where she was. She sat up and rubbed her eyes, realizing she no longer wore her glasses. She found them beneath her. One of the lenses had popped out and one earpiece had broken off.

Great! Just what she needed—to start the day off blind as a bat. She had a pair of contacts upstairs in her bathroom, but she rarely wore them. The prospect of sticking anything in her eyes on a daily basis held no appeal, but it was better than bumping into the furniture.

She sat up and brushed the hair from her face. She could imagine what a mess she looked like after spending half the night in here bawling her eyes out. She hadn't done that since she was a child, wept as if her world were ending. The cry had been cathartic on a number of levels, primarily as a reliever for all the stress she'd been under lately with the anniversary coming up.

But she'd also come to a decision last night, one she intended to honor this morning. She still had no idea how, but that didn't change her resolve. It was time for Carly to reclaim a little bit of herself, although she had no idea who that self was anymore.

She stood and stretched. Jackson was somewhere in her house. While she appreciated that his words had spurred her to examine her situation, she didn't necessarily want to bare to him the physical results of that examination, either. She still had some dignity left. With any luck, he was still asleep and she could make it upstairs to her room unnoticed.

She unlocked and opened her door and poked her head out. There was a man on her sofa playing solitaire with a deck of red-backed cards, but it was Drew, not Jackson. He noticed her before she had a chance to withdraw. "Morning."

Oh, hell. He'd seen her, so there was no point in playing coy. She stepped into the room, stopping to the left of the coffee table. "Where's Jackson?"

"He had to go out for a moment."

Lacking anything more intelligent to say, she said, "Oh." She blinked, still trying to banish sleep. "Are you hungry? If you give me a few minutes I can make you some breakfast."

He grinned. "Never ask a man my size if he wants food, ma'am. The answer is always yes."

She smiled back. "I don't mind, really. I rarely cook for anyone besides myself. I'll be right back."

She went to her room, showered, and dressed in a pair of khaki shorts and a black T-shirt. She put in the dreaded contacts and blinked them into place. As usual when she wasn't working, she didn't bother with a bra. She didn't have anyone to impress, not that what she had up top would impress anybody anyway. She brushed her hair and twisted it into a sort of ponytail, stuck her feet in a pair of black slippers, and declared herself ready.

Drew was already in her kitchen by the time she got there, his head stuck in the refrigerator.

As she approached, he straightened. "How does steak and eggs sound?"

He held a platter in his hand that contained the steaks she'd intended to fix for herself and Jackson last night but never cooked. "Sounds great. I'll put them under the broiler."

He lifted the platter out of her reach as she went to take it. "If you don't mind, I'll handle it. I'm no free-loader."

She shrugged. "Suit yourself. But if you poison me I will sue you."

"Fair enough." He winked at her. "I'll treat you to my famous secret marinade. I think the paper should be here by now."

That was a first—her getting kicked out of her own kitchen. She supposed Drew wanted to keep his secret sauce a secret. "Call me if you need anything."

She got her copy of the *Times* and settled on the sofa. Usually when the paper came, she turned to the business section first, the fashion section second, and ignored most of the rest. But today she was the new and improved Carly. She found the magazine section and turned to the puzzle page. When she'd been a girl, she and her mother had spent many Sunday afternoons lying on her parents' bed working on the puzzle. Carly hadn't known many of the answers, but the shared time together had kept them close. God, she missed those days when she and Charlotte could while away an afternoon together without the underlying rancor coming between them.

She retrieved a pencil from her study and started filling in answers. By the time Drew called her from the kitchen, she'd already figured out the quotation that ran through the puzzle, but little else.

As Drew helped seat her at one of the kitchen chairs she caught a whiff of his cologne, a woodsy scent that suited him. She watched him as he took the seat across from her. He was an attractive man in a big bear sort of way, with deep dimples in each cheek and twinkling brown eyes. He didn't have Jackson's raw sex appeal, but a girl could do a lot worse.

"Why are you looking at me like that?"

"Like what?" She feigned innocence, but she knew she'd been staring at him.

He put his fork down. "The last woman who looked at me like that took me for half of everything I owned."

"You were married?"

"I guess you could call it that. We had a license and a minister, but that was about it." He lifted one shoulder in an offhand gesture. "Chalk it up to being young and stupid." His gaze strayed downward from her face, over her body to her left hand, and back again in a lingering way. "How about you? Any disasters in your past?"

Carly swallowed. She knew exactly where his gaze had lingered: on her breasts. Drew hadn't been obvious about it, but it was so unusual for a man to pay any attention to her anatomy whatsoever that she'd noticed. Shocking! Was the man too blind to notice there wasn't much to see in the first place, let alone linger over? But he gazed back at her with an appreciative glint in his eyes.

Was this man actually flirting with her? Since the last time such a thing had occurred was when she was in college, she couldn't gauge. And what was she supposed to do about it? She didn't know what the old Carly would have done, but the new Carly she was this morning wanted to know for sure if he was attracted to her. She had little experience at flirting herself, but she'd seen Charlotte besot a man enough times to make a decent go of it.

She returned Drew's smile and lifted her left hand, and tapped her thumb against her ring finger. "Fortunately no." She brought her hand down and grasped one of Drew's in a sympathetic way. "I'm sorry things didn't work out for you, though."

Drew's Adam's apple bobbed and his thumb rose to brush her knuckle. Then he blinked and pulled his hand from hers. "How's the steak?"

For a moment, she focused on her plate, cutting off a small piece of meat while willing the smile of satisfaction that sprang to her lips to settle down. She couldn't help it, though. She'd barely touched him and he'd responded. Of course, he'd snatched his hand away from her. So maybe she'd overdone it a bit, but still. How long had it been since a man had any reaction to her at all?

When she looked up at him, a more benign expression covered her face. "Want me to try to guess what's in your secret sauce?"

He flashed her a boyish grin. "If you think you can."

She brought the piece she'd cut to her mouth, though she already knew what her answer was going to be. The steak was delicious though, juicy and flavorful. "Let me see." She made a show of savoring the bite she'd taken, an action she hoped he'd find stimulating. "I taste lemon, Worcestershire sauce, oregano . . ." She rattled off a few more ingredients. "Am I right?"

For a moment he looked at her with a stunned expression. Then he swiveled his head around to look at the counter where all of the ingredients she'd mentioned still sat. He offered her a sheepish grin. "Seems like if a man wants to keep a secret he should learn to clean up after himself."

She nodded. "Could be."

His expression turned serious. "Uh, you don't have anything going on with Cousin Brucie, do you?"

Was the man insane? Jackson didn't even like her. Still, she had no intention of answering that question when she wasn't sure why he'd asked it. "Would it bother you if I did?"

"I wouldn't want to step on Jackson's toes."

"Glad to hear that, cousin."

Her eyes flew to where Jackson stood, just inside the kitchen. She hadn't heard him come in and didn't know how he'd gotten in. He answered at least part of her question by walking forward to drop a set of keys, the ones that belonged to her mother, on the edge of the kitchen table.

"How'd it go?" Drew asked.

Jackson ignored the question. Instead he focused his scowling gaze on her. "Carly, go upstairs and put on a sweater. The air-conditioning must be on too high in here."

She stared at him, not having the slightest clue what he was talking about. The temperature was fine. But she didn't want to argue with him in his present mood. She wasn't really hungry anymore anyway. She rose from the table. "Excuse me."

As soon as Carly was out of the room, Jackson punched Drew in the shoulder, hard. It was the only way to get through his thick hide. "What the hell is wrong with you?"

"There's nothing wrong with *me*. What's your problem?" Drew threw his napkin onto the table and rose to his full height, which topped Jackson's by about three inches. It was an intimidation tactic left over from their youth, one that Jackson had learned to ignore a long time ago.

"I'm looking at it. I left you here to take care of her."

Drew grinned. "And if you'd come back an hour later, I'd have taken care of her real good."

Yeah, right. Like Miss Priss 2004 would have gone along with that. Besides, Drew might have gotten her stirred up a bit, but he wasn't that much of an opportunist. Not usually.

"She's an innocent, man." Anyone who was around Carly for five minutes knew that. She didn't even have enough sense to know why he told her to get a sweater. Even from the other side of the room he could see the shape of her nipples beneath her T-shirt.

"And I've always wanted to be an educator."

"Have you always wanted to be six feet under? Leave the girl alone."

"Why? So you can have her all to yourself?"

He shot his cousin a droll look. "Why would I want to do that?"

Drew shrugged. "I don't know? Maybe because she's sweet and funny and kinda cute in an Uma Thurman sort of way."

Jackson leaned against the counter. Maybe he had it wrong. It looked like Carly had addled Drew's brain. Without those Coke-bottle glasses of hers, her eyes were huge and luminous, and as she'd retreated from the room he'd noticed that her legs were proportionately as long and shapely as her mother's.

He shook his head to clear that image from his mind. "I don't have time for this." He gave Drew the *Reader's Digest* version of what Charlotte had told him.

Drew's first response was a high-pitched whistle. "What do you need me to do?"

He handed Drew a slip of paper on which he'd written the name and number of the detective who was now in charge of the Sharon Glenn case. "See if you can get him to talk to you. Professional courtesy or whatever. Let me know what he says. See if you can do the same at the Five One. I don't know who's handling Duke Anderson's case but it's got to be someone out of that house."

Drew nodded. "What are you going to do?"

"I'm going to get her out of here, up to the Vineyard. She's scheduled to go up tomorrow night, but I figure it will give us at least one day without anyone knowing where she is. If it turns out Duke's death was an accident, then I got a free day at the beach."

Drew stood and Jackson walked him to the door. But the bigger man surprised him by grabbing him in a bear hug. "Watch yourself, man," Drew said on releasing him.

Jackson understood how he felt. They were the only family either of them had left. Neither of them believed he could afford to lose the other. "You do the same."

"Don't I always?" Drew let himself out and strolled down the walkway toward his car.

Jackson closed the door and leaned his back against

it. He'd told both Drew and Charlotte that he'd take Carly out of the city, but truthfully he had no idea how he was going to get that accomplished. She was stubborn and headstrong, and short of telling her the real reason he wanted her out of New York, he had no logical reason for getting her to go.

He pushed off the door and walked the short distance to the staircase. He couldn't hear a sound coming from upstairs and wondered what she was up to or if she'd welcome his presence up there. He decided to chance it, as he didn't have much choice.

There were four bedrooms at the top of the staircase, two on each side. First, he tried the room that appeared to be the largest. He paused in the doorway, finding Carly leaning over a suitcase on her bed. Her shorts had ridden up enough to show a hint of derriere.

Jackson swallowed. For a girl that was supposed to be homely, she sure managed to rev his motor at the moment. "Carly."

She spun around, obviously surprised. She clutched some article of clothing to her chest. Even so, he noticed she must have figured out what he'd meant by the sweater comment, because she'd put on a bra. *Damn!*

"What are you doing up here?"

Remembering his words to Drew, he was seized by an idea. "I wanted to ask you a favor."

"What's that?"

"The day your mother walked into my office was going to be my first day off in a long time. I was hoping to spend the day outdoors, enjoy a little sunshine . . ." He trailed off, trying to gauge her reaction to his story.

She tossed the garment she held into the bag and turned back to him with her arms crossed in front of her. "And?"

"And I wanted to know if you wouldn't mind heading up to the Vineyard a day earlier. I'll buy you an ice cream cone at Mad Martha's."

A hint of a smile turned up her lips. "So you've been before?"

"A few times." It occurred to him that maybe he ought to confess to his knowing Sam and Adam then, but decided to skip it. He needed her acquiescence first. "So what do you say?"

"We'll have to drive up."

"That's not a problem. It'll give me an excuse to take the Caddy out."

She shrugged. "I'm almost through packing. Is half an hour okay?"

"That's fine," he said cautiously, wondering what he'd done to gain her consent so easily. "I'll be downstairs." He turned to leave when she called him back.

"If I wanted to ask you for a little favor later, would that be all right? You know, a little quid pro quo?"

"What's the favor?"

"I'll tell you later, okay?"

He didn't like the sound of that but he agreed. "I'll need to stop by my apartment too."

"I figured." She shooed him away with a flick of her wrist. "The quicker you leave, the quicker I can finish packing."

Jackson left the room mentally shaking his head. It wasn't supposed to go like this. He thought for sure Carly would balk at leaving a day early, thereby leaving someone on her staff to pick up the slack of whatever she was supposed to do Monday morning. That didn't seem like her at all. And she wanted to ask him a favor? He loped down the stairs wondering exactly what he'd just gotten himself into.

Chapter 10

"Hush, you antisocial little beast," Charlotte fussed at Mr. Jingles. Every time the phone rang, which was often, Mr. Jingles went into a snarling fit. He didn't like the phone and when visitors showed up he hid under the bed. The only person other than her the dog seemed to like was John, and that was probably because John fed him.

Charlotte picked up the cordless phone and brought it to her ear. "Hello."

"Hi, Mom."

"Carly?" She recognized her daughter's voice, but it held a different quality she couldn't identify. "Sweetheart, are you all right?"

"I'm fine. I just wanted you to know that Jackson and I are heading up to the Vineyard a day early. The Wesley said it was fine, so that's where we'll be. You have the number, right?"

"Yes."

"And you'll be on the plane Tuesday morning?"

"Of course, darling."

"I'll call Nora tomorrow and make sure she has everything in place. See you when you get up there."

"Have a safe—" The line went dead before she had a chance to finish her sentence. Charlotte leaned back against her pillows and pulled the now-quiet Mr. Jingles onto her lap. What on earth had gotten into Carly? Even though Jackson had gotten her daughter to do exactly what she wanted, a feeling of unease gripped her.

"He'd better take care of my baby," she told Mr. Jingles, stroking the fur between his ears, though she didn't really doubt for a moment that he would. Aside from keeping Carly safe, she knew he wouldn't take advantage of her as another man might. For one thing, Carly would never allow it. The last time Charlotte had hired an investigator, it had been a man barely older than Carly in order for him to fit in on the campus of the college she attended.

When Carly came to her later, furious because she'd discovered that the man she was dating turned out to be a man she'd hired, Charlotte had tried to downplay Carly's anger by saying at least she hadn't slept with the man, considering he was such a lousy lay to begin with. Not that she had slept with him to know. It was Charlotte's way of telling Carly at least she hadn't gotten in too deep before she found out. But she'd watched Carly's face crumble and knew any words of warning came too late.

Charlotte hadn't had to go looking for that young man to fire him and sue the pants off his firm. He'd come to her, not to defend his actions, but to confess that he'd only behaved so unprofessionally because he'd fallen in love with her daughter. Carly wouldn't listen to him, though. She wouldn't listen to Charlotte either, not only that she'd never been to bed with the man, but also refusing to believe that he cared for her at all.

That was the last time Charlotte had hired anyone to look after Carly, until Jackson. And that was the last time Carly had ever mentioned any man to her mother. For all Charlotte knew, that was the first and last time

Carly had ever been with any man at all. Guilt ate at her now, as it often did, fearing that her own actions had cost her daughter any chance at happiness.

Or maybe she was simply out of sorts because John hadn't come back yet. When Jackson had phoned early that morning to say he was coming over, she'd sent John on some fool's errand that she doubted fooled him. She suspected he knew she wanted him out of the way, but it wasn't like him to stay away to punish her.

The sound of the outer door opening reached her and she relaxed. That is, until John appeared at her bedroom door bearing an expression on his face almost as determined as Jackson's had been.

"We need to talk," he said in a quiet voice. "There's something I need to tell you."

Dread flooded through her, knowing she didn't want to hear anything he might say with that look in his eyes. He took what looked like a wallet from his back pocket and tossed it to her. She picked it up and opened it. Inside lay a gold policeman's shield. Although she already knew the answer, she asked, "Whose is this?"

"Mine. I retired from the force seven years ago."

"You were a police officer?"

Pride flashed in his eyes. "I was a lieutenant."

Charlotte shook her head. "If you were a policeman, why did you become a chauffeur?"

"I didn't become *a* chauffeur. I became *your* chauffeur." He sat on the bed near her and shooed Mr. Jingles to the floor. "Five years ago a friend of mine heard you were looking for a driver. He knew I had a thing for you from way back. He suggested I interview for the job, as it was probably the only way I'd ever meet you. It was a lark, Charlotte. I never believed you'd hire me, and when you did I figured once you did a background check on me you'd discover I'd lied to you and fire me just as quickly. But you never checked on me, did you?"

She shook her head. "I told Carly I would, but I never did. I liked you and thought that ought to be enough. Why didn't you ever tell me?"

"Because I hadn't been working here a week before I realized I was falling in love with you. I overheard you talking with some woman about how the police treated you after your husband died. I figured you'd send me packing and I didn't want to go." He laced his fingers with hers. "I understand if this changes things between us."

Charlotte closed her eyes and pressed her lips together. So much about him was explained by his admission: his no-nonsense demeanor, his refusal to talk about his past. She had assumed that he'd led a hard life and out of respect for his privacy she'd never pried. She opened her eyes and gazed at him levelly. "If I wanted you to go, you'd be willing to walk away?"

"No, Charlotte, I wouldn't, but I would understand if you were angry with me."

"I am angry with you."

"Then we are in the same boat, since you've been lying to me from the first day Jackson walked in the door."

"Yes."

"There weren't any notes."

"No. How did you know?"

"For one thing, I'm the one who picks up the mail. I would have noticed. Second, although I'm retired, I still have my sources. I know about the phone calls, I know about Duke Anderson. You were right to get Carly out of town."

"I'm sorry, John."

"I know. Come here, baby." He pulled her onto his

lap and held her in a way that let her know everything
would be all right.

She burrowed closer to him, needing his warmth
and his security. "I'm so scared," she whispered against
his neck.

He pulled away from her and tilted her chin up so
that she looked at him. "Understand two things, Charlotte. I'm never going to let anything happen to you.
And you are not going anywhere without me."

Jackson lived in an apartment building on the
Bronx/Yonkers borderline, across from the Bronx
River Expressway. His apartment was furnished barely
enough to make it habitable: a sofa, the obligatory
manly-man big-screen TV, a coffee table. There was a
line of boxes stacked by the door, but there was enough
dust on them for them to have been standing there for
months.

When Carly glanced at him, he shrugged. "Maid's
year off. Why don't you have a seat? I won't take that
long."

Aside from the boxes, the rest of the apartment was
neat from what she could see. Unless he hoarded them
all in the bedroom, there wasn't a personal item, a me-
mento, a photograph in the place. She sat on the edge
of the sofa, wondering what the sparse furnishings in
his apartment said about him. Not much of a decora-
tor? That he didn't spend much time here? That he felt
little attachment to this place? Maybe he was moving,
as the packing boxes suggested, or more likely he had
never quite moved in.

Sighing, she sat back on the sofa. She didn't understand him, not that her understanding him was a
prerequisite for anything. But to herself she questioned
his motivation for sticking with this case when he

clearly didn't believe her mother was telling him the truth. Or why suddenly he wanted to get out of the city while Charlotte remained. It fit in with her plans, so she wasn't complaining, but one of these days someone was going to have to explain this whole mess to her.

Unable to keep still, she rose from the sofa and paced along the area behind the sofa. She had to be out of her mind contemplating what she was contemplating. The idea hadn't even occurred to her until she'd caught Jackson watching her pack in the reflection of her bedroom mirror. His gaze had been glued to her butt and her attention had been so focused on watching him that when he'd called her he'd startled her.

As shocking as that thought might be, he was attracted to her, at least a little bit. Or maybe he was just horny as hell. Either way it didn't matter too much, since that fit in with her plans, too. The new Carly wanted to experience all those things she'd denied herself for so long for no good reason. That included making love to a man she could at least pretend desired her. She didn't want any hot and heavy emotional scene. She doubted she could handle that. All she wanted was the proverbial fling, a few days to get her toes wet, not dive headfirst into the water. And as she figured it, that's all she would have with Jackson anyway.

What she saw in his apartment convinced her of the rightness of her rationale. He was a transient sort of man. He wouldn't hang around or want anything more from her. He'd take what she offered and not balk when she took it back. She could do this. If she ever got up the nerve to ask him, that is. She smiled to herself, wondering what Jackson would think when she called in her favor.

"What's so funny?"

She'd been lost enough in her own thoughts not to

hear his approach. She shook her head. "Nothing important." She glanced down at the black bag he held. "Ready to go?"

"Just as soon as we get the car."

Her brow furrowed. They'd left the car right outside the building. But once out on the street, he got her suitcase from the trunk and led her to a private house down the street.

He set both bags on the curb. "My neighbor lets me keep it here."

She followed him to the garage door, which he lifted easily. Inside was a large vehicle covered by a tarp. She stood to one side as Jackson removed it, revealing a fire-engine-red Cadillac convertible that must have been made in the fifties, tail fins and all.

He grinned at her. "You like?"

After seeing his apartment, she was surprised he had one possession he seemed to treasure. "Where did you get it?"

"It used to be my father's. Get in."

He held the passenger-side door open for her. She slid in across leather that felt like butter to her bare thighs. "Where are the seat belts?"

"There aren't any." He closed her door. "They didn't make seat belts in the fifties and they don't make any to fit the car."

She clamped her lips together. The old Carly would have balked at riding in a car without the proper safety equipment. But as big as this thing was, it would have to get hit by a semi to even feel an impact.

He must have read her thoughts on her face because he said, "Don't worry. I'm an excellent driver."

She'd seen that in the couple of times she'd ridden with him. Most New Yorkers drove by riding the horn and giving people the finger. By comparison, he drove like the fabled little old lady from Pasadena.

After stowing their bags in the trunk, he started the engine. "Ready?"

She nodded. In a way she felt as if she were embarking on an adventure, flying high without a safety net. But what if Jackson turned her down? She hadn't considered that possibility before, but he might. He more than might, he probably would. Just because a man stared at a woman's butt for a few seconds didn't mean he was hot to jump into bed with her. Maybe it just meant that said woman should have done a better job of keeping her butt covered.

She'd gone crazy, that was the answer. She'd lost her mind to come up with such a plan in the first place. Maybe she should just ask Jackson to take her home and she'd get on the plane tomorrow like the good little girl she was and forget this foolishness. Maybe she should just go back to her sane boring life where everything made sense and she risked nothing, not even the embarrassment of having a man who attracted her turn her down.

But she couldn't do that. She couldn't go back to being what she was, because she no longer wanted to be that person. In truth, she didn't know what she wanted, but she had to take the chance to find out.

Jackson turned onto the New England Thruway, trying to keep his mind on the road, rather than the long expanse of Carly's legs. She'd never changed out of the shorts she'd had on. There was no reason to. It was a seasonably warm June day, and the few clouds in the sky above did nothing to block out the sun.

Besides that, Carly hadn't said one word to him since he pulled out of the garage fifteen minutes ago. She stared off facing away from him, leaving him no clue as to what she was thinking.

He tried the same tactic he'd used before. "Dollar for your thoughts."

She turned to face him. A slight smile played on her lips. "Actually, I was thinking about you."

"Me? What were you thinking?"

"I was wondering if you'd always been a private investigator."

"No, I was a cop first."

"Really? What made you want to be a policeman?"

He lifted one shoulder. "I don't know." He'd never really thought about it much. When he was a kid, he'd thought his father's job was like being a cop, junior grade, like a minor league player waiting to move up to the majors. Even when he was old enough to know better, the job had still held some appeal. He'd graduated from college with a B.A. in criminal justice and had briefly thought about a law career. But in the end, he'd landed in the first job he'd ever really contemplated—being a policeman.

"Why did you leave the force?"

"I wasn't as well suited to the job as I thought I'd be."

"So you became a P.I.?"

"Yeah. The hours were worse, the pay was lousier. What can I say? I'm a glutton for punishment."

She laughed, a tinkling sound that pleased him. "But you still get to carry a gun."

"You've been watching too many TV shows. Not all P.I.s carry."

"Why don't you?"

He chose the most innocuous answer to the question. "I'm not interested in shooting anybody." He snuck a look at her. He couldn't tell if she was appalled or flabbergasted.

"What do you do if someone tries to shoot you?"

"I duck. Besides, most of the people I run into aren't interested in shooting me, either."

"Thank goodness."

At least she didn't want to see his hide get nailed to the wall. But he'd had enough of her twenty questions and decided to turn the tables on her. "How did you and Charlotte get into the cosmetics business?"

"It all started with a lipstick. Charlotte's favorite color got discontinued by a cosmetics company. I found the manufacturer and convinced him to sell us a limited quantity just so Charlotte would stop complaining. But so many women loved that color that they started to write to Charlotte, asking her where they could get it. We repackaged it and began selling it out of this little cosmetics boutique on Fifth Avenue. It sold so well, the next thing we knew we had several shades of lipstick and some blush that didn't look chalky on black women's skin. Most of the items were production overruns from other companies that were put into our packaging. Charlotte had some perfumier who was madly in love with her. I convinced him to create a fragrance for her, which was how Scarlet was born. Now someone else buys the overruns from our factory."

She sounded proud of herself, which he supposed she should be. How old could she have been ten years ago? Seventeen, maybe? And she, more than her mother, had started what had grown into a multimillion-dollar company. Amazing. At seventeen he'd been busy getting himself into trouble.

"Did you always want to be a successful businesswoman?" he asked, mimicking her earlier question to him.

"No."

"Then what?"

"It's silly."

She seemed determined not to tell him, which made him all the more determined to know. "Tell me."

She huffed out a breath. "If you must know, I wanted to be a singer."

"Have you got a voice?" She warbled a few off-key lines of "The Star-Spangled Banner." "Okay, keep the day job."

She smacked him on the shoulder, which surprised him. At no point before had she ever made a move to touch him in any way. In fact, she'd been different all day, not in any way he could put his finger on, but he knew it was true. Not that he was complaining. He appreciated the change in her, even if he didn't understand it.

The Steamship Authority at Wood's Hole, Massachusetts, was a madhouse of cars, pedestrians, and bicycles. Since they'd decided to come up to the Vineyard at the last minute, they had to wait on the standby line to see when they could get a ferry over. As it was a Sunday afternoon, with most people coming off the island rather than going on, the line moved quickly.

Once they'd parked in the hull of the ship, Jackson cut the engine, his gaze on Carly as she got out of the car. She stretched her back in an exaggerated way. "Now I know what you meant the other day about your sacroiliac. You may be used to sitting in a car for hours, but I'm not."

They had driven straight through to ensure that they had enough time to get on a ferry that night. Jackson's spine wasn't singing any hallelujahs either. Upstairs in the interior of the ship, they waited in line at the small concessions stand where Jackson bought a ham and cheese sandwich for each of them, a beer for himself, and a ginger ale for Carly. With their purchases in hand, they went out on the deck and found an unoccupied spot at the railing. The sun was beginning to go down, casting rays of crimson and gold on the water.

"It's beautiful, don't you think?" Carly said, tucking a strand of her hair behind her ear. The setting sun took most of the heat of the day with it and stirred up a strong, chill ocean breeze. "Mother Nature in all her glory."

"Mmm," he agreed, but his mind was more on his sandwich. He hadn't eaten at all that day. But while he devoured his meal, Carly fed most of hers to the gulls that flew alongside the ship.

He rinsed down the last of the sandwich with a swig of beer. "How long is this trip again?"

"Forty-five minutes. Just when you start to get bored you see land on the other side." She took a sip from her straw. "Have you made any headway in figuring out what my mother is up to?"

It was the question he dreaded her asking, but he knew she would get around to it sometime. "Don't worry about your mother, Carly. She's in good hands."

"That's not what I asked you."

He didn't want to lie to her, but he didn't see any way to tell her the truth without telling her everything. He decided to take another approach. "There's something I need to tell you before we get on the island."

She cast him a skeptical look. "Yes?"

"Adam and I are old friends from our days on the force together. I know Sam, too."

"Why didn't you tell me this before?"

"At first I was supposed to be *Bruce*, not myself. After that it never came up."

She shrugged. "That's no big deal."

The wind whipped up again, blowing tendrils of her hair around her face. He tucked a strand behind her ear. He felt her shiver beneath his touch. "Almost everyone has gone in."

"Chickens!"

He nodded in the direction of the interior of the ship. "Sure you don't want to head back to the coop?"

"And miss this glorious sunset? No way." She smiled up at him with her lower lip caught between her teeth. "Can't we stay out a little longer?"

"Is this the favor you wanted to ask me before?"

"No. Not yet."

He didn't know why he did it, but he pulled her in front of him and wrapped his arms around her. "Better?"

She nodded and settled against him. "Much better. Thank you."

Jackson smiled, glad Carly couldn't see him. She sounded as if he'd lent her his jacket rather than his body to keep her warm. He inhaled, breathing in the tang of the ocean and a delicate floral scent that was all Carly. She heated him as well, though if anyone had told him two days ago that holding this woman would give him a raging hard-on he'd have told them they were nuts. But here he was getting all turned on by the little pixie in his arms. Now what did that say about him?

He didn't know, but for the moment he felt contented to have her there while they watched the sun sink behind the horizon.

Chapter 11

"I think we have a problem here."

As Jackson stepped aside to let Carly enter the room she saw to what he referred. She'd booked a one-bedroom suite and when she'd called to say she was coming earlier, she hadn't bothered to change the reservation, figuring that with one bedroom and a living area, each of them would still be afforded a bit of privacy. But this suite consisted of a ground-floor living area and a bedroom loft to the rear and up a few steps off the main area. No privacy for either space.

"Do you want to try to get another room?" she offered even though she knew the prospect was unlikely. The man at the desk had already complained to them in a good-natured way about a lack of space due to the expansion of the season. "Folks," he said, "used to come Fourth of July and stay till Labor Day. Now they start showing up in May and don't seem to ever want to go home." Carly hadn't bothered to inform him that most of the overcrowding was due to her own guests.

Jackson set the bags down by the door. "I think we can make do. The sofa opens out, doesn't it?"

"If it does, I'll take it. You probably wouldn't even fit in it. Or we can do the mature thing and each of us take one of the twin beds up there."

"I suppose we could do that." Though the idea

sounded as appealing to him as sticking his hand in scalding water. "Dibs on the bed by the window."

She couldn't argue with him, as he'd insisted on paying for the room. He claimed he intended to put it on his expense report to Charlotte. So be it. She hadn't wanted to argue about it anyway. "Whatever," she said. "I'm going to freshen up and then I suggest we get something decent to eat."

"Sounds like a plan."

She carried her suitcase into the bathroom, rather than rummage through it on the outside. She set the case on top of the closed commode and turned to look at herself in the mirror. "You must be the most pathetic seductress that ever walked the planet," she whispered to her reflection. Here she had Jackson in one little room where they would have to practically be on top of one another just to exist, and she'd actually suggested changing it. Her own lack of ingenuity boggled the mind.

But how to actually tempt him? When the time came, she had to make him want to accept her proposal. Since he didn't seem terribly excited by the Carly she was, maybe it was time to be the most different Carly she could be.

A plan formed in her mind. She turned on the shower faucet and as the water heated she looked through her bag for the sundress she'd packed. Charlotte had bought it for her, but she'd never worn it. Holding the white sheath with little spaghetti straps up to her body, she knew it would fit.

That settled, she washed her hair, leaving it to dry in its naturally curly state. Rather than pinning it up, she parted her hair on the left side and left it down. She applied a minimum of makeup and added a pair of white sandals that had a low but narrowly sexy heel. When she was done, she surveyed herself in the mirror.

Maybe she should announce to Jackson that she was stepping out of the bathroom, because she looked nothing like the Carly he'd first met.

What did they say about women willing to change themselves around just to please a man? Nothing good, but it was a temporary displacement that would last for one night only or as long as it took for this fling with Jackson to run its course. There would be plenty of time after that to decide which Carly she wanted to be.

Jackson was sitting on the sofa when she emerged from the bathroom. He had his head back and his eyes closed, and for a fleeting moment she wondered if she'd taken so long getting ready that he'd actually fallen asleep. "Still hungry?"

He opened his eyes and did a double take. "What did you say?"

"I said, are you still hungry?"

He stood, his face bearing a bemused expression. "I thought your hair was straight."

She didn't know what to make of that comment. "I usually blow it dry."

"You don't wear makeup."

"I do sometimes, when I'm out in public. You can't own a cosmetics company and not wear makeup. In this case, just a little mascara and a new lip gloss that smells and tastes like strawberries. Want to try it?"

"You want me to put on lip gloss?"

He sounded so incredulous that she giggled. "No, silly." She moved closer to him so that a scant couple of inches separated their bodies and touched her index finger to her lower lip. "Here." With one hand braced on his chest she rose on tiptoes to touch her finger to the same spot on his lip. "How's that?"

Satisfaction rippled through her as he rolled his lips inward, issuing a low savoring sound. "Not bad."

But as if he realized what he'd done, he set her away

from him with his hands on her waist. "Maybe I'd better change."

She didn't bother to tell him she was severely overdressed for where she wanted to go. Most people showed up in jeans or shorts or whatever they had on at the moment. The only prerequisite was that you had to wear a shirt and shoes at all times.

When he emerged from the bathroom ten minutes later, carrying both of their suitcases, she realized he'd both showered and shaved. He set the bags down by the sofa. "Ready?"

He'd changed into a pair of black linen pants and a short-sleeved black and white shirt that clung to his physique in an appealing way. Carly took a deep breath. "As ready as I'll ever be," she said, but to herself she added, *to put my seduction plans into motion.*

He opened the door for her and pulled it closed when they were both on the other side. "Do you want to walk or take the car?"

"Let's walk. It's only two blocks away, the night is warm, and the moon is full." She linked her arm with his.

"All right."

As usual, there was a line to get into the restaurant, but once they were inside, the service was quick and the food was delicious. But more diverting than the food or even the bottle of wine they ordered with dinner was Carly herself. Somehow she charmed him into telling stories about his work he rarely spoke about. Her laughter delighted him and her pathos when he told him about one particular runaway he hadn't been able to find touched him deeply.

A man could easily fall for a woman like that. Not him, but someone. As the waitress cleared their dishes from the table, he watched her, wondering why no one had.

"Would you like dessert?" the waitress asked, pad in hand.

"I'm afraid the gentleman has promised me ice cream from Mad Martha's."

"I said I'd buy you an ice cream cone. I didn't say it had to be now."

There was laughter in her voice when she said, "Please. And then a walk on the beach. I want to look at the moon."

"Okay, then consider that your favor."

"No. I still get my favor or there's no deal."

"Whatever you want, Carly."

"Whatever I want? Hmm, I'm going to have to think on that a bit."

He chuckled. "Maybe I should have specified. Anything you want for dessert."

"Fair enough."

After paying the check, he took her hand and led her out of the restaurant. Mad Martha's was just up the block a little bit. As they waited their turn in line, he turned to her and asked her what she wanted.

"A chocolate ice cream cone. Two scoops."

As the line moved, he guided her forward with his hands on her waist. "A chocolate ice cream cone? You can have a frappe, you can have a shake, you can have a float with whipped cream or a banana split with jimmies and you pick a chocolate ice cream cone? Live a little."

"I am. Usually I order one scoop of nonfat vanilla in a cup."

He couldn't argue with that. When it was his turn to order, he said. "Two two-scoop chocolate cones."

"What happened to living a little?" she asked him.

He shrugged. He was already living dangerously, letting her get to him in this way. He was hired to do a job, and regardless of the fact that he had no intention of taking a cent of Charlotte's money, he ought to keep his mind more on protecting her daughter than on how much he enjoyed being with her. Maybe he ought to remember that the only reason he was there would hopefully be over soon enough.

He paid for their ice cream and the two of them left the store. Despite what he'd told himself, he kept his hand on her waist, holding her beside him. He told himself it was to keep them from getting separated in the crowd that was out that night, but he knew that was a lie. One little lie couldn't hurt, could it?

By the time they reached the entrance to State Beach, he had finished his ice cream cone, but Carly still had most of hers. He rolled up his pants legs a bit and they left their shoes to the side and walked down the path to the sand. He took Carly's hand because he couldn't seem to keep himself from doing otherwise.

They walked along for a while in companionable silence. He noticed her looking out at the water and stopped. Smiling, he asked her, "What do you find so fascinating about the ocean?"

"Aside from its beauty? I don't know, it calls to me. I think it was JFK who said that when we return to the ocean we return from whence we came. Or something like that."

"So you were a sea anemone in another life?"

"Maybe. Or a shark."

"You couldn't have been a shark. All they do is eat and you can't finish an ice cream cone."

"My eyes were bigger than my stomach. After the wonderful dinner." She shrugged.

He pulled her closer. "Let me help you out with that." He nibbled the little bit of cone left from her fingers.

"You," she said, and there was a catch in her voice.

"You could have been a shark. You've eaten everything in sight since we got here."

No, not everything. There was one morsel he'd never get to sample, and for better reasons than Charlotte's faith in him. *Damn!*

His gaze met hers. He knew he should look away, because what her gaze reflected was too telling.

"About that favor I wanted to ask you . . ."

He knew he should put an end to this before it began but he heard his mouth say, "Yes?"

"I was wondering if, well, when we get back to the room, if you wouldn't, well . . ."

"Yes?"

She looked up at him in obvious distress, unable to vocalize what she wanted. Since he already knew, he decided to put her out of her misery. "Are you talking about making love?"

"If you wouldn't mind."

A rush of heat instantly suffused his body. Would he mind making love to her? He wouldn't mind if someone gave him a million dollars, either. Heaven help him, he wanted her. Especially after the day they'd spent today. He wanted to teach her exactly what to do with that luscious mouth of hers and what his could do for her in return.

But would he make love to her? Absolutely not. For one thing, she was his client's daughter, the woman he was sworn to protect. For another, if she was as innocent as he suspected, he'd be taking something not meant for him to have.

She looked up at him expectantly, waiting for his answer. "It's not that hard a question, Jackson. Yes or no would do nicely."

But he couldn't be that stark about it. "Are you a virgin, Carly?"

She crossed her arms in front of her and sputtered, "Is-is that what you think?"

"Answer my question."

"If you must know, there was one man."

"What happened?"

"Do we have to talk about him?"

"Yes."

"I was madly in love; he was working for and bedding my mother. According to her he was a, quote, 'lousy lay,' but I was too stupid to know the difference."

She bit her lip and started to walk away from him, back toward where they'd left their shoes, making him regret he'd pushed her so hard. But that revelation explained so much about her and her relationship with Charlotte that it took him a moment to realize she wasn't just putting some space between them. Carly intended to leave without him.

He caught up with her and spun her around with a hand on her arm. "I can't, Carly, you know I can't."

"I wasn't asking you for any strings or any promises. We have one night before the others start showing up. I thought . . ." She shook her head.

"You wanted to use me."

"With your full knowledge and permission."

Damned if that didn't sound like a worthwhile arrangement. He couldn't offer her anything but the here and now—the night as she put it. But he knew she'd want more, if not before, then after. And the one thing he couldn't bring himself to do was disappoint her. "I can't."

She lifted one shoulder in a shrug. "Well, then that settles that." She sounded as if he'd just denied her a dinner reservation, but even in the dim moonlight he saw the hurt in her eyes. She turned away from him, resuming her walk down the beach.

He caught up to her and caught her wrist, "Carly, please—"

She went rigid but she didn't pull away. "I understand, Jackson. I really do. Just don't touch me, okay?"

He released her because there was nothing else for him to do. He followed her back to the side of the road and put on his shoes as she slipped into hers. Without waiting for him, she started across the street, only to be driven back by the blare of a car horn. He had obviously upset her so much all she wanted to do was get away from him—to the point she wasn't looking where she was going.

Whether she liked it or not, he would not allow her to injure herself. He took her hand and when she tried to pull away he held fast. So they walked the short distance back to the hotel with her trying to ignore the fact that he held her hand. She didn't say one word to him until they got back to the room.

"Good night, Jackson." She walked up to the loft, kicked off her shoes, and without taking off another article of clothing, got into bed and pulled the covers over her head.

Jackson's chin dropped to his chest. How to feel like a first-class heel in one easy lesson. He wanted to go to her, to make everything right with her. But he couldn't think of a single thing to say or do to accomplish that. Instead he took a long cold shower more to punish himself than for any other reason. He changed into the lone pair of pajamas he owned and got out Charlotte's records and his laptop from his suitcase and arranged them on the coffee table. He called Drew's cell number and waited for him to pick up.

"There better be a damn good reason for this phone call."

"Nice to hear from you, too, cousin."

"Jackson. Damn! Hold on a minute."

Jackson heard Drew's muffled voice and an equally distorted female voice. Good to see Drew had recovered from his flirtation with Carly this afternoon. Jackson should have known he was in trouble then, because he'd walked into that kitchen and wanted to brain his own flesh and blood for talking with Carly in such an intimate way.

"You still there?" Drew said finally.

"No, I'm on a slow boat to China. What have you got for me?"

"Don't pull that sarcasm crap with me—"

"Drew," he said in exasperation, "what did you find out?"

"This is interesting. Anderson died of alcohol poisoning. The stiff reeked of it. There was some of it in his lungs, too, but not enough to kill him."

"What was he drinking?"

"Gin."

That didn't make sense. He said as much to Drew. Most of these old rummies found one drink they liked and stuck with it. The night he'd met Duke he'd been drinking Old Turkey. Then again, if someone had given him a bottle he'd probably have downed it if it was rubbing alcohol. "I need to think about this."

"I figured you might."

"Anything else?"

"How's Carly?"

"Don't you already have one woman in your bed?"

"Don't bite my head off. I'm not trying to get greedy. She's a sweet kid. I just wanted to make sure you're treating her right."

"I'm treating her fine," he said, but he knew Carly wouldn't agree with that assessment. Feeling tired beyond words, he rubbed his eyes with the thumb and forefinger of his left hand. "Anything else?"

"Tell Carly I say hello."

Jackson clicked off the phone. That last comment was intended to annoy him and it succeeded. He sat back and looked in the direction of the loft. Carly hadn't bothered to turn out the light, so he had a clear view of her. The parts of her not buried under the blanket, anyway. In her sleep she had turned to face him. Her face looked soft and peaceful in sleep, except an occasional hitch in her breathing.

Carly had been crying. He'd made her cry. He hadn't thought he could feel any worse where she was concerned, but he did. He'd never be able to work like this. He switched off his computer and walked up the few steps to the loft. He stopped by her bed and peeled back the bedspread so that she wouldn't get overheated during the night. She stirred a little, but didn't wake. When she settled down again, he leaned down and kissed her forehead. "I'm so sorry, Carly," he whispered.

He turned off the light and got into bed, but for the most part he stared up at the ceiling wishing sleep would come.

The next morning he awoke to someone shaking his shoulder. "Jackson, wake up."

"Carly?" She stood next to his bed, already fully dressed in a pair of slacks and a long-sleeved shirt. Her hair was bone straight and pulled back into one of those dreadful buns. She probably would have had on her glasses if she had a pair to wear. Her face bore not a smidgen of makeup. Her mouth was twisted into a frown.

He sat up, instantly awake. "What is it, baby? What's wrong?"

She took a step away from him, about all the distance that separated the two beds. "Nothing. But if you want breakfast, you'd better hurry up."

She walked away, rapidly as if she weren't sure if someone was chasing her. He called to her but she didn't stop. She let herself out of the room and closed the door behind her with a soft click.

Jackson threw off the covers, intending to go after her. But then he heard her voice. He went to the window and parted the curtain. She was sitting with a couple of old biddies in the rockers that lined the porch. She would be fine for a few minutes, while he showered and dressed. He did both in record time.

He pushed open the screen door to be greeted by brilliant sunshine overhead and an excellent view of the marina before him. Boats of all sizes bobbed in their moorings or traveled across the deep blue water closer to the horizon. He inhaled, breathing in the clean island air. He could definitely get used to this.

"Is that your young man?" he heard one of the biddies say.

"That's him," Carly said in a droll voice and her gaze on him left a lot to be desired.

"And a handsome one he is, too," the biddie on the left added.

All three women stared at him, but Carly's gaze was the least welcoming. Obviously she had told them some sort of story to cover his being in her room. He walked up to her, put his hands on her shoulders, and leaned down to kiss her cheek. "Morning, sweetheart."

"Well," the biddie on the right said, "we're going to leave you two young people to yourselves. We're off to tour the island."

After good-byes and promises to see each other later, the two older women left, heading in the direction of town. Jackson slid into the seat the biddie on the left had vacated. "What was that about?"

"They saw us checking in. I had to tell them something. Too bad it didn't occur to me to tell them you were my brother."

She was still angry with him, and despite what she said, she didn't understand. On top of that, she seemed determined to take it out on him. "Don't punish me because I can't give you what you want, Carly," he said in a quiet voice.

Her gaze flew to his. "That's not what I'm doing."

"Yes, it is."

She shook her head. "No. I don't throw myself at men every day. Hell, I've never thrown myself at a man before last night, ever. I don't know how to be around you anymore."

"Just be yourself."

"Who's that?" She stood, grasping the cup at her feet. "I'm going to get some more coffee." She bolted before he had a chance to answer or try to stop her.

"I'm sorry, Carly," he whispered, but he had a feeling that wouldn't be the last time he'd say those words.

Chapter 12

Jackson wasn't sure what state he'd find Carly in when he returned to their room, but he didn't expect what he found. She was sitting calmly in one of the overstuffed chairs perpendicular to the sofa reading a copy of the island paper.

"Anything good in there?" he asked, closing the door behind him.

"There's an article about the shoot on Wednesday. They're predicting quite a few people will come out to see Sam. She helped me convince Jarad Naughton to direct the commercial for us. Do you know him, too?"

He eased into the chair across from her. "Yeah, his wife's a shrink, isn't she?"

"Yes."

She lowered her paper and looked at him. "What have you got against shrinks?"

"Nothing, if you actually need your head shrunken."

She shrugged, as if dismissing the subject. "I need to go over to Sam and Adam's this afternoon to make sure everything is okay. That's where the clambake will be Wednesday night."

That suited him fine. If anything was to go down while they were here, he might need Adam's help. "What time do you want to leave?"

She checked her watch. "Another couple of hours.

They're barbecuing this afternoon." She lifted the paper again, signaling, he supposed, that the discussion was over.

He sighed, not knowing what to make of her detached attitude. Last night she'd cried, this morning she'd been angry. Now she seemed as interested in him as a ball of lint. Maybe that was for the best. Maybe he could manage to do what he was supposed to do in the first place. Find out who might want to hurt her.

"How do you know Paul Samuels?"

She lowered her paper again. "He was my father's law partner for a brief time."

He knew that already. He'd checked Samuels out two days ago, and hadn't liked everything he'd found. Samuels had been a power twenty years ago, a candidate for Manhattan City Council from a wealthy Upper East Side district. At the time, it was speculated that the lowly position he sought was merely a stepping stone to higher office. Something or someone had derailed his prospects of that; exactly what, Jackson hadn't been able to figure out yet. "Why do both you and Charlotte keep in touch with him? I notice he's on the guest list for Wednesday night."

"He also happens to be my godfather and Charlotte's friend."

Jackson frowned. Something about Samuels didn't add up to him. "I want you to introduce him to me."

"You think Uncle Paul has something to do with the trouble my mother is in?"

"I have no idea."

That wasn't a complete lie. He didn't know anything for sure, but he did know that Samuels and Duke Anderson knew each other. Anderson had testified once on behalf of one of Samuels's clients, a high-level drug dealer, who was accused of sticking a shiv in another inmate. Anderson had said the client didn't do it, but there had been some speculations as to whether Anderson could have seen anything at all. If Anderson had been willing to lie for Samuels once, why not twice?

"Charlotte probably called him for legal advice and a boost to her feminine ego. Uncle Paul is one of the legions of men who are madly in love with my mother."

Enough in love to kill her husband to get him out of the way? But if that was the case, why hadn't he made a move on Charlotte twenty years ago?

"How does Charlotte feel about him?"

Carly lifted one shoulder in a shrug. "I don't know. She thinks of him as her friend, I guess. I remember for a while after Daddy died he came around a lot. Then he just stopped. Over the years they started seeing each other socially again."

So maybe he made a play and Charlotte rebuffed him. Jackson noticed Carly watching him closely.

"I can assure you Uncle Paul would never hurt my mother. He loves her."

"All men kill the things they love, by all let this be heard."

She smiled. "Oscar Wilde. 'The Ballad of Reading Gaol.' The coward does it with a kiss. The brave man with a sword."

He grinned. "Never let it be said that I'm not edumacated."

She smiled, the first one he'd seen on her face since last night. He couldn't have hurt her too badly if she could find humor in one of his jokes. "Is there anyone else you can think of who might want to get back at your mother?"

She shook her head. "Not anyone that makes sense. Not even a disgruntled employee. She's always left the firing up to me. Unless you want to start checking out her assistants, but that would take forever."

Abruptly she sat up and put her feet on the floor.

"You know, there is one man she dated that will be at the shoot. Gary Vespers. He works for the security company that will be handling the shoot. As I remember it, he wasn't too happy when Charlotte gave him his walking papers."

That was an interesting bit of news, but he didn't see how Vespers could fit in with Duke Anderson and his father's trial. That didn't mean he wouldn't check Vespers out or satisfy himself that the man in question wasn't giving Charlotte any other trouble.

"You wouldn't happen to have Vespers's Social Security number, would you?"

"No, but I can get it from personnel. I need to call my office anyway."

Carly got her cell phone from her purse, gathered some papers from her suitcase, and went to the "bedroom" to make the call. In the meantime, Jackson booted his computer and within a few moments called up Vespers's address and phone number. Considering the Upper East Side location, Vespers must be doing well for himself to afford that neighborhood.

Noticing a movement in his periphery, he focused on Carly. She held up a piece of paper on which she'd written Vespers's Social Security number. He keyed it in first to run a credit check, then the New York State Department of Motor Vehicles. At least Vespers was consistent. He didn't work for the security company; he owned it. And there was his picture, big as life on the Web site for Axis Security. He drove a Porshe, paid his bills on time, and didn't have a criminal record as far as Jackson could determine. But something about his profile bothered Jackson. He'd skimmed over some of the personal data, but he went back over it now. Then he noticed it. Vespers's mother's maiden name was Glenn. Veronica Glenn. That name sent a chill of recognition down Jackson's spine. He called up an article on Sharon Glenn's death and found what he was looking for. Sharon Glenn had been Gary Vespers's aunt.

Jackson had barely pulled to a stop in the drive in front of Sam and Adam's house when the door opened and Samantha and Ariel, Jarad's wife, came out to greet them. Sam was nearly six feet tall with auburn hair, amber eyes, and a slender, long-legged figure. Ariel was more Carly's height with jet-black hair and the sea-green eyes that ran in her family. Both of them made Carly feel as adequate in the looks department as an ugly duckling at a swan convention.

As Carly got out of the car, Ariel came around to her side of the car to embrace her.

"Long time, no see, stranger," Ariel remarked.

Carly hugged her back. "Unfortunately that is too true." Back in the city, she and Ariel lived less than fifteen minutes from each other but rarely saw each other off the island. "Let's fix that, okay?"

"Fine by me," Ariel said. "What are you doing here, with Jackson of all people?"

Carly had discussed with Jackson what cover story they would give their friends, but somehow she couldn't make her mouth form the lie.

Jackson saved her from having to. "Charlotte hired my company for some added personal security. Since Carly was coming up early, I came up with her to check things out."

Ariel eyed him skeptically. "You don't do personal security."

"For an old friend I do."

Ariel opened her mouth to say something else, but Sam cut her off. "I hope you guys are hungry. Adam is grilling enough steaks to feed a small army."

Sam casually draped her arm around Jackson's waist, leading him toward the house. Jackson reciprocated by looping his arm around Samantha's shoulders. Inwardly Carly groaned. She must really be losing it if a harmless friendly gesture could make such white-hot jealousy shoot through her, first because she knew nothing could be going on between Sam and Jackson since Adam would kill him if there was, and second because Jackson wasn't hers to get jealous over to begin with. Not even temporarily. He'd made that clear last night.

From beside her, Ariel said, "Okay, what are you really doing here with Jackson?"

Carly laughed. You could fool some of the people some of the time, but fooling Ariel any of the time was almost a miracle.

"Get over here, you pain in the ass," Adam called to Jackson once they emerged from the back door that faced onto the beach. Adam stood at a massive grill set at the end of the patio with a pair of tongs in his hand. Jarad stood next to him, a bottle of beer in his hand. "And get your hands off my wife, while you're at it."

Laughing, Sam pushed him forward. "It's too early in the day for making threats, Adam. Wait until after lunch."

Jackson walked to where the men stood, shook Jarad's hand, and braced himself to endure Adam's bear hug. Like Drew, Adam topped Jackson's height by a few inches and had an unfortunate tendency to be affectionate. "How was the trip up?"

"Not bad. I brought the Caddy."

Adam elbowed Jarad. "You have got to see this car. What year is it, 1954?"

Jackson nodded.

"Everything new under the hood but all the original hardware, dash, whatever. And the ride is sweet. We should take it out while you're here."

"Any time you're ready."

"We'll sneak out after lunch. For some reason the women expect us to feed them."

Jackson glanced over his shoulder, just then noticing that none of said women had followed them. "Where did the girls go to?"

"Don't let Ariel hear you say that. She'll never let me hear the end of it."

Adam added, "Who knows? Inside having some hen party, no doubt."

"Talking about us, no doubt."

It occurred to them that just now they were doing the same thing in reverse.

"Wait a minute," Adam said, "you got Carly to ride in a car without seat belts? What did you do, drug her?"

"What do you mean?"

"Don't get me wrong, she's a sweet kid," Jarad put in, "but when you look in the dictionary under uptight, her picture is there."

Jackson accepted the beer Jarad handed him. "She's not that bad." In fact, last night she'd been soft and feminine and so damn alluring it had taken every bit of his willpower to refuse her.

"No? Then someone must have been slipping her some happy pills in with her morning coffee."

Adam cast him a hard look. "Or maybe slipping her something else."

Jackson recognized the protectiveness in Adam's gaze and the censure in his voice. He didn't blame Adam. Adam knew his track record with women, and if he were in Adam's shoes he wouldn't approve either. He didn't approve himself.

Jackson raised both hands in surrender. "Not me,

man. I haven't laid a finger on her." Adam seemed mollified by that, but he continued, "The real reason I am with her is Charlotte hired me to look after her. It seems that someone might have murdered Duke Anderson."

"Who?" Jarad asked.

Jackson ran down the whole story, starting with Sharon Glenn's death to what he'd found out about Gary Vespers that morning. Jarad's response was the same as Drew's, a low whistle. Adam's was to shake his head as he turned the meat. "Poor kid. How is Carly taking it?"

"She doesn't know and I want to keep it that way. She's under enough pressure getting this shoot off tomorrow without having to look over her shoulder for bogeymen that might or might not be there."

"If that's how you want it, man. What do you want us to do?"

"Just keep an eye out for her. Let me know if you see anyone suspicious hanging around. From what I understand, there will be at least a hundred people up here between the crew, the caterers, the photographers, and the press."

"Not a problem," Jarad said.

But as the conversation switched from the upcoming party to the ubiquitous question of which team was better, the Yankees or the Mets, Jackson only half paid attention. The rest of him wondered what Carly was doing inside.

"I hope you don't mind us hanging out in here awhile," Sam said once the women had settled in the solarium with white wine for Carly and Ariel and a glass of orange juice for Sam. "I figured we could stand to miss the testosterone festival going on in the backyard."

"Amen to that," Ariel said, lifting her glass in salute to Sam. "When those boys get together, it's like someone let open the cages at the zoo. I'm surprised they're not eating the meat raw instead of putting it on the grill."

Sam laughed. "What do you think they're talking about now? Who's better—the Mets or the Yankees or who's headed to the playoffs?"

"Either that or they're talking about us." Ariel fastened a hard look on Carly. "And speaking of the men, don't think it's slipped my mind that you never answered my question."

"What question was that?"

"What are you really doing here with Jackson?"

Carly countered with a question of her own. "Why do you really want to know?"

Ariel shrugged. "When the two least likely people to be together drive up in an automobile, you wonder."

"You have to excuse Ariel," Sam said. "She's been on Jackson's case ever since he said the psychiatric profession bred nothing but neurotics and crybabies rather than curing anyone who actually needed fixing."

Carly hid a smile behind her hand. She could imagine Jackson saying that and she could equally imagine Ariel not being amused.

"And you think every word that comes out of the man's mouth is pure gold."

"I admit it. I have a soft spot for Jackson. Adam wouldn't be here if it wasn't for him."

Sobering, Carly asked, "What do you mean?"

Sam took a deep breath and let it out. "Adam and Jackson were part of a narcotics task force several years ago. They were trying to roust the drug dealers from one particular housing project in the Bronx. So they did a lot of buy-and-bust operations, you know, where they try to buy drugs from someone and if the other guy comes through they arrest him. A lot of knocking down doors and seizing whoever and whatever they found inside."

Carly nodded, urging Sam to go on. It all sounded terribly dangerous to Carly and a wonder that they had both come out alive.

"On one raid, they got a tip that someone was dealing drugs out of a particular apartment. They show up, bust down the door, swarm inside, and find nothing. No one is there, there are no drugs, it's just a regular apartment. At first they assume the tip must have been bad, either someone messing around with the police or someone had tipped the dealers off and they left.

"But my darling husband notices that there's a large picture on the wall above this beat-up sofa that's askew. He goes over to check it out, thinking it's nothing. But when he takes down the picture, he sees that it concealed a large hole in the wall. It turns out the dealers had rented two apartments. One was a cover for the other. If the police raided the apartment everyone knew to be the drug location they would find exactly what they found. Nothing."

"What happened?"

"As soon as the dealers realized their lair had been breached, they started shooting. Considering the number of cops in the building and on the ground, they were just as trapped as if they'd gone to the right apartment in the first place. Adam was caught between the wall and the sofa. As big as he is, crouching in tight places is not his specialty. The first bullet hit him in the side, went right through his vest. God knows what would have happened if Jackson hadn't pulled him down, out of harm's way.

"They tell me after that it was chaos, with police swarming into the other apartment and shots being fired. Jackson killed the one who had hurt Adam." She pointed her index finger at the center of her forehead.

"I can't say I'm sorry he did, but one of the bullets, his bullet, went through the window into another apartment across the way. It hit a ten-year-old boy in approximately the same place."

Carly covered her mouth with her hands. "Oh, no." She could imagine how Jackson had felt learning that he'd killed an innocent child. Beneath his gruff exterior lay a sensitive man. He'd proved that to her last night when she'd seen both his impotence and rage at not being able to locate a young child until it was too late.

Sam shifted and took a sip from her glass. "After that Adam transferred out of that unit, but when Jackson got back to the station and they took his gun, he handed them his shield as well. He quit. He just walked out. He got a citation for bravery for saving Adam's life, but he never accepted it. He says no force on earth could ever possess him to pick up a gun again."

He'd told her he had no interest in shooting anyone, and she supposed she had her answer why not.

For a moment they all lapsed into silence. Then Sam sat forward with an entreating look on her face. "Don't give up on him, Carly, please. He needs somebody, someone who will bring some joy into his life. He may not know that, but everyone who cares about him does. It's not just that kid, but a lot of other things as well, including his father's death. He hasn't had an easy time of it. He may not show it, but that doesn't mean it's not true."

"There's nothing to give up on, Sam. There's nothing going on between Jackson and me."

Sam sat back. "There's no way on earth you could get me to believe that."

"Why not?"

"Because I know both of you. You forget Ariel and I were watching from the window for you to arrive. When you pulled up, he had a look on his face that could freeze water and you were sitting so far on the other side of him you were practically out the door."

"What do you want me to do, Sam? I already made a fool out of myself once over that man. He already told me he's not interested. That much of a masochist I'm not."

"And you didn't see the way he looked at you when you weren't paying attention. I did, and it was not the look of an uninterested man. In his own way he's hurting, too. If you knew him better you'd know that. I don't want to get too much into your business, but have you told him how you feel?"

"Maybe I would if I knew what that was."

"Then how exactly did you make a fool out of yourself with him?"

"I sort of asked him to make love to me." Carly covered her face with her hands, mortified to confess she'd done anything so stupid.

Ariel, who had remained silent during Sam's story, said, "*Jackson* said no?" She and Sam exchanged a glance that Carly couldn't begin to comprehend.

"Why is that so shocking?"

"Don't get me wrong," Ariel continued. "All comments about my profession aside, I think Jackson's a great guy. But where women go . . ." She trailed off, shrugging.

"I wouldn't call him the love 'em and leave 'em type," Sam continued, "because that implies the man in question made some promise in regard to longevity."

"He's more like 'I'm not promising you a thing except a few great moments in the sack and then I go home. If you can handle that, then come on. If not, see you around.'"

Sam nodded in agreement. "That's him to a tee."

"That's what I offered him. One night. Last night,

and he turned me down. He seems to think I'm some fragile flower that will break if he touches me."

Sam and Ariel exchanged another of those unfathomable looks.

"What?"

"Take it from a couple of old married ladies. He's probably kicking himself right now for that lapse in judgment. And there's only one thing more certain than the fact that every man makes mistakes."

"What's that?"

"The fact that no man wants a woman telling him he's made one."

Carly chuckled. "So what do you do?"

Ariel said, "You don't tell them they made a mistake, you show them."

"With great delicacy," Sam added. "If necessary."

"With a sledgehammer when it's not," Ariel added.

"Which do you think is required in this case?"

In unison, Sam and Ariel said, "Sledgehammer."

Carly laughed but Sam grew serious for a moment. "I know we're joking here, but don't hurt him, Carly, not if you can help it. Promise me that."

Carly nodded. She didn't want to hurt him; she wanted to understand him. Sam's story proved to her that he was a more complex man than even she had imagined. A good man whom she realized she was coming to care for in more than simply a superficial manner. That's not what she'd bargained for when she decided to seduce him, but that's what she'd ended up with. Now what was she going to do about that?

Chapter 13

Jackson glanced over at Carly, who sat beside him in the car as they drove back to the hotel. "Did you have a good time?"

She turned her head to look at him. "You know I did."

He smiled to himself. He guessed he did know. Once the women had joined the men outside, she'd seemed different, relaxed maybe, and definitely not disinterested or angry as she had been with him earlier in the day. Half of him wondered what the women might have told her about him during their "hen party," as Adam called it. The other half didn't want to know.

But the six of them had spent a pleasant afternoon and evening stuffing themselves on steak and salad and the other trimmings Sam had made to go with the meal and enjoying each other's company. As usual, when he and Adam got together, the conversation turned to their exploits on the police force while the others listened, equally fascinated and appalled by what they had to say.

"Do you miss it?"

"Miss what?"

"Being a policeman, a cop, whatever."

He snuck another glance at her. When had she learned to read his thoughts so clearly? Yeah, he missed it. He'd found a way to make a living doing something else. He was good at it. Still, there were parts of being on the job he missed. But no police department on earth wanted a man who refused to carry a gun.

"It's part of my past," he said in a way that he hoped would end the conversation.

"That's a shame."

He snorted. "What makes you say that?"

She shrugged. "It's obvious both you and Adam miss being in the thick of things. Adam 'rides a desk' as he puts it because that's the way Sam wants it, but I think that's a mistake."

"Why?"

"People should do what they love, don't you think? It makes them happier in the long run."

True, but he also understood Sam's fears for Adam's safety. "If you were in Sam's place, married to a cop, you wouldn't ask your husband to accept a safer assignment."

"I would never expect a man to give up what he wanted for me."

There was something about the way she said that and the silence that followed that he found disconcerting. He wondered if she meant that she was easygoing enough not to ask a man to change for her or that she lacked the power to get a man to do so. More than that, he wanted to see the smile return to her face. "You know, you're starting to sound like Ariel with all that pop psychology babble."

She slapped her palms to her face comically. "Heavens no. Not that."

He chuckled. "Better watch yourself." He pulled into a spot behind the hotel and cut the engine. "Home again, home again, jiggedy gig."

She rolled her eyes. "More poetry. I don't know how I can stand it." She extended her hand toward him, palm up. "If you don't mind, I'm going to go in. These shoes are killing me."

He pulled the key from his pocket and gave it to her. "I'll be in in a minute."

They both got out of the car, she to head inside, he to pull a protective tarp over the car. It only took him a minute, but by the time he got to the porch steps, she must have turned on the radio. He paused a moment, listening to her singing along to a Whitney Houston track and outdoing the diva. Then what was that butchering of the national anthem about? He thought to ask her about it, but by the time he got to their room she'd already disappeared into the bathroom.

Carly surveyed her image in the bathroom mirror. She'd been doing that a lot lately, staring at her reflection, wondering who the woman who stared back at her was. She had had no better answer now than she had two days ago. At least tonight she hadn't done anything she could look back on with complete mortification.

Despite what Samantha and Ariel told her, she had no intention of embarrassing herself further where Jackson was concerned. Any man you had to hit over the head to make him interested in you was a man not worth having. She meant what she said to Jackson about not expecting a man to change what he wanted for her, and that included whether or not he wanted her. Besides, she'd already hit him with the best sledge-hammer in her arsenal and she hadn't even dizzied him a little.

The only thing she'd really succeeded in doing was crying her eyes out and taking her frustration out on Jackson. Her tears had solved nothing and she vowed that no matter what, she was done with that. He'd bruised her ego, that's all. She should be beyond that by now, letting what others thought of her get to her. If she paid attention to every comment overheard by her mother's friends who lamented that she was definitely not her mother's daughter, or every slave-driver complaint from her employees, she'd be too depressed to get out of bed.

But she did regret the way she'd treated Jackson. He hadn't deserved either her anger or her aloofness. The man had a right to turn her down. She never should have put him in the position of having to reject her in the first place. But she recognized in herself the need for some human connection, even if it was mostly a sham. It was a need she'd felt for a long time but never acknowledged in any real way. She'd given her entire life to her company, but it was a poor companion and a sterile lover. There wasn't one single person in her life whom she loved and trusted absolutely or anyone who she believed was unconditionally on her side. That was a lot to lay at the doorstep of a man she'd known less than a week.

She took out her contacts, changed into her nightgown and robe, and brushed out her hair. It was late and she was tired, but there was one more thing she needed to do before climbing into bed.

Jackson was sitting on the sofa, playing a game of solitaire on his computer for want of anything better to do, when Carly came out of the bathroom. She'd changed into a lavender silk robe and slippers. She stood by the chair nearest the bathroom, her fingers gripped together, a troubled expression on her face. "Jackson, can I talk to you for a minute please?"

He shut the computer and sat back. "Of course, sweetheart." He patted the spot next to him, but she ignored the gesture.

"I owe you an apology."

His brow furrowed. "For what?"

"Last night. I'm sorry about the way I treated you. Last night and this morning. I never should have asked you that stupid question in the first place."

"Why did you?"

She shrugged. "Plain stupidity, I guess."

He shook his head. Stupidity had nothing to do with it. He understood the feelings that she didn't want to voice better than she thought. He knew about loneliness and the desire sometimes to reach out to someone else, anyone else for a little relief. In a way, each of them had built solitary lives for themselves, and sometimes the confines chafed more than either of them was willing to admit.

And he knew with absolute certainty that if they'd met under any circumstances other than the ones in which they found themselves, she wouldn't have had to go begging.

"Come here, sweetheart." He reached for her hand and pulled her closer until he could settle her on his lap. She didn't exactly resist, but she didn't come to him eagerly either.

"Jackson . . ." she said in warning.

He pressed her cheek against his shoulder. "Shh, Carly." His hand stroked over her back in a gentle motion. Gradually she relaxed against him. Her breath, warm and fragrant, fanned his cheek. One of her hands was trapped against his body, but the other gripped his biceps as if she didn't want him to let her go. He didn't want to let her go, either. But he doubted he'd last long before doing something stupid. Already, his body had hardened in response to her. He only hoped that she didn't notice or maybe she assumed he'd have the same reaction to having any woman sit on his lap.

He didn't know why she picked that moment to lift

her head and gaze up at him. Maybe she sensed the restlessness in him. He didn't know. She looked at him with such an expression of longing that he couldn't hold her gaze, not because he didn't want what she wanted, but because her eyes reflected the ache he felt within himself. Instead he focused on his own hand that rested on her thigh above the soft silk of her robe. "Carly—" he started, not knowing what, if anything else, to say.

Sighing, she shifted her position to free her hand. "I know, I know," she said, cutting him off. "You're only here to protect me from Charlotte's invisible monsters. I'll try to remember that in the future." She slid from his lap and stood. "Good night, Jackson." She turned and headed toward the stairs leading to the loft.

He couldn't let her go like that, thinking she was the only one affected by the chemistry between them. Despite her lack of rancor, he knew she viewed what just happened between them as another rejection, though truth be told, he wanted her now more than ever.

He'd lied to her about everything else, according to Charlotte's wishes. Didn't he owe her what little bit of honesty he could give her? He could only hope she wouldn't use what he was about to tell her against him. He caught up with her as she paused to turn off the upstairs light. "Carly, look at me."

She spun around, her surprise at him having followed her evident on her face. "What now?"

He stroked an errant lock of hair from her face. "Understand something, Carly. I never said I didn't want you. That would be a lie." He tugged on a strand of her hair. "But considering I've been hired to protect you, I can't afford the distraction."

She said nothing for a long while, considering him with her teeth clamped on her lower lip. "Do I distract you?"

"Big time. If I'd been thinking clearly, I never would have let you come into this room alone without checking it first." But the day they'd spent alone together with no one knowing their whereabouts had lulled him into thinking they were safe, when that could be far from the case.

He touched his lips to hers, intending only to give her the barest of kisses and send her to bed. But the moment his mouth claimed hers, he knew he'd miscalculated. God, she tasted sweet, and her lips beneath his were so soft. He squeezed his eyes shut from the sheer pleasure of the contact. But it was her low, throaty moan that did him in. His tongue plunged into her mouth to seek and find her own. And damned if she didn't kiss him back. Her arms wound around his neck, drawing him closer as she angled her head to give him better access to her mouth. Not the response of an innocent, but of a woman who knew how to please a man, this man. A groan rumbled up from somewhere deep in his chest.

He had to stop, now while he still could, before he did what he really wanted to do: carry her up to one of those narrow beds and take all she wanted to offer him. He broke the kiss and slid her arms from around his neck. "Go to bed, Carly."

She leaned back against the wall, her eyes closed, her breathing as labored as his own. When she opened her eyes, her gaze held equal parts of amusement and desire. "Is that what you really want me to do?"

"No, but it's for the best."

She smiled. "All right, Jackson. I'll see you in the morning."

He nodded, careful to keep his hands behind his back as she moved away from him. "Sweet dreams," he whispered, then returned to the sofa to endure his own tortured ones of her.

* * *

Carly woke early the next morning, stretched, and looked over to Jackson's bed to find it empty. Rising on her elbows, she looked down into the living room. Jackson, still fully clothed, lay sprawled on the sofa. She flopped onto her back.

He'd truly shocked her last night by admitting that he wanted her. And that kiss! It surpassed every fantasy she had imagined. She supposed she'd surprised him a little too, by the way she responded. Despite what people thought, she wasn't a prude or a kid who didn't know what to do in a man's arms. She'd enjoyed sex, what little sample of it she'd had. But it wasn't something she couldn't do without if getting her heart broken was the cost for having it.

She closed her eyes and replayed the kiss in her mind, the taste of him on her tongue, the scent of him mixed with the ever-pervasive tang of the ocean, the heat that had coursed through her. Still, it wasn't enough. Maybe a day ago, she would have been content to accept a purely physical relationship with him. It was what she herself had thought she wanted. But after being with him the day before, hearing the others talk about him, and mostly the tender way he'd held her before he'd made his revelation changed her mind.

A girl could easily lose her heart to a man who treated her with kindness and deference and who dedicated himself to her protection on top of it. He'd told her he wanted her, but never one word that he was beginning to care for her in any way. She didn't expect that, considering the short time they'd known each other. Yet, if Sam and Ariel were right, he never would. In fact, he'd probably head for the hills if he knew how strongly she was beginning to feel for him.

She heard Jackson stir and made herself a hasty

promise. He would never know that she felt anything
more for him than a severe case of lust. It was what she
needed for her own self-protection. But she sighed remembering how long the last promise she made to
herself in regard to him had lasted.

Later that morning they drove out to the Edgartown
Airport to pick up Charlotte. Carly knew Charlotte intended to leave Mr. Jingles behind, but she hadn't
expected her to pick up a different traveling companion. Carly slid a questioning glance at Jackson. "I
thought Johnny wasn't coming."

Jackson's only answer was a disinterested shrug, leading her to believe that he knew more than he was
telling.

The first thing Charlotte said when she saw the car
was, "Why, Jackson, I didn't know you cared."

Laughing, he opened the passenger-side door to let
Charlotte and Johnny sit in the back. Once they were
all seated and Jackson had pulled onto the highway,
Charlotte said, "What have you two been up to by your
little lonesomes? And what happened to your glasses,
Carly?"

"I fell asleep on them and they broke."

"Wonder how that happened."

Carly didn't say anything to that. Let her mother
speculate awhile if she wanted to. When they got out of
the car at the hotel, Charlotte linked her arm with
Carly's. "What do you say you help me settle in and
then we get an early lunch? I'm famished."

"Fine by me." As they approached the reservation
desk, a thought occurred to her. "You didn't happen to
book a room for Johnny, did you? They're full here as
far as I know."

Charlotte dismissed Carly's concern with a wave of her hand. "Johnny will have to stay with me, I guess."

No doubt she'd make the poor man sleep on the sofa. "If that's how you want it, but the suites here don't have a separate bedroom. It's only a loft."

"Don't worry yourself, Carly. I assure you that we are both adults and can cope with a little lack of privacy. By the way, how are you and Jackson handling that, or does he have his own room?"

There was Charlotte again with her one-note song, but Carly had no intention of dancing to its tune. There was no way she'd tell her mother one thing that happened between her and Jackson, especially since as far as Carly was concerned they wouldn't be taking it any further. "Better yet, why don't we give one room to the guys and we take the other one?"

"Why? So they can kill each other after fifteen minutes? You never put two men in the same room. It's a territorial thing."

Carly turned to cast a glance at Jackson and Johnny, who were coming in the door each bearing a piece of Charlotte's luggage. They looked pretty chummy to her, but she could see the wisdom of not putting them together considering her suspicions that Johnny harbored feelings for her mother and Jackson reputedly slept with her. But Johnny must know the truth since Charlotte had referred to him as Jackson, not Bruce, when she got off the plane.

Carly shook her head. It was too convoluted to sort out. She only knew she felt sorry for Johnny, trapped in the same room with a woman he loved who didn't know he existed except as a means of providing her with what she wanted. To Charlotte, she said, "I thought Johnny hated the ocean."

Charlotte shrugged. "It turns out he likes the ocean fine. What he detested were my friends accompanying me when I asked him to drive us out to Sag Harbor. You know Leslie and Marc Harper."

Carly smiled, appreciating Johnny's good sense. She wouldn't have ridden anywhere with that buppie nightmare couple either. "I guess it's settled then. You stay with your man and I'll stay with mine."

Charlotte clapped her hands together in excitement. "Carly!"

"Calm down, Mother. It was only a joke."

Charlotte made a put-out face. "Next time tell one that's funny."

"I'm going to tell her, Charlotte." Jackson leaned back against the booth's cream-colored upholstery, waiting to see what her response would be. After Charlotte and John got checked in, he'd called Drew to find out if any progress had been made in the Anderson investigation. Duke had been strong-armed out of his hole-in-the-wall hangout by another man, the same man a witness claimed to see with him minutes before his death. No one had seen this man do anything to Duke, but it didn't look good.

To Jackson's mind, that changed things. If someone actually did do in Anderson, that same person could be after them as Duke had warned Charlotte. Carly needed to know that, for her own protection. He couldn't put it off any longer.

Now they sat in Linda Jean's, one of the diners on Circuit Avenue. After they'd finished lunch, John had asked him to keep an eye on Charlotte long enough for him to rent a car for them. Carly had excused herself to go to the ladies' room. Jackson figured it would probably be the only moment he'd have alone with Charlotte to tell her.

Charlotte glanced in the direction of the ladies'

room, probably trying to make sure Carly wasn't on her way back. "You absolutely cannot do that, Jackson. The shoot is tomorrow, for heaven's sake."

"Is that all that concerns you, Charlotte, getting the commercial done for the company?"

"That's not fair and that's not what's uppermost in my mind. There will be over one hundred people on that beach tomorrow, one of whom might want to hurt my daughter. That is not the time to have her angry with us, and she will be angry when she finds out we kept this from her. I'm prepared to deal with that when the time comes. Are you?"

In truth, he dreaded telling her as much as he wanted to get it done. But he hadn't created this situation, Charlotte had, by insisting he say nothing. But he answered her question honestly. "No."

"Then trust me when I say this isn't the right time. I do appreciate your loyalty to my daughter and I do understand your desire not to lie to her, but please, Jackson, wait until this is over."

He realized Charlotte wasn't telling him what to do, but asking him not to do what he wanted. *Damn!* Undoubtedly, Charlotte knew Carly better than he. He had to bow to her better judgment about what was best for her daughter. But he didn't feel good about it. Not one little bit.

Chapter 14

By the time they got back to the hotel, Nora was waiting for them. Carly had barely made it up the steps to the front of the hotel when Nora rushed out and embraced her. Nora stood over six feet tall in her bare feet and had excelled on her college's volleyball team. When Nora hugged you, you got hugged. "God, do I love this place!" Nora enthused.

Smiling, Carly stepped back. "How was the trip up?"

Nora rolled her eyes. "Not as bad as I thought. What room are you in?"

"We're right here on the first floor."

Nora's eyebrow rose a notch, as she turned to survey Jackson. "We?"

Now she'd gone and done it. It hadn't occurred to her to invent some sort of cover story for the others about what Jackson was doing in her room. As far as she knew, Nora was the only one he'd actually met before. "Long story."

"I bet. And probably juicy."

"Nora—" Carly warned. If the office grapevine had a hierarchy, Nora was queen grape.

Nora held up both hands, as if to protest her innocence. "You don't have to tell me anything if you don't want to. Just glad to see you get a little of your own, if you know what I mean."

"Nora!"

"Okay. I'm shutting up."

They reached the door to Carly and Jackson's room. "This is us," she said.

"Okay," Nora said. "I have to go finish checking in and then I'll come collect you. Brenda says there's something wrong with the bags and she wants you to check them."

"Give me a few minutes, okay?"

"You're the boss." Nora glanced over at Jackson and wiggled her fingers at him. "Bye, Bruce."

"Uh, Nora. His name is Jackson."

Nora laughed. "I know, long story. I'll see you in a few minutes."

As Nora walked off, Carly slid her gaze to Jackson, who looked as if he was about to laugh. "What?"

"Does she always talk that much?"

Carly tilted her head from side to side, considering the question. "Pretty much. Why?"

"No reason. Just wondering if I should send my ears out for that lube job now or wait until later."

"Do not pick on her. Not only is she the most efficient secretary I've ever had, I think she's the only member of my staff who actually likes me."

"That's because you're probably the only one who can stand to listen."

"I overheard one of the marketing people call her Big Bird minus the feathers. I fired him."

"Point taken," Jackson said, opening the door to their suite. "Wait here."

Jackson disappeared inside, for his room check, she supposed. When he emerged a few moments later looking none the worse for the experience, she asked, "Is this truly necessary?"

He stood aside to let her in and closed the door. "Let's hope not, but we're here on the first floor where anyone with a little ingenuity could get into the room without notice."

Carly sat at one end of the sofa and slipped off her shoes. "Then why didn't we change rooms?"

Jackson sat in the chair closest to her. "Because we can get out of the room without notice, if we have to. In case you didn't notice, the upstairs gallery is closed off. The stairs are being repaired."

No, she hadn't noticed. She hadn't even thought to look. "Is that why you closed all the windows and turned on the air conditioner?"

"No, I did that because you can hear just about everything we say on the porch and vice versa."

That hadn't occurred to her either. But she didn't want to dwell on that, too long. She had a more pressing concern. She tucked her feet underneath her and brushed her hair from her face. "Do you think something is going on between Johnny and my mother?"

"What makes you say that?"

"He shows up here with her in the first place. Then she doesn't bat an eye about sharing the same room with him. On top of that, I caught the two of them making goo-goo eyes at each other in the backseat of the car when they thought I didn't notice."

"Would it bother you if there were something going on between them?"

"Of course not. I adore Johnny, and they're both adults, thank God. And who knows? It might mean my mother has gotten over her teenybopper phase."

Jackson shrugged. "Could be."

Sighing, she realized he hadn't answered a single one of her questions, merely asked a new one of his own. For the second time that day, she suspected he hid more than he told. Or maybe she was simply getting paranoid. Why would Charlotte have told Jackson and not her? Keeping quiet about her conquests was definitely not one of her mother's strong suits.

She slid her shoes on and stood. "I'm going to freshen up before Nora gets here."

He grasped her wrist as she tried to pass him. "Fine. But from now on, I don't want you going anywhere without me or John with you, and I certainly don't want you going anywhere alone."

The somber tone of his voice and the serious look in his eyes caused a shiver of apprehension to run up her spine. Whatever Charlotte was up to, Jackson obviously took it seriously, so she did, too. "What do you know that I don't know?"

"Nothing."

The quickness of his response and the fact that he didn't quite look her in the eye made Carly suspect he dissembled at best. Maybe he didn't *know* anything, but he suspected. "Jackson, if my mother really is in some sort of trouble I need you to tell me. Not just because I'm her daughter, but because we'll be in the middle of a madhouse tomorrow. If I need to be on my guard or look out for her, I need to know now."

Jackson, who'd remained seated, stood. "Look, Carly, I . . ."

He sighed and the indecision she sensed in him surprised her. Up to now, he'd seemed nothing but sure of himself. That in itself concerned her. What was he keeping from her? "Tell me."

For a moment, their gazes locked. Under other circumstances, she would have found the intensity in his eyes arousing, but now it sent alarm racing along her nerve endings. "Tell me," she whispered.

"Carly—"

The sound of a knock at the door cut off whatever else he might have said. Then Nora's voice reached them. "You guys ready in there?"

Carly ground her teeth together in annoyance. Nora's appearance, even if it was on the other side of the door, killed the moment. She could sense Jackson withdrawing from her inch by inch though he didn't take a step away from her. *Damn!*

"Be right there," Carly called back, wishing for once that her assistant wasn't quite so good at keeping her word.

Carly hadn't lied when she said the following day would be a madhouse. Jarad's production company, the security staff, and the people from the advertising agency had been out here on this stretch of sand below the clay cliffs of Gay Head, setting up, shooing off curious onlookers of the human and animal variety, and scarfing down the offerings from the craft services table. Everyone seemed to be in a rush, laying down wires for one thing or another, setting up monitors, rolling in the dolly camera, and adjusting lights and boom microphones. Several young men and women with no obvious purpose except to scurry from one person to the next dashed around the set.

There must be almost a hundred people here already, and the fans expected to come see Sam hadn't shown up yet. Could a would-be attacker wish for a more perfect setting to harm a victim or perhaps snatch her during the chaos? Jackson doubted it. Though a cadre of thick-necked men guarded the perimeter of the barricaded set, their presence did nothing to allay the bout of disquiet that addled his stomach and inspired a heightened sense of awareness in him. Call it a case of cop's intuition that hadn't bothered to quit the force when he had. But he didn't feel good about this shoot.

Jackson shifted his position, leaning his back against

An Important Message From The ARABESQUE Publisher

10 ANNIVERSARY 1994-2004

Dear Arabesque Reader,

Arabesque is celebrating 10 years of award-winning African-American romance. This year look for our specially marked 10th Anniversary titles.

Plus, we are offering *Special Collection Editions* and a *Summer Reading Series*—all part of our 10th Anniversary celebration.

Why not be a part of the celebration and let us send you four more specially selected books FREE! These exceptional romances will be sent right to your front door!

Please enjoy them with our compliments, and thank you for continuing to enjoy Arabesque.... the soul of romance bringing you ten years of love, passion and extraordinary romance.

Linda Gill
PUBLISHER, ARABESQUE ROMANCE NOVELS

P.S. Don't forget to nominate someone special in the Arabesque Man Contest! For more details visit us at www.BET.com

SPECIAL OFFER! 4 BOOKS FREE!

ARABESQUE ★BET BOOKS

A SPECIAL "THANK YOU" FROM ARABESQUE JUST FOR YOU!

Send this card back and you'll receive 4 FREE Arabesque Novels—a $25.96 value—absolutely FREE!

The introductory 4 Arabesque Romance books are yours FREE (plus $1.99 shipping & handling). If you wish to continue to receive 4 books every month, do nothing. Each month, we will send you 4 New Arabesque Romance Novels for your free examination. If you wish to keep them, pay just $18* (plus, $1.99 shipping & handling). If you decide not to continue, you owe nothing!

- Send no money now.
- Never an obligation.
- Books delivered to your door!

We hope that after receiving your FREE books you'll want to remain an Arabesque subscriber, but the choice is yours! So why not take advantage of this Arabesque offer, with no risk of any kind. You'll be glad you did!

In fact, we're so sure you will love your Arabesque novels, that we will send you an Arabesque Tote Bag FREE with your first paid shipment.

* Prices subject to change

THE "THANK YOU" GIFT INCLUDES:

- 4 books absolutely FREE (plus $1.99 for shipping and handling).
- A FREE newsletter, *Arabesque Romance News*, filled with author interviews, book previews, special offers, and more!
- No risks or obligations. You're free to cancel whenever you wish with no questions asked.

INTRODUCTORY OFFER CERTIFICATE

Yes! Please send me 4 FREE Arabesque novels (plus $1.99 for shipping & handling). I am under no obligation to purchase any books, as explained on the back of this card. Send my free tote bag after my first regular paid shipment.

NAME _____

ADDRESS _____ APT. _____

CITY _____ STATE _____ ZIP _____

TELEPHONE ( ) _____

E-MAIL _____

SIGNATURE _____

Offer limited to one per household and not valid to current subscribers. All orders subject to approval. Terms, offer, & price subject to change. Tote bags available while supplies last.

Thank You!

AN064A

ARABESQUE

Accepting the four introductory books for FREE (plus $1.99 to offset the cost of shipping & handling) places you under no obligation to buy anything. You may keep the books and return the shipping statement marked "cancelled". If you do not cancel, about a month later we will send 4 additional Arabesque novels, and you will be billed the preferred subscriber's price of just $4.50 per title. That's $18.00* for all 4 books for a savings of almost 40% off the cover price (Plus $1.99 for shipping and handling). You may cancel at any time, but if you choose to continue, every month we'll send you 4 more books, which you may either purchase at the preferred discount price. . . or return to us and cancel your subscription.

* PRICES SUBJECT TO CHANGE

THE ARABESQUE ROMANCE CLUB: HERE'S HOW IT WORKS

THE ARABESQUE ROMANCE BOOK CLUB
P.O. BOX 5214
CLIFTON NJ 07015-5214

PLACE
STAMP
HERE

the wardrobe and makeup trailer into which Sam, Charlotte, and Carly had disappeared. When he'd tried to follow her inside, not knowing the purpose of the vehicle, Carly had informed him that if anyone tried to impale her with an eyebrow pencil, he'd be the first to know. Although she'd asked for answers from him before her assistant showed up, she hadn't picked up the subject again once they returned to their room, which led him to believe she'd drawn her own, correct conclusions.

He didn't mind that one bit. It protected him from divulging information his client had sworn him not to share and also put her on her guard at the same time. Besides, if it came to it, she wouldn't resist any efforts he might have to make to protect her.

But why would he? That question nagged at him from the beginning. He could understand it better if someone were after Charlotte, perhaps fearing that she might know something or be able to provide some sort of damning information that a killer might want to silence. Or maybe he hoped to guarantee her cooperation by threatening to harm her daughter. Somehow Jackson didn't think so, though. When Charlotte told him that she didn't know much about the case, he believed her. Maybe someone else didn't.

And then there was Drew's suggestion that perhaps whoever had killed Duke Anderson hadn't been looking to silence him but to exact revenge for his role in the trial. That same person might want to exact retribution against Charlotte or maybe even Alex through their daughter. But why now, after twenty years had passed? When he'd asked that question of Drew, he'd replied cryptically, "Revenge is a dish best served cold." That might be true, but until Charlotte started getting phone calls, the case had been in a deep freeze.

What bothered him most is that he might never

know the answer to that question unless someone made a move on Carly. Or him. Duke Anderson had warned him not to go looking for trouble, but he'd done a good job of not following the older man's advice. He wasn't worried about his own safety. He could handle himself. Carly shouldn't have to.

Hearing the trailer door open, he turned to see Carly descending the three steps to the sand. She wore a beige sundress that molded to her curves and ended well above her knees. Somehow the dress still looked professional, or it would have except for the thick-soled black and white flip-flops on her feet.

She beamed up at him. "How do you like the drive-by makeover they did on me in there? They insisted on giving me the full treatment, hair, makeup, clothes, the works. What do you think?"

She made a slow turnaround, giving ample time to drink in every inch of her. Her hair was loose and curled around her shoulders. Her makeup had been applied to emphasize her best feature, her large, almond-shaped eyes. The dress accentuated her slim figure. She took his breath away, but most of all it was her smile that knocked him sideways.

He swallowed. "Is that the latest fashion for cosmetic company moguls? Linen and flip-flops?"

She folded her arms under her breasts, which only succeeded in deepening her cleavage. "Come on, Jackson, tell me what you think."

If he'd been with any woman but Carly, he would have assumed the woman in question was flirting with him. But the earnestness in her voice told him she sincerely expected an objective answer from him. Fat chance. Since he sincerely doubted she wanted to hear what he was really thinking about, which involved a big bed and the ruination of the cosmetologists' handiwork, he took a page from the psychologists' handbook and turned her question back on her. "What do you think?"

She lifted one shoulder. "The makeup is a bit much, but I like it."

He brushed back a strand of her hair that the breeze had picked up. "You look beautiful, sweetheart."

For a moment her humor-filled gaze met his hot one. Slowly the mirth slipped from her face to be replaced by a sloe-eyed temptress's smile. "Glad you approve."

She was definitely flirting with him now. He wished his brain could come up with something snappy to say, some bit of witty banter. But his thought processes seemed to have stalled the moment his libido kicked into overdrive.

"Carly! Carly, is that you?"

They both glanced in the direction of the voice, the moment between them gone. A look of recognition came into Carly's eyes a second before she turned more fully to greet the man striding toward her. Jackson had never met him but recognized him from pictures—Paul Samuels. In person, he reminded Jackson of the Jack Lalanne of his youth: as old as the hills, but possessing a body that remained muscular from a lifetime of exercise.

Samuels embraced Carly in a bear hug that lifted her off her feet. He spun her around once before setting her on her feet. "You're looking wonderful, my dear." He took Carly's hand in his and took a step back to survey her. "I think the Vineyard agrees with you."

"I think so, too. But what happened to you yesterday? I thought your flight got in last night."

"I couldn't get out of the office until it was too late to make the plane. I hope I didn't worry you."

"Not really. I figured that's what happened."

Samuels draped his arm around Carly's shoulders

and nodded toward the craft table to his right. "Why don't we catch up over a cup of coffee?"

Carly nodded, and as the two of them started to walk away, Jackson coughed exaggeratedly. Carly's head whipped around and she looked at him as if she just remembered he existed. "Oh, Uncle Paul, this is Jackson Trent. Jackson, this is my godfather, Paul Samuels."

Samuels turned and extended a hand toward him, which Jackson shook, but something in the older man's eyes told him that Carly's introduction had been wasted.

"It's a pleasure to meet any friend of Carly's," Samuels said.

Not much of one, Jackson assumed, given the look of disdain on the other man's face. Especially considering the death grip Samuels tried to exert on his hand. Of all the juvenile maneuvers. Jackson squeezed back, until the other man let go. Jackson suppressed a grin. "The pleasure is all mine."

"Yes, well," Samuels said, rubbing one hand with the other. "You do owe me that cup of coffee, Carly."

"Of course." Carly looked from Samuels to him in a way that told him both that their contest hadn't gone unnoticed and she was annoyed at him for competing. Not Samuels, just him. He couldn't fathom the reason for that and didn't bother trying.

"Are you joining us, Jackson?"

"No, you go on ahead. I'm sure you two would rather do your catching up alone."

She cast him a look that said she suspected he was up to something, which he was, so he only offered a blank stare that told her nothing. After a moment she turned and walked away.

Carly accepted a paper cup of coffee from Paul and took a dainty sip from it. She didn't usually drink it black, but she didn't feel like fiddling with milk or sugar either. Although a canopy had been set up above the table to keep the sand out and prevent errant seagulls from swooping down and carrying off the food, everything was covered with scarlet plastic lids.

"What has been going on with you lately?" Paul asked her, but immediately launched into a monologue about his latest business venture. Although she tried to pay attention, her gaze and her thoughts kept drifting back to Jackson. He stood leaning against the trailer, his arms and ankles crossed. Most people would mistake that for an indolent stance, but she also noticed how intently he watched her. Even when Johnny and Adam drifted over to join him, his attention didn't waver.

So why had he stayed behind? Probably because he wanted to see Paul in action, to get a bead on him. Jackson had questioned her about him, implying that Paul might somehow be involved in what was going on with Charlotte. She couldn't fathom that. Or maybe she didn't want to consider that a man she'd known all her life wanted to harm her mother.

"That's unseemly, my dear."

She blinked and focused her gaze on Uncle Paul. Disapproval hardened his features. "What is?"

"Gaping at a man the same way a mongrel covets a piece of steak."

Carly ground her teeth together. As long as she'd known him, Paul Samuels had been a man more impressed with his own importance than anyone else was. She put up with his pretentiousness because he'd always been very good to her and because of his relationship with Charlotte, but his snobbishness wore on her nerves.

Undoubtedly his comment had been sparked, not by the way she looked at Jackson, but by the fact that she looked at all. Without question Paul would consider a man like Jackson beneath him. The urge to tell him how ridiculous he looked on the beach dressed in Armani and wing tips tempted her, but she curbed her tongue. Antagonizing him wouldn't serve any purpose on a day when she wanted everything to run smoothly.

But like a dog with a bone, he wouldn't let it go. "I hear you're sharing your room with him. That can't possibly be true."

She wanted to know why that possibility shocked him so, but she suspected she knew at least three-quarters of the answer. And it wasn't only him. Half the people that worked for them had been around long enough to still remember her as little more than an awkward teenager who nonetheless had run the company from her dorm room. She knew how people thought of her, at least when it came to personal matters, as a sweet kid who needed someone to look out for her.

She doubted anyone would have seen anything amiss if she'd brought around some nerdy guy whose best friend was his pocket protector. Nobody expected her to attract a man like Jackson, whose appeal could be described many ways, but never as sweet. She'd seen how some of the women, Nora included, looked at him and when they looked at her she saw envy.

She wasn't quite sure what she saw in Uncle Paul's eyes, aside from his obvious disdain for Jackson. She knew she could tell him that nothing was going on between her and Jackson, nothing worth stressing himself over, anyway, but she wouldn't give him the satisfaction.

"That's none of your business."

He sputtered, taken aback by her bluntness. Maybe a week ago she would have tried to smooth things over for him, but this was the new Carly and she refused to suffer his nonsense. "After all these years, you're finally turning into your mother's daughter."

Uncertain whether he meant that as an indictment or a compliment, she decided to take it as the latter. "It's about time, don't you think?"

She never got to hear his answer, as Jackson came up beside her, draping his arm around her and placing his hand on her hip in a proprietary manner. He bent down to whisper in her ear, but spoke loud enough for Paul to hear, "Sweetheart, your mother is looking for you."

She cast him a skeptical look. "Really?" And the Tooth Fairy had left her a quarter, too. Unless Jackson had gone blind in the last half hour, he had to have picked up on Uncle Paul's dislike of him and his perceived unsuitability as a beau for her. Undoubtedly, he chose to rub it in the older man's face. But why at this particular moment? Even though Charlotte was at that moment scheduled for an interview with a reporter from *Essence* magazine, she was probably still in the trailer deciding which shade of blush best coordinated with her outfit.

Even so, he'd provided her with a hasty means of escape and she planned to take it. "Thank you, Jackson. Excuse me please, Uncle Paul."

She didn't get a chance to hear whatever his response might have been, as Jackson started leading her away with an arm around her waist. When they were out of Uncle Paul's earshot, she said, "Okay, what was that about?"

"That what?"

"I know Charlotte isn't looking for me, so why did you come over there?"

"Why are you annoyed that I did?"

She stopped walking and turned to face him. "We're not playing Socrates anymore or whatever you call it where I ask you a question and you ask me another one. I'll tell you why you came over there. To tweak Paul's nose because he doesn't like you."

"And that would bother you if I did? Not to sound like a two-year-old, but he started it."

She took a deep exasperated breath. "I know, but I expect that sort of nonsense from Paul."

"But you expect better from me?"

"It would be nice to have one man around whose ego doesn't govern his actions."

"I came over there because I didn't like the way he was talking to you. And since I didn't think you'd want me to feed him the knuckle sandwich he deserved, I figured I'd just get you away from him instead."

She lowered her head to hide a smile. His protectiveness charmed her, though his concern was misplaced. She could handle herself with Uncle Paul or anyone else. "Knuckle sandwich? I don't think I've heard anyone use that expression outside of a Popeye cartoon."

"I was going for the clean version. Would it have made you feel better if I'd said I'd been two seconds away from kicking your friend's ass?"

Paul wasn't her friend, he was Charlotte's, and he'd been her father's. But she wouldn't argue semantics with Jackson. "It would have been honest."

He snorted. "Well, I'd honestly like to know when all this is supposed to get started." He gestured in a way that encompassed the whole scene around him.

"As soon as Sam is ready, I guess. This isn't my show, it's Jarad's and the agency people's."

"The advertising agency?"

She nodded. "My mother and Brenda, she's the publicity director you met yesterday, handle the press."

"And what do you do?"

"Stay out of the way, mostly. The agency is excellent and I trust Jarad implicitly." She pointed to where a monitor was being set up. "I get to watch what's going on over there."

Hearing the sound of applause, Jackson turned in the direction where everyone else stared. Sam was coming down the dressing room stairs.

Beside him, Carly said, "Now the real madness will begin."

Jackson swallowed. That's exactly what he was afraid of.

Chapter 15

By two o'clock that afternoon, Jackson's sense of apprehension hadn't eased any, despite the uneventfulness of the day. Gary Vespers hadn't made an appearance and Samuels had kept his distance, preferring to wander over to the tented area where Charlotte held court over the reporters. Undoubtedly, Carly was right about Samuels being jealous, but Jackson suspected his bout of the green-eyed monster had nothing to do with Charlotte.

Time after time, Samuels's gaze followed Carly, not her mother. Jackson wasn't sure what to make of that, he only knew he didn't like it. But when Charlotte left with the press to take the tour around the island, Samuels went with her. Fine. Let John deal with him for a while.

In the meantime, Sam's crowd of adoring fans, secured behind the barricades and the guards, had hung on her every move as she'd been filmed in a variety of positions, sporting a variety of outfits, wearing different shades of makeup that, according to Carly, would all be sifted through later to decide which images were best to use. At the moment Sam was walking along the shore while her motions were tracked and filmed by a cameraman on a dolly. He stood next to Carly as they watched the feed from the camera on the monitor.

"Cut, cut, cut," the woman he had come to know as

the AD or assistant director said in a carrying voice. For the third time in three takes, a seagull had flown past in the background, when they wanted the background seagull-free. "Can't someone do something about these birds?"

Carly cast him a humorous look. "A bit high-strung, isn't she?"

"A bit."

"What does she expect someone to do? Shoot them?"

The words were barely out of Carly's mouth when a series of loud sharp pops filled the air and a collective cry of fear and surprise issued from the crowd. Jackson had Carly on the ground with his body covering hers by the time the second pop sounded. She trembled beneath him, but he couldn't address her fear, not yet, when he wasn't certain the danger had passed.

Glancing around, he saw that just about everyone had hit the deck, as well, including all the muscle hired to keep everyone else safe. Damned amateurs. He caught Adam's eye and motioned in the direction from which the sound had come. Adam nodded. Jackson shifted enough so that he could see Carly's face. She looked back at him with wide, frightened eyes. "Don't move, okay? I'll be right back."

She surprised him by not arguing about him leaving her unprotected. She simply nodded and whispered, "Be careful."

He winked at her and moved off to join Adam. They were in a natural curve of the cliff wall, which afforded the shot some privacy but made it impossible to see who might be lurking on the other side. It also put the shooter, if that's what this was, at a disadvantage. The only person they might have had a clear sight for had been Sam down at the water's edge, and the cameraman.

Silently, Jackson edged along the cliff wall, behind

Adam, who already had his gun drawn. For the first time in a long time, he wished he had one, too, if only to have something handy to beat the crap out of whoever had done this. He hated seeing that look of panic in Carly's eyes, even though it only lasted a second. But if this turned out to be what he thought it was, he wouldn't need one.

Once they got as far as they could go without being seen, Adam counted to three by raising three fingers one at a time, then in a flash he whipped around the corner, his gun trained on whoever might be waiting there.

Almost immediately Adam's shoulders relaxed. "Oh, for heaven's sake."

Only after Jackson saw Adam lower his gun and reholster it did he venture around the corner. Three terrified kids, probably no more than twelve or thirteen, huddled around a box full of firecrackers. The detritus of the string they'd already lit lay burnt in the sand next to them.

"He made me do it," the youngest-looking of the three said, pointing to the boy next to him, who was clearly his brother.

Jackson exhaled as relief flooded through him and the rush of adrenaline subsided. "What did you boys think you were doing?"

"We didn't want to hurt anyone. We were just . . ."

The boy trailed off, probably realizing that telling an armed man you had scared the bejesus out of the better of two hundred people just to get your kicks was probably not the best way to go. Especially considering the murderous expression on Adam's face and the fact that at no time did he identify himself as a policeman.

"Let's go, all of you," Adam said, motioning back the way they had come.

Jackson helped the youngest to his feet and grabbed

the box of fireworks in the other hand. In the distance the sound of sirens approaching reached them over the sound of the crashing surf. The island police would be there any moment.

"My mom is gonna freak," the boy beside him wailed.

Despite himself, Jackson empathized with the boy. He'd gotten into enough scrapes himself to know the feeling. "Come on," he said gently, urging the boy forward with a hand on his arm. The boy nodded and trudged alongside him around the corner to where the others, realizing there had never been any real threat, began to rise and dust themselves off. He scanned the crowd, but he didn't see Carly. That didn't alarm him at first. As petite as she was, he'd have a hard time finding her in a crowd anyway.

One of Vespers's men had corralled the other two kids and motioned for the third boy to join them. "Think you can handle them?" Jackson asked, not bothering to fight the urge to taunt the man. The guard had the good grace to look contrite.

But Jackson wasn't worried about the kids, the guard, or the crowd. He needed to find Carly. Scanning the area, he found Adam with his arms around Sam, Ariel and Jarad huddled together, the crew picking up fallen equipment and beginning to indulge in a little gallows humor now that the danger had passed, but no Carly.

Alarm ricocheted through him, tautening his nerve endings. This was the situation he'd dreaded. Carly in danger because everyone's attention was diverted, especially his. He threaded his way through the throng of people, hoping to spot her. Bile rose in his throat, as bitter as the knowledge that by leaving Carly he'd put her in more danger than she would have been if he hadn't done anything at all. But letting other people do his job wasn't in his nature. He only hoped his miscalculation didn't cost Carly her life.

He saw her then, standing beside the dressing room trailer. For the second time that day, relief washed through him—until he realized she was arguing with a man who had his back to him and his hand wrapped around Carly's wrist.

He pushed the rest of the way through the crowd and grabbed the man by the back of his clothing and shoved him up against the trailer with his face pressed against the structure. A second later he had the man's hand, the one that had grabbed Carly, twisted up behind his back in what he hoped was a painful position. He leaned into the man and in a low, mean voice, he said, "Who the hell are you and why were you touching her?"

The man sputtered something, but with his face mashed up like that it was impossible to make out.

"It's not what you think, Jackson. Let him go."

He heard Carly's voice, full of urgency and entreaty, but he didn't feel like easing off just yet. "Why were you touching her?" he repeated.

"For heaven's sake, Jackson. That's Gary Vespers. He was trying to keep me from going after you."

Vespers? Revealing his name was supposed to make him want to squash the guy less? Nonetheless he pushed away from him and glanced at Carly. She'd been coming after him? Why?

Immediately Vespers flipped around to lean his back against the trailer, breathing heavily, with his hand at his throat. Jackson looked him over, taking satisfaction that the imprint of the trailer's siding was visible on Vespers's pale skin. In person he appeared much lankier than he had in his promo photo, almost effeminate. What had Charlotte ever seen in this man?

"Nice security force you've got here, Vespers. Seems all they know how to do is duck and cover."

"We're only being paid to handle the crowd."

So that's all they did? And not even a great job of that. A few of the spectators, as well as a few of the crew, had gotten injured when either the barricades or some of the equipment had fallen. "Why'd you take such an interest in Carly?"

He darted a look at Carly before answering. "Ch-Charlotte asked me to keep an eye on her if I could."

He'd give the guy credit for this, at least. He hadn't spilled the beans to Carly about her mother's deception. Although he wanted her to know, he didn't want her to find out from this little weasel. He wanted to tell her himself, or make sure Charlotte did. He was grateful that at that moment, the account manager of the agency and some of his underlings came over to check on Carly and lament the ruination of the shoot.

He pulled Vespers to the side, out of Carly's earshot but where he could still keep an eye on her. "What did Charlotte tell you?"

"Only that she'd been receiving notes threatening Carly's life."

The same nonsense she'd told him. "What is your relationship to Charlotte?"

"We don't have one, exactly." Sighing, he shifted against the trailer. "Look, I'm not proud of it, but I kind of blackmailed her into loaning me the money to start my agency. I think she told Carly we were lovers to cover the fact that I kept coming around pestering her, but we never were."

"And now?"

"I paid Charlotte back every cent she gave me. With interest. However it was done, she gave me my start and I'm grateful to her for that. I would never do anything to hurt Carly or Charlotte."

Jackson exhaled, not sure whether to believe him. On the surface, he'd spat out everything he knew without too much provocation. That's what bothered

Jackson. It wasn't unusual for a subject to appear totally accommodating, and only later did you find out he neglected to tell you the murder weapon was at home in his closet. But he did find it telling that not one of Vespers's men had come over to investigate who was roughing up the boss.

"Can I go now?"

Jackson nodded. He'd had enough of this gutless wonder anyway. He needed to talk to Carly to make sure she was okay and to find out what had possessed her to try to come after him.

She watched him with a wary expression as he walked toward her. He supposed she had a right to. He admitted to himself he might have gone a bit overboard in the way he'd handled Vespers, but when he'd seen that man's hand on her, he'd seen red and nothing else.

He stopped at the perimeter of the group of people surrounding her. "Can I speak to you for a moment?"

She nodded and excused herself from the group. He took her inside the trailer, which was thankfully empty, and pulled her into his arms. For a moment, he simply held her, realizing that she still trembled slightly from the ordeal. "Are you all right?"

"It's about time you asked me that question."

He pulled back from her, enough to see her face. A slight smile turned up the corners of her lips. He didn't resist the urge to lower his head and claim her mouth. His tongue met hers for a dance that started slow and sweet, but gradually picked up the tempo. She trembled again and a certain amount of satisfaction filled him, knowing this time passion, not fear, caused the tremors.

But this wasn't the time or place for that. He pulled away from her by slow degrees, not wanting to, but knowing he had to. He set her away from him and took a step back, widening the gap between them. He needed distance from her and a moment to settle his own emotions. "What was the confab out there about?"

She blinked, surprised by his question. "Nothing important. Just trying to figure out how many of those people will want to sue me. Are you all right, Jackson?"

"I'm fine." His own mental state didn't concern him. Hers did. "You tried to come after me. Why would you do that?"

"I wasn't *coming after you* coming after you. Not the way it sounds. The minute you left, I tried to call you back but you didn't hear me." She shook her head and lowered it, avoiding his gaze. "I was worried. It didn't occur to me at first that you were unarmed. And when it did . . ."

She crossed to one of the chairs where her purse sat, reached inside, and pulled out a little .22 S&W, a model with a pearl handle designed to fit a woman's hand. "I was trying to come in here to get this to give to you."

He stared at the gun in her hand as if it were a snake prepared to strike. In a way, that's what it was, as the barrel pointed at him. He took the weapon from her by the handle, pointed it toward the floor, and flicked open the cylinder. All six chambers were filled. "What are you doing with this, Carly?"

"Someone tried to mug me two years ago. I live alone. I thought I ought to be better prepared."

He shook the bullets into his palm, put them in his pocket, and clicked the cylinder closed. "That's not what I meant. Are you prepared to use this thing?"

She crossed her arms, rubbing one hand over the opposite shoulder. "I've had lessons."

"But are you really ready to point this at someone and take their life if you have to?" Unbidden, his finger curled around the trigger, not enough to fire, just enough to spark a muscle memory of times past. He tucked the gun in the back of his waistband, equally stimulated and repulsed by the familiar weight of having a weapon in his hand.

"I don't know, Jackson. I've never been in the situation to have to decide."

"Pray you never are." He opened the door to the trailer. "Let's get out of here."

Chapter 16

The incident with the firecrackers put a damper on the day and called the shooting to a halt, as both Sam and, oddly, Adam seemed too shaken up to continue. It was decided that the ad agency would make do with what they had rather than try to get permission to shoot for another day. Carly was grateful that no one outside of a few people with minor cuts or scrapes needed medical attention. In fact, the crowd seemed to be the only ones jazzed by the events of the day. Maybe they figured they got a lot more excitement than they'd planned for that day.

As the production company folded up its equipment, Carly collected her things and the few items her mother had left behind from the trailer before joining Jackson, who waited for her outside. Ever since they'd left the trailer together the first time, he'd been subdued and mostly silent. She had no idea what was going on in his mind right now, but his uncharacteristic moodiness tore at her. She knew to some degree that having her gun or any gun in his possession must upset him. But he hadn't seemed himself to her from the moment he'd squished Gary Vespers against the side of the trailer. Or maybe she didn't know him as well as she thought she did.

She descended the stairs watching as Jackson turned

to look at her with such a bleak expression in his eyes that her heart went out to him. As she approached, he put his arm around her waist to pull her closer to him.

Adam said, "Sam and I are going to head over to the house. Jarad said not to wait for his guys, so we'll see all of you over there."

"Just like a man," she said to Jackson, trying to lighten his mood. "Leave them alone for five minutes and they take over everything." Carly's shoulders slumped as neither man's expression showed the slightest trace of humor.

Jackson squeezed her side. "Ready to go?"

She nodded. So maybe he acknowledged her attempt to pull him out of his mood even if he wasn't ready to respond to it. For now, that would have to do.

Out in the massive parking lot, Carly waited for Jackson to open the door for her before sliding across the smooth leather seat. He walked around the car and got in, slamming the door. He unlocked the glove compartment, pulled the gun from his waistband, and tossed it in. He snapped the door shut and relocked it, all without saying a single word to her.

"Jackson, would you please say something to me?"

"What would you like me to say, Carly?"

"Something other than 'ready to go?'"

"Everything that needs to be said today has already been said."

What was that supposed to mean? "Who said what?"

"You did and you're right. I have no business calling myself anyone's bodyguard if I don't have the guts for the job."

Her mouth dropped open. "When did I say that?" He didn't answer her, but she knew. He viewed her attempt to arm him not as concern for his safety but doubt over his ability to do his job. He had to be out of his mind. She felt safer with him than she did with Adam, even though Adam was six feet seven, weighed 250 pounds, and, more often than not, kept a cannon strapped to his hip.

"Sam told me what happened with you and Adam and how you left the force."

His jaw tightened. "What did she say?"

"That you were given a commendation for saving Adam's life, which you never accepted."

"That's not all she told you, is it?"

"No."

"You don't have to gloss it over, Carly. I know what happened. I killed a ten-year-old kid."

"It was an accident."

"That doesn't make the kid any less dead."

No, she supposed it didn't. "How long do you intend to punish yourself for that?"

He darted a glance at her. "Is that what you think I'm doing?" He shook his head. "The department shrink they make you see said I should 'forgive myself' for what happened and move on, but how am I supposed to do that? I was supposed to be the one who catches the bad guys. I wasn't supposed to be one of them. I wasn't supposed to hurt the innocent, and that's what I did."

"So you left out of guilt over the boy's death?"

"I left because I was scared, Carly. Scared I'd make another mistake. In my line of work, I can't afford mistakes."

His candor surprised her, as did his reference to his occupation. He still thought of himself as a cop even though he no longer wore a badge. And worse yet, he viewed himself as a coward because he no longer had the stomach for the job. "Everybody's scared, Jackson."

He tucked a lock of her hair behind her ear and a tender look came into his eyes. "Even you? You start a business when you're only seventeen and turn it into a major corporation. While grown men are cowering in fear, you go looking for your gun." He offered her a lopsided grin, but the intense expression in his eyes told her he was only half teasing her about the last part.

"Pretty dumb idea, huh?"

"Pretty much. Next time I tell you to stay put somewhere, you stay put."

"Yes, sir."

"I'm not kidding, Carly. You could have been hurt."

"But I wasn't."

"But you could have been."

"But I wasn't. Look, Jackson, we could argue this all day if you want, but frankly I'd rather go to Sam's house and eat shrimp."

He shook his head, looking at her with an expression she didn't understand. "Whatever you want, baby." He gunned the engine and pulled out of the dirt parking lot onto the narrow road ahead.

Charlotte watched anxiously from the window of Sam and Adam's house, waiting for Carly and Jackson to show up. Although Adam told her Carly hadn't been hurt in any way, she wouldn't be able to truly relax until she saw her daughter with her own eyes to make sure she was all right. This time, even John's arms around her did little to comfort her.

Jackson's big red monstrosity of a car pulled up in front of the house. She glanced at John over her shoulder. "They're here."

Left on her own, she would have run outside, but John held on to her. "They'll be inside in a minute, baby," he said gently.

She nodded, seeing the logic of his words, but that didn't lessen her feelings of anticipation. It seemed to take forever for them to get out of the car and walk the short distance to the front door. But she did notice the way Jackson slipped his arm around Carly's waist, not in a protective way but an affectionate one. And Carly allowed it. In fact, she seemed to move closer to him. Hope stirred in Charlotte, a long-buried dream she'd crushed long ago in both Carly and herself with her own foolhardiness. Maybe . . .

The front door opened and this time John let her go. She rushed to Carly and embraced her. "Darling, I heard what happened. Are you all right?"

Carly hugged her back briefly, then pulled away. "It was just some kids with firecrackers, Mom. Although Jackson nearly crushed me when he threw himself on top of me."

She wasn't sure whether Carly said that to provide proof of Jackson's bravery or to divert her attention elsewhere, but she succeeded in both. Charlotte turned to Jackson. "Thank you."

Jackson nodded, but said nothing. He looked at John and for a moment the two of them seemed to communicate something she didn't understand. How did men do that?

John said, "Good to have you back in one piece, Miss Scarlet."

"Thanks, Johnny."

"Sam was looking for you. She's upstairs."

"Thanks. But before I go and while I have both of you here, I just want to say that you two can quit pretending there's nothing going on between you. I know and I approve, so you can stop sneaking around on my account."

Carly leaned up and kissed Charlotte's cheek, then patted John's shoulder as she passed him on her way up the stairs.

Charlotte, who'd been too stunned by the revelation that Carly knew about them to really react, turned to John. "How did she know?"

But it was Jackson who answered her. "You said it yourself, Charlotte. Your daughter's not stupid. And I hope she's given you a clue as to how easily secrets can be dispelled. When do you plan to tell her?"

She had rarely seen such a look of coldness in a man's eyes as she saw in Jackson's now. Rather than face him she turned to John. In his eyes she saw a disappointment so profound she couldn't bear his gaze either. She turned back to Jackson, wishing she could find some words to make him, make them both, understand why she had done what she did.

"Never mind, Charlotte," Jackson said. "You just answered my question. You never intended to tell her, did you?"

She shook her head. "I hoped you'd find out who was threatening her quickly enough that I wouldn't have to."

"You don't have to worry about saying anything to Carly anymore. I'll take care of that." He shook his head, his derision clear in his eyes. "You led me to believe this shoot today was some big damn deal and, fool that I am, I believed you. She could have stayed home and the outcome wouldn't have been any different. If you want to lie to your daughter, that's your business, but you made me a party to that, too, and for no other reason than you're too much of a coward to level with your own daughter. What did you think she would do? Run off and try to find out who was after her by herself? She's too level-headed for that. Or is keeping her a little girl under Mommy's thumb what's important to you?"

"That's not fair. Carly is her own woman."

"It's about time you noticed that." He looked from her to John. "Excuse me, will you?"

He walked away without another word. For a moment Charlotte could only stare after him, nonplussed by both his anger and by the fact that every word he'd spoken to her carried the ring of truth. John's arms closed around her from behind, steadying her. "Did you hear what he said to me?" she asked him, not as an indictment of Jackson, but to find out if John agreed with him.

"Cut the boy some slack, Charlotte. He's in love with your daughter and he has every right to be angry with you."

She didn't waste time considering what Jackson did or did not have a right to. "John, do you really think so? Is he in love with Carly?"

"Yes, I do. When I found out he used to be a cop, I checked his record. Do you know he never received a complaint for excessive force? Not one. Yet according to Adam he nearly wrenched some poor guy's arm out of the socket today for daring to touch her. I'd say he's a goner or very close to it."

And if Charlotte weren't mistaken, Carly had feelings for him, too. Charlotte had never seen her daughter behave around a man the way she did with Jackson—open, smiling, allowing him to touch her in ways that bespoke a growing intimacy. She doubted Carly had taken him to her bed yet, but she suspected she wanted to. Then again, she'd been wrong the last time, too.

She pulled John's arms more tightly around her. "I've been such a fool, John." She'd wanted to save her daughter from ugliness in the present and an equally ugly past, but what if she'd ruined Carly's chance for a future with Jackson? "She's going to hate him for keeping this from her."

"That's where you're wrong, Charlotte." John's breath fanned her cheek as he brushed his lips across her temple. "She's going to hate all of us."

Carly found Sam and Ariel in the little anteroom to the bedroom she shared with her husband. Sam lay on a divan, her feet and head propped up with pillows. "God, Sam, are you all right? You weren't hurt today, were you?"

"I'm fine actually, though I wish someone would tell Adam that. He dragged me up here, fixed me up like this, and told me to stay put."

Carly took a seat next to Sam. "You're not sick, are you?"

Sam grinned. "Not sick, no."

Ariel groaned. "What Sam isn't telling you is that she and Adam are expecting another baby."

"Congratulations." Carly leaned over to embrace Sam. "Why didn't you tell me?"

"She just told me fifteen minutes ago. Don't think I'm going to forget that."

"I'm sorry, guys," Sam said. "Adam and I decided to keep it a secret until the three-month mark passed. We had a little trouble conceiving this time and we didn't want to jinx ourselves in case this one didn't take."

"That's understandable," Carly said. And it explained why both Sam and Adam seemed so shaken by the incident with the firecrackers. Undue stress could definitely have an adverse effect on a pregnancy. "When is the three months up?"

"Next week, so I think we're safe. Besides, I figured someone ought to explain why my husband is downstairs acting like the bear whose paw got stepped on."

"He's worried about you," Ariel said.

Sam rolled her eyes. "You're not married to a cop, so you don't know this, but they worry about every little thing you do, but whenever there's an opportunity to throw themselves into danger, they're right there."

Carly smiled to herself. Jackson hadn't behaved any better, but at least Adam had a gun and a badge to back up his impulses. Jackson had neither.

"What are you grinning about?" Sam asked. "Jackson was right there with him. Doesn't that bother you?"

"Why should it? Don't get me wrong, I was terrified for his safety. But did I expect him to cower in the sand next to me? No way. They're protectors, Sam. That's what they do. I'm not saying all cops are like that. Some are simply on a power trip. Some are corrupt enough to sell their own mother for a buck. Even as a child, I remember my father complaining about cops who would lie on the stand or plant evidence just to convict a person they believed to be guilty or to clear a case. Not every cop is one of the good guys, but the ones we know are. Asking either one of them to be any different is like asking us regular humans not to breathe."

Carly hadn't intended to lecture Sam on her husband's character or to upset her further, but seeing the distraught look that came over Sam's face, she realized she'd done both. In a small voice, Sam said, "Jackson's not a cop anymore."

"Maybe not on paper."

Sam didn't say anything else after that and Carly searched her mind unsuccessfully for something to say to dispel the tension in the room.

Ariel saved her. "Somehow I remember coming up here with the intention of putting on my bathing suit and going for a swim."

"That sounds like a plan," Sam said, offering them a watery smile. "Let's go."

"You ladies go on ahead," Carly said. "I didn't bring a suit."

"Nonsense," Sam said, rising. "I'm sure I've got something that will fit you."

That's what Carly was afraid of. Sam's taste in clothing could be a bit more daring than anything Carly would consider suitable to wear. Then again, what had she told herself about being more adventurous? Was she giving up on the new Carly so soon? No way. Carly grinned. "Let's see what you've got."

But when Carly surveyed herself in Sam's full-length mirror wearing the tiny fuschia bathing suit Sam had given her, she said, "I cannot wear this." Carly might not have had much to conceal in any garment, but the suit barely covered any of it.

"Why not?" Sam protested. "You look smashing in it."

"Jackson's eyes are going to pop when he sees you," Ariel added.

That might be true, and any other time that would have been her only concern. "You don't understand. My staff is downstairs, some of them anyway, and the people from the advertising agency. I'm the boss. If they see me like this they'll think . . ." Carly trailed off, uncertain how to end that sentence. More than likely, the people who thought they knew her best would probably think she'd lost her mind.

"They'll think you're human?" Ariel supplied. "That you've got a great guy you want to impress? That you don't have an ounce of cellulite? And believe me, I'm jealous."

Carly laughed. "All right, all right. I'll wear the suit."

"If you're really stuck on this modesty thing," Sam said, "here." She pulled a matching shawl from one of her drawers and tied it around Carly's hips. "Voila."

Carly couldn't see how this helped much. The lacy material hid absolutely nothing and lent her an exotic look the suit alone did not. But she wasn't going to complain about it. Who knew what Sam would pull out of her wardrobe next?

Once the other women had donned their own cover-ups—a sheer black jacket to match Sam's tiny black bathing suit and a white lace one for Ariel—the three of them headed downstairs, each of them wearing a different pair of Samantha's high-heeled sandals.

They were halfway down the stairs when Adam appeared at the lower landing. "Now, isn't this a sight?" he said. "I'm used to having only one lovely lady in the house at a time. Now I've got three." He held out his hand to his wife and after Sam descended the last few steps he pulled her to his side.

"Flatterer," Ariel accused. "But don't stop. We like it."

But it was evident to Carly that Sam and Adam wanted to be alone, for a few minutes at least. As she and Ariel continued through the house, Ariel leaned closer to her and whispered, "At least someone will be having great make-up sex tonight, if the two of them last that long."

Carly giggled, but as they passed the front door, it opened and Jarad's crew poured in. Ariel excused herself and went to her husband. Carly stood in the center of the floor feeling abandoned. She hadn't planned on making a solo appearance in the backyard. She'd counted on the other women, particularly Sam, to deflect whatever attention she might have gotten by showing up in this skimpy outfit.

Carly sighed. There was no hope for it. She continued to the back of the house and slid open the back door. The music didn't immediately stop playing and all conversation didn't die, but surveying the patio, she noticed several heads turn in her direction and several faces registering everything from shock to frank approval. There was only one person's face that mattered to her, but she didn't see him, not at first. Then the crowd shifted and she found him, standing next to Nora. The woman was talking his ear off about something, and he looked ready to bolt at the nearest opportunity.

Maybe he sensed her presence or maybe he was looking for an escape route, but his head turned and his gaze settled on her. The glazed expression fell away from his face to be replaced by a look of such intense desire that she felt his gaze rush over her body like a wave of heat. She swallowed and licked her lips. No man had ever looked at her like that before and the effect was a little heady. A lot heady. Her breasts felt heavy and somewhere deep in her body an ache throbbed, demanding release.

She had made the decision to leave this man alone, that he would only offer her heartache, but she'd already broken that promise to herself. She'd break it again if she got the opportunity. She knew that as sure as she knew her own name. Heaven help her, she'd fallen in love with him. That realization had nothing to do with the way he looked at her now or even her own reaction to his gaze. She should have known it upstairs while she was defending him to Sam. Maybe it took seeing him to bring the point home. But she knew with a certainty that was absolute that if the chance ever came to be with him, she would take it and worry about the consequences later.

Chapter 17

By the time the sun started to set, most of the guests had already left for the hotel. In the meantime, they had scarfed down every morsel of food provided, swum in the ocean, and rehashed the day's events ad nauseam. The only people who seemed dissatisfied with anything were the reporters, who bemoaned the fact that they were touring the island when all the chaos started. Only reporters or cops would lament not getting a chance to have the bejesus scared out of them.

And then there was Carly. She blew Jackson away in that barely-there outfit. And he wasn't the only one. By all accounts she was the hit of the party while Charlotte remained in the background. He'd bet usually their situations were reversed, with Carly being more comfortable letting her mother have the limelight. And it wasn't just the outfit. She exuded an aura of new-found confidence that captivated him.

Watching her now as she stood with John and Adam, a laughing smile on her face, he wondered how what he was about to tell her would affect her. He'd told Charlotte he would simply because he knew she never would, but he didn't want the news to come from him. It was bad enough that he'd kept the truth from her, but she'd blame him even more if the words came from his lips.

He couldn't think about his own wants, though. Carly needed to be told and he wanted to do it at a time when there were others around who might buffer her reaction or at least provide her with someone else to turn to if she turned away from him. But not at the house.

He walked to where she stood and placed his hand on the small of her back. "Can I speak to you for a moment?"

She offered him a beaming smile. "Of course." She excused herself from the other men and followed him to the edge of the patio. "What do you want to talk to me about?"

"Come take a walk with me first." He nodded toward the shore.

"All right." Using his shoulder for balance, she slipped off her shoes and left them at the corner of the patio. She took his hand. "Let's go."

For a long while, they walked in silence, while Jackson tried to formulate the words he would use to tell her. That wasn't the only reason he remained silent. He wanted to enjoy a few moments alone with her with the ocean lapping at their feet and the warmth of her palm in his hand when he was sure she didn't hate him.

Finally, they came to a stone jetty. Either they had to stop or they had to climb over it. Jackson tugged on Carly's fingers to draw her to a stop. She looked up at him expectantly. "Looks like this is the end of the line."

"Looks that way." In both a literal and metaphoric way. He couldn't put it off any longer. But first he wanted to hold her, even if it was for the last time. He pulled her into his arms, crushing her to him with one hand at her nape and the other low on her back. Her arms came around him, her fingers splaying across his shoulders, holding him just as fiercely. He buried his nose against her neck, inhaling the floral scent of her perfume and the tang of the ocean. The waves crashed beside them and for a moment he had the feeling of being suspended in time where nothing stood between them and nothing mattered but the strength of their embrace.

But Carly started to stir. He lifted his head to look down at her and knew she'd misinterpreted the reason for this excursion along the shore. Before he had a chance to react, she cradled his face in her palms and brought his mouth down to hers.

He shut his eyes and let her passion flow over him, tightening his groin and hampering his breathing. His brain told him to behave, but his body had a will of its own. His hands roved over her back, over the softest skin he'd ever felt on another human being, and lower, to cup her derriere in his palms. She made a sound, not quite a moan, but the most erotic sound he'd ever heard. His pulse raced and his body ached with the need to be with her.

Always before with her, he'd been able to hold back from her, maintain some control, but this kiss was different, wild, out of control. This time something flowed between them, as potent and inexorable as the waves rolling onto shore. And in that moment he admitted to himself the one truth he'd tried to keep even from himself. He was in love with her. He knew it by the novelty of the emotion. He was in love with her and he was about to break her heart.

That thought sobered him enough to pull away. She gazed up at him with bemused, expectant eyes. "What is it, Jackson?"

He didn't know how to begin. Especially not now when he could still taste her kiss on his lips. For want of anything better to do, he ran his hand along her collarbone, to brush back one of the strings that held her top in place, but he only succeeded in trapping the material between his fingers. "Carly, I need to—"

She silenced him with a finger against his lips. "You don't have to say it." She covered his fingers with hers and gave a tug. The material covering her parted and fell away, baring her breasts to him.

He sucked in his breath, his attention riveted to her newly exposed flesh. Her breasts were small but firm, tipped with coral-colored areolae and prominent nipples. The urge to bend and take one of those nipples into his mouth assailed him. But he knew if he did that, he'd really be lost. This wasn't the time or place for them, aside from the fact that he'd never perfected the art of sleeping with a woman while deceiving her.

He pulled her toward him, holding her tight enough to feel the peaks of her breasts against his chest through his shirt. "I did invite you down here for a reason, but this isn't it."

She stiffened, then pushed away from him, turning her back to him to begin retying her top. "This is absolutely the last time I make a fool of myself over you, Jackson. Absolutely the last. No need to wait for three strikes. Two is enough."

Having refastened her top, she started off in the direction of Sam and Adam's house.

He caught her with his arms around her waist, trapping her arms against her sides. She struggled against his grasp, but in this position there was little she could do about it unless she really decided to hurt him. He leaned into her to whisper in her ear, "Baby, think of what you're asking. Is this what you really want from me? A quick tumble in the sand?"

She stopped struggling. "Right now, I don't want anything from you except to be let go."

He released her because he sensed the restlessness

in her and he didn't want to hurt her just to hold on to her.

She stumbled forward and kept going. When he tried to come after her, she turned around to face him. "Stay away from me, Jackson. I mean it. Just leave me alone."

He knew he'd hurt her, but he couldn't let her go like that. He searched his mind for something to say that would make her want to stay and hear what he had to say. In a carrying voice, he said, "Carly, your father didn't die of a heart attack, he was murdered."

Carly whipped around to face Jackson. Why would he say such a thing to her? How would he even know? "What did you say?" This time when he approached her, she didn't back away, but she crossed her arms in front of her and glared at him when she thought he'd gotten close enough.

"I'm sorry, Carly. It was the only thing I could think of to say to get you to listen to me."

"Then it's not true?"

"No, it's true. Your father did suffer a heart attack, but only because someone was trying to run him and your mother off the road. When they succeeded they left them there for dead."

She shook her head. "Even if that's true, what has that got to do with anything?" He reached for her, but she smacked his hands away. "Just tell me."

She listened to his story of the death of Sharon Glenn, a woman she barely remembered from so many years ago, Duke Anderson's testimony, and how her parents had been chased down by some man and a woman who looked like her mother.

She didn't realize he'd drawn close enough to close his arms around her or that she'd been crying until he moved to brush the tears from her face. In a quiet voice, he said, "I'm sorry, Carly."

She knew he referred to her finding out about her father in this way. It was shocking to think that someone for whatever reason had wanted her father dead. And for the moment, she couldn't argue with having Jackson's arms around her, as she doubted she'd still be standing.

But she knew there had to be more to this story that he hadn't told her, something that made it imperative for her to know. "What else hasn't Charlotte told me?"

He sighed, pulling her closer, until her cheek nestled against his heartbeat. "A few days ago, Duke Anderson resurfaced. He warned me that I should stop investigating Sharon Glenn's death in order to try to clear my father's name, and he warned Charlotte that you were in danger as well."

"So she hired you to take care of me, is that it?"

"Partly. I think she also hired me to divert me from what I was doing by feeding me the same crazy story I told you."

She pulled back from him, needing to see his face when she asked the next question. "How long have you known the truth?"

He shook his head. "Is that impor—"

"How long have you known?"

"Almost from the beginning."

She withdrew farther from him, so that their bodies were separated by a few inches. "So you mean all those times I asked you if you knew what was going on with my mother, you lied to me when you said no?"

"Yes."

"Why, Jackson? Why would you do that to me?" Instantly she knew the answer. "That's the way my mother wanted it, isn't it?" He said nothing and she took his nonanswer for assent. She laughed bitterly. "You'd

LADY IN RED   197

think I would have learned my lesson the first time about throwing myself at one of Charlotte's investigators, but I have no one to blame but myself since I did it with my eyes open this time. I want to thank you for having the decency not to sleep with me before letting me know your first allegiance is to my mother."

She turned and ran back to the house, fighting tears. She didn't mind crying for her father, but she'd be damned if she'd cry for herself. She was done with that, done with everything and everybody. All she wanted was to get her things and get out of there. She'd walk if she had to.

The others were still on the patio. She brushed past them without answering any of the questioning glances thrown her way. She hurried up to Sam's room, changed back into her dress, grabbed her purse, and headed toward the stairs. She halted on the top step. A sea of faces awaited her at the bottom of the steps. Neither her mother nor Jackson met the damning looks she sent them. And then it occurred to her: they all knew. Ariel and Jarad and Sam and Adam, even John, all had to know if they'd rallied around her in this way. They'd all known, and not one person had felt enough loyalty to her to tell her. Not until Jackson did, and she still wasn't sure why he had.

To hell with all of them. She didn't have to answer to anyone anymore. She stalked down the stairs, stopping on the third step from the bottom. "What's with all the long faces, people? Disappointed poor little Carly didn't fall into a frail heap finding out some old drunk thinks she's in danger? Don't hold your breath waiting for that to happen."

"Carly, please come into the great room where we can talk."

Carly looked into her mother's imploring face. "Why, Mother? So you can spoon-feed me some more of your pap about strange note writers? Haven't you heard? Jackson over there spilled the beans on you."

"Carly, don't act like this. Please, darling."

"Oh, cut the drama, Mother. I'm immune to that by now. If all of you will excuse me, I'm getting out of here. And by the way, Mother, I quit. Find some other lackey to run your company for you because it won't be me."

She marched past them, head held high and a defiant look in her eye. She heard her mother call her, but the only person who tried to stop her was Jackson. As she passed him, his arm shot out to capture her waist, but she pushed him away. "Don't you touch me," she said in the lowest, meanest voice she could muster.

He lifted both hands, as if to prove his compliance with her wishes. "Carly, please stay. There's something I haven't told you yet."

"Something else? Write me a letter." She pivoted and hurried out the front door. She could feel Jackson behind her coming after her, but she didn't care. She just had to get out of there, away from all those she had believed cared for her, at least enough to be her friends, but did not. Mostly she wanted some time alone to lick her wounds and kick herself a few times for ever letting Jackson close enough to break her heart.

Jackson caught up with her just outside the front door. With a hand on her arm, he swung her around to face him. "Damn it, Carly, where the hell do you think you're going?"

"What do you care? Afraid you won't get paid if I fall in a ditch somewhere?"

"I haven't taken one dime of your mother's money and I don't plan to."

"Then what's in it for you, Jackson? You get a thrill out

of making out with Charlotte Thompson's ugly duckling daughter or did you lose a bet?" She shook off his grasp and started walking in the direction of the main road.

Inwardly, he cringed at her definition of herself. He remembered the confidence he'd seen in her earlier that day and knew the seeming betrayal of everyone she knew must have devastated her in more ways than one. But if she thought he intended to let her leave here by herself, she'd lost her mind.

He caught up with her again and with no ceremony whatsoever, slung her over his shoulder. She shrieked and hit him with her fists, but that he assumed was only because he startled her. After that she went completely stiff, until he plunked her down on the hood of his car. He braced a hand on either side of her, boxing her in.

The first thing she said to him was, "You do realize you have left yourself in a particularly vulnerable position."

Her legs were trapped between his thighs. If she wanted to she could lay him low, but if she wanted to she'd already have done it. "Go ahead. And when I pick myself up off the ground, I'll still come after you."

"Why can't you leave me alone?"

A variety of answers spun through his head, the foremost of which was that he was in love with her. But he doubted she'd appreciate that response or even believe him. He settled on the answer he thought would have the most effect on her. "Because two days after I spoke with Duke Anderson, he turned up dead."

He felt a tremor pass through her. "Was it an accident?"

"The police don't believe so, though they have no proof yet it wasn't."

She trembled again, and he had to fight the urge to pull her into his arms. She'd probably fight him anyway. But he knew he'd scared her. Maybe he'd scared her enough that she would accept his protection without balking. But for now he'd change the subject to give her time to adjust to what he'd told her.

"By the way, that was a lovely scene you pulled in there. You reduced your mother to tears, which is probably what she deserved, but you were wrong about the others."

"Was I? How would you feel if all of your supposed friends kept something that important from you?"

"They didn't say anything because I asked them not to, but both Adam and Jarad said I should level with you. And the only reason I told them anything was so that they would look after you in case I couldn't."

"So we're back to you, Jackson. I can understand my mother's behavior. That's nothing new. I can even understand Johnny. I wasn't wrong about him being in love with my mother. I never suspected she returned his feelings, though. Why would he risk his relationship with my mother for me? But you?"

Using her hands she pushed off the hood of the car, into his waiting arms. But she quickly extricated herself from him. "I'm not stupid enough to believe that you care anything about me. Not anymore. So you can can the Romeo routine. But considering I'd just as soon not end up dead, I hope you don't mind if I avail myself of your services until I can hire someone else." She walked away from him, got into the car, and shut the door.

Jackson huffed out a breath. He supposed that was something in his favor. She'd at least gotten in the damn car. That only left him with the task of winning back her trust, if he were able to do that. The only problem was she was right. If he cared for her, he should have told her, no matter what Charlotte said. He only wished right now he had a better reason why he hadn't.

Chapter 18

After another sleepless night on Carly's sofa, Jackson rose at dawn, showered, shaved, and dressed in a pair of jeans and a cotton shirt. As far as he knew, he and Carly had nothing in particular on the agenda. Even if they did, he wouldn't know a thing about it. She'd been extremely uncommunicative from the moment he got into the car beside her. She tolerated his presence, but that was it.

He got out his cell phone and called Drew, figuring the other man would still be in bed. The answering machine picked up and issued the same message Drew did in person. Jackson hung up. So maybe Drew was still in somebody else's bed. He tried Drew's cell and got no answer at all. That wasn't like Drew, but maybe he was busy at the moment and didn't feel like answering the phone. Or maybe Jackson should add his cousin to the growing list of people who didn't want to talk to him.

He called his office next and let Peggy catch him up on what everyone was up to. Since the roof didn't seem to be caving in on his business in his absence, he hung up satisfied about that at least. Then he heard Carly stir. She sat up in bed and stretched. She looked toward the bed where he was supposed to have slept, then her head pivoted around and she stared directly at him.

"Good morning," he said.

She cast him a sour expression and got out of bed.
She slipped on her robe and came down the stairs. She
stopped directly in front of him across the coffee table.
"I would think you'd be packing. Your replacement
should be here by eight o'clock."

His eyebrows lifted. "Excuse me?"

"I told you I intended to hire someone else."

Yes, but he'd assumed she'd said that because she
wanted to hurt him back, not because she actually intended to do it. Whom could she have gotten on such
short notice anyway?

She rummaged through her suitcase, pulling out articles of clothing. "If he gets here before I get out of the
shower, please let him in." She disappeared inside the
bathroom and shut the door.

Yeah, Jackson would let him in all right. Then he'd
send his butt packing back to wherever he belonged.
When a knock sounded at the door not five minutes
later, Jackson checked the peephole just to get a look
at whoever Carly had thought she'd hired. Surprised,
Jackson pulled back and opened the door. "Drew!
What the devil are you doing here? I tried calling you
this morning."

"I was on the road. You going to let me in or what?"

Jackson stepped aside to let his cousin enter, then
shut the door. Once the two men had seated themselves on the sofa Jackson said, "Seriously, what are you
doing here?"

"Didn't Carly tell you? You're out and I'm in."

For a moment he just stared at Drew. "You are kidding."

"Nah, man. She called me in the dead of night and
asked me if I could help her out since you would be
leaving. I figured I'd take a couple of days. I gather
that's not what's happening."

"Not exactly." He told Drew what had happened the night before.

"So she's pissed at you and called me in to get back at you."

Jackson propped his feet on the coffee table, leaned back, and closed his eyes. He rubbed his temples with his thumb and forefinger. "Hell, I don't know what's going on in her mind right now. I don't know if she's mad at me, hates me, or would rip my guts out given half the chance." All he knew was that before last night, she'd been coming to care for him, too. A woman like Carly didn't offer herself to a man she didn't have strong feelings for, very strong feelings.

He didn't count the first time she'd tried asking him to make love to her. He knew with everything that was in him that she never would have followed through with that. Last night, she would have let him take her, and part of him wished he hadn't refused her offer. If nothing else, he'd have that memory of being with her, while now he had nothing but recriminations for blowing things with her to begin with. By not being honest with her, he'd doomed himself from the beginning. He wished he'd seen that more clearly before now, but back then he hadn't imagined himself falling in love with her and needing her forgiveness.

"Someone around here's got it bad and it isn't me."

Jackson lifted his head. "That obvious, is it?"

Drew grinned. "You could say that."

"If you're so brilliant, tell me, what am I supposed to do?"

Drew tilted his head to the side, considering. "For the time being, give her what she wants. Maybe she needs some time to cool off."

"Maybe," Jackson echoed. He shook his head. "If you let anything happen to her—"

"I know, I know, you'll nail my big ugly carcass to the

wall. You've been threatening me with that for years. Haven't done it yet."

Jackson sighed. Nothing had ever mattered to him as much as Carly did, except perhaps clearing his father's name. "All right." He repacked what few articles he'd taken out of his suitcase and stacked his computer on top of the bag. "I'm going to check into another room. I'll be back."

Carly came out of the bathroom to find Drew on the sofa but no Jackson. Jackson's bag and computer rested on the coffee table as if he was preparing to clear out. She didn't know why she thought she'd find otherwise, considering that she'd told him to leave. She hadn't really expected him to do it without even a word of protest. She'd lain awake a long time last night, wondering if she'd been too harsh on him, wondering if she'd simply lashed out at him because she was hurt. She'd thought that maybe he'd told her the truth because he cared enough to do so and Charlotte wouldn't. But if he'd go without even trying to change her mind, didn't that say something, too?

She forced a smile to her face. "Hey, Drew."

"Hey yourself, pretty lady." He enveloped her in a bear hug that threatened to cut off her oxygen supply. "How's it hanging?"

"Mighty low. Give me a minute to put on some shoes and we'll go have some breakfast." She offered him a genuine grin. "I won't bother to ask if you're hungry."

"Shouldn't we wait until Jackson gets back to tell him where we're going?"

"I don't see why. He's not my bodyguard anymore. You are."

"Good point," Drew said. "Are you sure that's the way you want it?"

That was the rub. She wasn't sure what she wanted, but she wasn't going to sit around trying to figure out what Jackson wanted, either. She slipped on her sandals and turned to Drew. "Let's go."

They went to a little self-serve place on Circuit Avenue. You placed your order at the counter, got your own utensils, and waited for them to call you to pick up your food. Carly ordered coffee and a muffin for herself while Drew ordered three different meals. When she looked at him questioningly, he shrugged. "I couldn't decide, and luckily at my size, I don't have to."

Carly shook her head and allowed him to lead her to a table by the front window.

Once they had their food in front of them, Drew said, "Do you want to tell me what happened between you and Jackson? I've heard his version, but I'd like to hear yours."

"Why? So you can run back and tell him everything I said?"

"I'm not like that, Carly. I'm just curious. You're the one who put me in the middle of this. As long as I'm here, I'd like to know why."

"I don't know what to tell you." She liked Drew, but she wasn't about to pour her heart out to a man who owed his allegiance elsewhere.

"Then let me tell you something about Jackson, instead. This stays between the two of us. If he knew I told you, let's just say he wouldn't be pleased."

Carly nodded, wanting to hear whatever Drew might tell her. "Go ahead."

"You know Jackson's father was accused of murder, but you don't know the effect it's had on him. Even after the trial the police and everyone else were convinced that his father was really guilty and that he'd gotten to Duke Anderson to make him recant his story. They never looked for anyone else. So Jackson took it upon himself to do so. He spent years tracking down every lead, every person who might have known anything about anything.

"Frankly, I think he was obsessed with it, but I couldn't blame the guy. Especially since the one man who might have shed some light on what happened, Duke Anderson, disappeared off the face of the earth."

Drew sipped from his coffee cup. "You don't know the half of it. I mean, here he is a cop and the world believes his father, a former corrections officer, is a murderer. There are two things folks in law enforcement never forget, a rat and a screw up. As the rest of the guys saw it, Jackson's father screwed up and killed some girl with his bare hands. Some legacy to walk around with, and there were still some guys on the job who remembered Jackson's father who weren't above trying to rub his nose in it. He had to live with that, too, and as far as I know he never rose to the bait of those who wanted to get to him, never offed anybody for running their mouth. He never said a word."

Carly bit her lip. Her heart went out to Jackson. She never would have expected he'd suffered such cruelty at the hands of his fellow officers.

"Have you ever been to his apartment?" Drew asked.

"Once."

"He doesn't have one thing in there that's worth a damn. Does he still have the boxes by the door?"

"Yes."

"Those are his father's things. He keeps promising to donate them to the Salvation Army, but there's probably nothing but moth larva in there now."

She'd looked at his apartment and seen a man who couldn't settle down, but in reality he was a man who couldn't let go. A man who couldn't break free of a past he couldn't resolve. Such a life could make any man harsh and unfeeling, but she wouldn't use either word to describe Jackson. In fact, the opposite was true.

"He gave up, finally, you know. He gave up and I thought he would get on with his life, buy some decent furniture, get a girl who lasted more than a couple of nights, something. But there we are, hanging out at my place a month ago, and this show comes on, you know the one about unsolved cases? There's Jackson's father's picture right on the screen, the man who authorities believe killed Sharon Glenn, but no one has been able to prove it. And he was at it all over again. The only reason he agreed to help your mother is that he figured he owed her because of what your father had done for Donovan and maybe, just maybe she might remember something that might be able to help him."

Carly drew in a deep breath and held it. Such loyalty on Jackson's part didn't surprise her. He'd shown her similar devotion until she threw it back in his face. He might not have been truthful with her, but he'd done everything in his power to keep her safe. Wasn't that enough? Especially since she knew in her heart that Charlotte had convinced him to remain silent.

Letting her breath out on a sigh, she thought of what Sam had said about him needing someone, about not giving up. She didn't want to give up on him, she simply wanted some clue that he felt for her anywhere near what she felt for him.

"Want to tell me about you now?"

"Who, me?" Carly asked, sardonically. "I'm just an ingrate who has a mother that loves her, friends who support her, a good man who risked his life to protect her, and I treated them all like dirt. Well, my mother deserved what she got, and I'm not sorry I came down on her, but the others I owe a whopping apology."

"Even Jackson?"

"Especially Jackson." Carly inhaled and let it out on a sigh. "What I'm about to say stays between the two of us."

He crossed his heart. "Promise."

"I'm in love with him, Drew. That's why I overreacted. When I found out he lied to me, I assumed it was because he didn't care about me. I told him I wanted him to leave because I was angry, but I never really expected him to do so without putting up any fight at all."

"That's because I told him he should do what you asked. Me and my big mouth."

"He wasn't going to leave then?"

"No, he was going to check into another room in the hope that you would come around."

Carly laughed self-deprecatingly. "Tell me, is there a big sign on my forehead that says *idiot* or am I just imagining things?"

"There's no sign, but if you don't make things right with him, there will be."

"I will. Tomorrow. Tonight I have to do something I don't want him to know about."

Drew's eyebrows lifted in question.

"Don't worry, it's nothing illegal, immoral, or fattening. I just want to keep it to myself, okay?"

"Okay, but don't make me regret my promise."

"I won't."

Jackson paced around the small living room of the suite next to Carly's. It was an uncharacteristic action for him, but he couldn't seem to sit still or concentrate on anything. Drew had called him several times that day, letting him know what he and Carly were up to. After breakfast, he'd taken her shopping in Edgartown, then she'd gone to see both Sam and Ariel, he assumed to make amends for the night before. According to Drew, both meetings had ended in smiles and hugs, so at least Carly had made things right with the women.

She hadn't gone to see her mother, though. In Jackson's mind, that didn't bode well for him either. Even though Drew told him not to worry, he couldn't help feeling that he'd blown his shot with her, not to mention his concern for her safety. It had been hours since Drew called and it was nearly nine o'clock. Shouldn't Carly be back by now?

He wished he'd acted on his first impulse and followed them, but that would have been ridiculous considering the size and color of his vehicle. But at least he'd know where she was right now and that she wasn't in any danger. Or maybe she was, and that's why he hadn't heard from Drew. His thoughts went around and around and none of them were good.

When his cell phone rang he practically leapt on it, but relief flooded him at hearing Drew's voice on the other end of the line. But either there was a lot of static on the line, or Drew wasn't alone. "Where are you, man?"

"We're at the Star Chamber in Edgartown. Your lady's gone crazy and I can't do a thing with her. You'd better get down here."

Drew refused to elaborate, but he did give Jackson directions on how to find them. Twenty minutes later, he pulled up in front of the tiny club that sported a big yellow star on its awning. What had possessed Carly to want to come here?

Drew met him at the door. "Where's Carly?" Jackson asked.

Drew pointed. "She's right over there. I'm out of here, man. I'll see you back at the hotel." He slipped out the door and into the night.

Great! Jackson didn't see Carly, only a clump of men

standing around next to the bar. One of them shifted, and he caught a glimpse of a dark-haired woman who had her back to him. That woman with the wild hair and backless dress could not be Carly. No wonder Drew had said she'd lost her mind. He shouldered his way through the men, none of whom seemed too happy to let him pass. He came to stand in front of her, his eyes drinking in every inch of her from the wild mane to her face to the scarlet minidress she wore and onto the spike heels that encased her feet. The effect was stunning and he could tell he wasn't the only man there who'd been hit. Was that why she'd come here? To pick up some man, though there wasn't a decent one in the place?

The first thing she said to him wasn't hello or to register surprise or even to ask what he was doing there in the first place. Instead, she said, "That rat Drew called you, didn't he?"

He ignored her question, since she already knew the answer. "Would you mind telling me what you are doing here and why you are dressed like that?"

"I'm going to sing. It's open-mic night. I paid the manager fifty bucks to squeeze me in tonight. If I'm not mistaken, I'm next."

He could sense the anticipation in her laced with an undercurrent of dread. She'd told him that's what she'd always wanted to do with her life. The cosmetics company was something she knew she could handle, but she wanted something else instead. He admired her for reaching for that, even if it was in some seedy dive better suited to Times Square than Martha's Vineyard. He winked at her. "Break a leg, sweetheart."

Her response was to grab her glass from the bar and toss down the remains of its contents. "I'll try."

She left him to join a man at the front of the stage area who Jackson assumed was the emcee for the evening. He plunked himself down at a table in the front where he could see her and see everyone else and ignored the startled couple who had once been the sole occupants of the table.

Some toothpick of a kid was finishing up a painful rendition of some rap song Jackson had never heard before, accompanied by canned music. He left the stage to a smattering of applause from one corner of the room, probably his relatives.

The emcee hopped onto the stage and advanced toward the microphone. "We have a treat for you tonight, a woman of mystery. Please put your hands together for the Lady in Red."

Carly's advent onto the stage was greeted with the sort of enthusiasm usually reserved for waiting for a streetlight to change. That is, until she started to sing. Accompanied by a solo pianist, she launched into a rendition of "You Really Got a Hold on Me," but Smokey never sang it like that. Her voice, low and sultry, reverberated through Jackson, like a second insistent heartbeat. The others must have been similarly affected, as conversation stopped and the sounds of cutlery ceased. Then she looked directly at him as she repeated the title of the song, making him wonder if her feelings for him affected her choice of material. And if they did, what was she trying to tell him?

The end of the song was greeted with applause and catcalls. Beaming, Carly bowed to the audience, bowed to the man who'd accompanied her, and bounded off the stage. She came running toward him and threw herself into his arms. "I did it, Jackson. I did it."

He caught her to him and squeezed her tight. "You sure did, baby. You were wonderful." Before he could help himself, his mouth clamped down on hers. And she welcomed him, sucking on his tongue when it invaded her mouth. He groaned and pulled her closer, until he heard a coughing sound to his left. He broke the kiss and set her on her feet.

Carly stepped back from him and introduced him to the man who stood beside them, the manager of the club.

He extended a fifty toward her. "I wanted to give you your money back. I should be paying you. In fact, can you come in tomorrow night? I had a cancellation."

Carly shook her head, but she took the money. "I'm afraid this was a one-shot deal. I'm not going to be on the island that long."

The man shook his head. "Shame. If you're ever in town for a while, give me a buzz."

As he walked away, Jackson turned to Carly. "Why only a one-shot deal?"

"I wanted to see if I could do it. Get up in front of a crowd and really belt one out. I was so scared, I thought I was going to throw up. That's not how I imagine myself going through life, but I wanted to prove something to myself, and I did, so now it's over."

He tucked an errant strand of her hair behind her ear. "Does this mean we get to go home now?"

"Yes."

He wanted to ask her if that meant she'd forgiven him, too, but he figured that conversation was best left until they were alone.

"Tell me something," Jackson said later as they drove home. "Why didn't you want me to know you were singing tonight?"

"I never said that."

"You didn't have to. When I walked in you were upset that Drew called me."

"If you must know, I was afraid I'd bomb miserably. I didn't care if Drew knew that."

But she would have minded him knowing she'd fallen on her face. He didn't know whether to be pleased by that admission or not. He checked the rearview mirror. The same black truck was riding his tail. They'd picked up whoever it was almost as soon as they left the club. Granted, there weren't that many roads out here for anyone to travel, but something about this truck, an even bigger monster than the vehicle he drove, bothered him. Out of habit he memorized the tag number.

"What's the matter?" Carly asked.

He stole a glance at her. She still wore the same beaming smile that hadn't left her face since her performance. He placed a reassuring hand on her thigh. "Nothing. Just the idiot behind me drives like a New York cabbie."

He checked the rearview again, in time to see the truck speed up, but not enough time to react. The truck rammed them from behind, propelling them forward. Jackson threw his arm across Carly's chest to keep her in place. Without a seat belt, she had nothing to restrain her from going through the windshield or being thrown from the car.

Jackson gunned the engine, putting distance between them and the other vehicle. "Are you all right?" he asked Carly.

"I'm fine." She twisted around to look at the truck behind them. She held her hair back from her face. "Idiot."

Jackson inhaled. She still thought that bump had been an accident. He knew better. That bump was just the beginning. "Listen to me, Carly," he said in a voice he hoped held the urgency he felt. He wanted her down on the floor, but there wasn't time for that. "Hold on."

Immediately she straightened and grasped the arm

he planted across her, while he tried to concentrate on navigating the narrow winding road with his left hand. Gathering her closer, he gunned the engine again, but too late. Pain shot through his shoulder as the truck rammed into them again and Carly was thrown against him. He knew that must have hurt her, too, though she didn't make a sound.

He glanced in the mirror again. The truck was coming at them again, and this time he knew they weren't going to make it. The road curved too sharply. He could only hope the incline here down to the beach wasn't as sharp as it looked.

"Hang on, Carly," he said, as the truck plowed into them again, forcing them from the road, down the embankment at an odd angle. Carly screamed, echoing the panic in his own soul. They skidded to a hard landing, but she slipped from his grasp this time, falling forward against the passenger-side door.

"Carly," he called, pulling her back to him. "Baby, are you all right?" But her body was limp in his arms, and when he brushed her hair from her face, his fingers came back sticky with her blood.

Chapter 19

"Carly!" Jackson shouted. Although he knew better, he shook her. "Carly, answer me."

She batted at his hands on her shoulders. "Quit poking me," she protested.

They were the sweetest words Jackson had ever heard. He thanked whatever gods were available that she was alive and she was conscious, but blood flowed from a gash along her hairline. "Hold still, okay?"

She nodded and winced.

He pulled off his shirt, wadded it up, and pressed it against her temple to stanch its flow.

"Your hand is shaking."

"You scared the hell out of me."

"*I* scared the hell out of you? What about that lunatic in the truck? That wasn't an accident, was it?"

"No." A shiver passed through her, but he couldn't worry about her fear now. Though the truck had rambled on without stopping, that didn't mean the driver might not return to judge the success of his handiwork. He needed to get her out of there. He needed to get her to a doctor to look at her wound. "Do you think you can walk?"

She nodded, but he doubted either of them would know the answer to that until she stood. He took her right hand and arranged it so that she kept the shirt pressed to her forehead. "Hold on to that, okay?"

Sensing a vehicle stop up on the road in the periphery of his vision, he turned. A short, round man climbed out of the SUV. "Hey," the man called. "Do you need help down there?"

Jackson could have kissed the man full on the mouth. Until that moment, he'd had no idea how he was going to get Carly anywhere. "We're coming up," Jackson called back.

He unlocked the glove compartment and pulled out Carly's gun. He didn't intend to use it, but if they were to abandon the car he couldn't afford to leave it where it was. He fished around for the bullets, but only found five of them. That would have to do. He pocketed the bullets and his keys and tucked the gun at the small of his back. He'd have to hope it was dark enough and their Samaritan wasn't observant enough to notice.

He went around to Carly's side of the car, opened her door, and lifted her into his arms. "Hang on to me," he told her, and she leaned into him, resting her cheek on his shoulder and wrapping her free arm around his neck. She weighed absolutely nothing, but the imprint of her soft skin on his bare flesh started another kind of tension in him. He swallowed and started to make his way up the incline to the road.

"I saw the whole thing," the man said as Jackson emerged onto the road next to him. "I was on the other side of the road and came around." He opened the passenger-side door and stood aside to let them enter. "Damn drunk drivers!"

If that's what the man believed, Jackson wasn't going to argue with him. Jackson sat and arranged Carly on his lap before fastening the Seattle to cover both of them.

The driver slid in beside him. "How's she doing?"

Carly said, "She's fine. It's just a cut."

"A cut that needs to be looked at."

"The hospital isn't far." The man started the engine. "I'm Dave, by the way."

"Jackson."

Dave nodded and pulled off onto the road. While he launched into a monologue about folks who drank and drove and the stiffness of Massachusetts law concerning those activities, Jackson stoked his thumb over Carly's cheek. "How are you really, baby?"

"It hurts, Jackson. It really hurts."

He squeezed her to him, then shifted so that he could get to his cell phone. He called Drew and giving him as little information as possible asked him to meet them at the hospital. "And bring me a shirt," he said before disconnecting the call.

As he returned the phone to his belt, Dave said, "I wasn't trying to eavesdrop, but I have a shirt in the back you can use. It's probably a little dusty, but it's clean."

"Thanks." Considering that he wanted to attract as little attention as possible, showing up at the hospital shirtless and with a gun visible in the back of his pants was not the best way to go. He turned to see the shirt in question lying on the backseat. He had to adjust Carly to reach for it. At one of the few stoplights on the island, he slipped it over his head. They were as good to go as they would ever be.

Carly was seen by a doctor with striking blue eyes and a bit too much bedside manner to suit Jackson. It took six stitches to close the cut at Carly's temple, but it was so close to her hairline that no one would probably ever notice the scar. The doctor gave Carly a small supply of antibiotics, a couple of Darvons, and a prescription for each to be filled at a pharmacy in the morning.

Jackson helped Carly rise to a sitting position. "Ready to go, sweetheart?"

"Yup," she said in a sleepy, drugged voice. They'd given her something for the pain. She'd protested taking anything, claiming she'd be better off without it, but he was grateful the medicine finally seemed to have taken effect. "Where are we going?"

"I think you've already gone to la-la land."

"Could be." She slid off the examination table, but she swayed on her feet before Jackson caught her.

Sighing, Jackson swung her into his arms. Drew was waiting for them at the small emergency reception desk. "Pestering the nurses?" Jackson asked.

"Someone's got to," Drew said in a sour voice. "They wouldn't tell me anything."

Carly lifted her head. "Hey, Drew."

"Hey, Carly."

She tucked her face beside his neck again. When Drew looked at him questioningly, Jackson said, "Outside."

Once they were all seated in Drew's car with Drew behind the wheel and Jackson and Carly in the back, Drew looked over his shoulder at him. "Is this the point where you tell me what the hell is going on? What happened to Carly?"

"On the way home from the club a truck ran us off the road. Why didn't you make sure no one followed you before?"

"What are you talking about? Nobody followed me."

"Someone had to. We picked up the truck almost as soon as we left the club."

"Nobody followed me. Did you stop to think someone might have followed you?"

As Drew revved the engine, Jackson considered that

possibility. Of the two vehicles, the Caddy was more noticeable and more easily traced than Drew's Lexus. And Carly wasn't the only one whose life had been threatened lately. Maybe whoever had been after them was gunning for him and injuring Carly was simply a bonus. He had to admit that on the way to the club, he'd been more concerned with finding out what Carly was up to than monitoring who was behind him. Instead of protecting her, he might have led a killer right to her.

Drew pulled out of the parking lot. "Where are we going?"

"I don't know. Just drive." A third possibility sprang into his mind. Maybe no one had followed either of them. Maybe someone close to Carly had known where she was and had the patience to wait them out. That thought scared him most of all, because it meant that Carly trusted whoever it was that tried to kill them.

Samuels immediately sprang to mind. Had she called him to let her know where she would be? She didn't seem overly close with him, but he was her godfather. It wasn't inconceivable that she would have confided in him.

He shook her shoulder. "Carly, who did you tell where you were going tonight? Carly?"

She mumbled something incoherent. Great! She was out of it and he couldn't risk bringing her back to the hotel if he didn't know who might be waiting there to finish what they started. They needed to get lost until he could get some answers from her.

"Go into Vineyard Haven," he told Drew. "I think I know a place."

The diminutive bed-and-breakfast owner wasn't pleased to have them show up on her doorstep at two in the morning, but she did accept his cash for two rooms for a night. She showed them to opposite rooms on the floor upstairs, then left them alone.

"Nothing beats the incurious," Drew said. "You'd think two men and an unconscious woman showed up on her doorstep every day."

Jackson shifted Carly in his arms. "Be grateful. What were you planning to tell her if she asked?"

Drew yawned. "Me? Not a damn thing. I'm beat. You take care of Carly and holler if you need anything."

"Will do." Jackson stepped into the room the innkeeper had left open for him and surveyed the solitary big bed that dominated the room. He couldn't very well sign the register as Mr. and Mrs. John Anderson and ask for separate beds. Drew had gotten a bit more creative than Jackson with his moniker. He'd signed his name as Benjamin Gay.

Jackson kicked the door closed before heading over to the bed and laying Carly on it. She immediately rolled onto her side and tucked her hands underneath her cheek. He smiled. If it weren't for the remnants of her makeup and the killer dress she had on, she'd look like a little girl fast asleep on her parents' bed.

But she wasn't a little girl; she was a woman, the woman he loved. He could have lost her tonight. A tremor passed through him at the prospect. He couldn't dwell on that, though. He'd drive himself crazy. He emptied his pockets onto the nightstand and pulled the gun from where he'd left it. He didn't know why he did it, but he put the bullets back in the gun and put it in the drawer.

Yawning, he stretched, and for the first time he noticed the stiffness in his shoulder and a pain in the region below his sternum. Lifting his shirt, he explored the semicircular pattern of tenderness. He remembered being thrown against the steering wheel but hadn't paid it any attention. He let the shirt fall. He'd survive.

He sat on the bed to remove his shoes and socks. He

left on everything else. A little discomfort would help to keep him awake. The only reason the hospital was willing to release Carly so soon was that he promised someone would be around to check on her.

He removed her shoes and stretched out next to her. He should have put her under the covers. The room was cool and he could feel the tiny shivers in her body. But she rolled against him and laid her hand on his chest, seeking his warmth. He drew his arms around her as she burrowed closer. "Better?" he asked.

He hadn't really expected a response from her, and he didn't get one. Not a verbal one, anyway. Her hand slipped under his shirt, moving upward over his abdomen. He placed his hand over hers to halt her exploration, believing she didn't know what she was doing.

She lifted her head and regarded him with half-closed, dreamy eyes. "I want you, Jackson."

He knew it was only the painkiller talking, loosening her tongue and her inhibitions. They'd never gotten around to discussing what happened at Sam and Adam's house. For all he knew, she was still angry with him for withholding the truth from her. Still a shock wave of heat zinged through his body hearing that frank admission. He pressed her cheek against his chest. "Go back to sleep, Carly. You don't even know what you're talking about."

She settled against him and said in a solemn voice, "One of these days, I'm going to take no for an answer."

Jackson pulled her more fully on top of him and pulled the cover up to cover them both. Her body fit into his in a way that made him wish she were more lucid or he had fewer scruples.

One of these days, he was going to be able to say yes to her. He only hoped she wouldn't give up on him before then.

* * *

"Jackson?" Carly groaned. The right side of her head felt as if it had met with the business end of a sledge-hammer and her mouth felt as if someone had swabbed it with a giant Q-tip. Other smaller aches peppered her body, making it difficult to lie still. And what on earth was she lying on? Every inch of it was rock solid, but definitely not flat, and a steady rapid beat throbbed in her ears. She catalogued her body again, not looking for aches this time, but for a clue as to where she was. She shifted slightly, and the thing below her groaned. It wasn't a what she was lying on but a who. Her head snapped up and she looked directly into a pair of warm, brown, amused eyes. "Jackson!"

His fingertips brushed the temple that didn't hurt, then the back of his hand grazed her cheekbone. "Are you back among us, finally?"

She let her gaze wander over him. There were scratches on his arm and he wore a Nike T-shirt she'd never seen on him before that sported a stain that looked like blood. "What happened to you?"

"Don't you remember?"

She started to shake her head, but it hurt enough to make her stop. But it occurred to her that they couldn't be in their hotel room. This walls were painted a soft shell-white, not the blue of the other room, and they lay on one very large bed. She turned her head to survey the rest of the space. "Nice room."

He snorted. "How are you feeling?"

"I'll let you know when the little guy in my head puts his hammer down." She lifted her hand to touch the spot that pained her most.

Jackson caught her wrist and pulled her hand down. "Don't touch it, sweetheart. The doctor had to give you stitches."

She remembered that. "Turquoise eyes."

"I beg your pardon?"

"The doctor had turquoise eyes."

"Is that all you remember?"

Hearing the indignation in Jackson's voice, she answered, "Yes." But images started to flood her consciousness, bringing the remembrance of stark terror. Someone had tried to run them off the road, in the same manner that had killed her father. She shuddered thinking about it.

"You're safe, Carly."

"I know." But she hadn't been last night. Someone was out to kill her or Jackson or both of them and it scared her to contemplate what lengths a killer might go to to get to them and the lengths Jackson might go to in order to protect her. "Thank you."

"For what?"

She lifted her head. "For taking care of me last night. But I do remember telling you I don't have a good reaction to painkillers."

He smiled so wickedly she wondered exactly what she'd done to cause that reaction. "I didn't do anything stupid, did I? We didn't . . ."

He winked at her. "I would have woken you up for that."

She buried her face against his neck. So she must have said something stupid in her stupor. Had she been out of it enough to confess her feelings for him?

He stroked his hands over her back. "Would it have been such a big mistake if we had made love last night?"

The question reverberated in her ears and through her body and clear to her soul. She shifted to be able to see his face. He regarded her with hooded intense eyes. Considering how many times he'd pushed her away, she had no idea what he wanted her answer to be.

Still she could only respond with the truth. "No." To emphasize her point, she pressed her mouth to his.

Satisfaction rippled through her as he groaned and his embrace tightened. His tongue plunged into her mouth and she welcomed it, rubbing her tongue against his. She felt him turning her so that she lay beside him.

He pulled away from her, leaning back on one elbow to look down on her. "Are you sure, baby?" He trailed a finger from her collarbone down to the valley between her breasts. "This isn't another drug-induced come-on?"

She cradled his face in her palms. "Make love to me, Jackson," she whispered, then brought his mouth down to hers.

Chapter 20

Jackson's eyes squeezed shut as Carly's tongue delved into his mouth, seeking his. Her arms wound around him and her fingers splayed across his back. He groaned into her mouth. Truth was that she wound him up tighter, faster, than any woman he'd ever known. It hadn't helped that he'd spent the night wide-awake with her body nestled with his. But as much as he ached to be inside her, he knew he couldn't rush her. As long as it had been since she was with a man, he'd probably hurt her no matter what he did.

And he didn't want to hurt her; he wanted to please her. He'd always considered himself a generous lover, as concerned with his woman's pleasure as his own. But this was different, he was different because he was with her.

But he wanted to see her, to feel her soft, soft skin against his body. He tilted her toward him enough to rasp down the zipper at the back of her dress. He broke the kiss and pushed up on one elbow to look at her. She stared back at him with eyes already darkened in passion. "Carly," he whispered, as he pushed aside the straps of her gown. The flimsy material parted, exposing her breasts. He ran his hand over one globe and then the other, back and forth, until her eyes drifted shut and a tiny moan escaped her lips.

He lowered his head and did what he'd wanted to do since their encounter on the beach. He took one of her nipples into his mouth and laved it with his tongue. She arched into him, calling his name. He placed a steadying hand on her waist, then let his fingers trail downward on the outside of her thigh. On the way back up, his hand traveled between her thighs, brushing her dress upward and out of the way. He brushed his hand over her mons over the cover of her panties and was rewarded with a tremor that shook her entire body. He circled lower, pressing inward. A second, more violent shiver wracked her body. Her fingers gripped his biceps, fueling a greater urgency in him. He tilted her toward him, to bring her other breast in line with his mouth while he slid her panties from her body.

He lifted his head to gaze down at her. She was nude except for the circle of her dress around her waist. He didn't waste any time trying to remove it. He urged her legs open wider with his hand between her thighs. He let his fingers wander over her inner thighs, her mons, but not where she really wanted it. Her hips arched against his hand, demanding more, and he gave it to her. He explored the soft, slick flesh between her thighs, making her neck arch and her body shiver.

He inhaled, breathing in the musky aroma of her arousal. His body pulsed with his need for her, and a sheen of perspiration broke out on his skin. She clung to him, her breathing rapid and shallow, her body restless, and he knew she wasn't far from the brink. He stroked her with his thumb as he slid his finger inside her. She was so hot and so tight a shudder wracked his body with the strength of a tidal wave. He lowered his head and buried his face against the sweet valley between her breasts.

"Jacksss—" she cried, the last of his name lost in the

explosion of her orgasm. He covered her mouth with his own, absorbing her cries as her body convulsed around him. When her tremors subsided, he stroked her damp hair from her face. "How are you feeling?"

She turned the lower part of her body toward him, laying her knee against his thigh. "If you could manage to do that, say every fifteen minutes, I wouldn't complain."

She'd meant that as a joke, but he didn't see it that way. "Didn't that man of yours ever please you?"

"Not like that." She wiggled out of her dress and rolled on top of him. "Has it occurred to you that you've got too much clothing on?"

He supposed that was her way of telling him she didn't want to talk about the other man, which suited him fine. When her fingers delved under his shirt, he obliged her by lifting it over his head and tossing it onto the floor.

Her lips touched down at the center of his chest. His breath sucked in from the gentleness of her touch—not tentative, but tender, loving. Did she love him? It was too soon to ask that of her. In the meantime, he concentrated on breathing while her warm, wet tongue circled his nipple and her hand traveled lower down his body to cup his groin. "Carly," he protested, grasping her wrist, knowing he didn't have enough control to take that.

She wasn't deterred. She squeezed him and such pleasure washed up through him that he had to squeeze his eyes shut just to withstand it. Hearing her low, satisfied laugh, he opened his eyes.

She grinned down at him. "Seems some of us can dish it out, but we can't take it."

With one hand curled around her nape, he brought her mouth down to his. The other hand explored the soft, rounded flesh of her buttocks. He kissed her until she writhed against him and she moaned into his mouth. When her eyes flickered open, he winked at her. "What were you saying about people who can't take it?"

She offered him a lopsided grin. "Damned if I know. The real question of the hour is, when do you plan to take off your pants?"

He turned them so that they lay side by side facing one another. He stroked his hand down her body, from her breast to her hip and back up, grazing her mons. "Getting impatient, are you?"

"Just a teeny bit."

Laughing, he rolled her off him and rose from the bed. She watched him avidly as he shed his remaining clothes, retrieved from his pocket one of the condoms Drew had forced on him last night, and rolled it on.

He rejoined her on the bed, lying on his side facing her. "Better?"

He barely got the word out of his mouth before her lips found his. Her tongue darted in and out of his mouth in imitation of the act to come. A groan rumbled up in his chest, as he rolled her onto her back and covered her. He rubbed himself against her and she moaned. "Is this what you want, baby?"

"Don't toy with me, Jackson."

No, he agreed, the time for games was over. He lifted himself, then sank into her by slow degrees until he was fully inside her. She wrapped her legs around him, taking him even deeper. He shuddered from the sheer pleasure of having her body wrapped around his. He settled against her, keeping most of his weight on his elbows so he wouldn't crush her.

"Better?" he asked, but he already knew the answer. Her face wore a bemused expression and her legs tightened around him. He withdrew from her as slowly as he'd joined himself with her and thrust into her. She made a small sound, not quite a whimper, but definitely not a moan. "Baby?"

Her eyes flickered open, and the vague expression in them gave him his answer. He definitely hadn't hurt her. In fact, she rocked her hips against him, urging him on. He thrust into her again, and again. She whimpered and clung to him. He buried his face against her neck, raining tiny kisses along her throat, while her hands roved over him, exciting him further.

He moved inside her with increasing urgency and she met him with every thrust, driving him to the brink of his control. "Carly," he called, wanting her to join him. She shook her head, obviously beyond words. He covered her mouth with his for a wildly erotic kiss that rocked him to his core. His hand slid to mold her breast in his palm. He rolled her nipple between his thumb and index finger, and she bucked against him, her neck and back arching, her legs tightening around him. He drove into her, again and again, himself beyond any restraint he'd wanted to show her. His own back arched as the most intense explosion of ecstasy he'd ever known spiraled through his body.

Panting and perspired, he sank against her. Her hands moved over his back as they had before—gentle, soothing, like a balm for his tortured soul. There had never been much tenderness in his life. His mother had died too soon to imprint on him anything of her temperament. His father had been a good man, a loving father, but undemonstrative. His aunt had barely exercised any parental influence of any kind except to make his life miserable. Carly was the first person, man or woman, he could remember ever touching him as if he were someone precious to her.

As much as he wanted to have her keep on holding him like that, he knew she couldn't bear his weight much longer. He rolled over, pulling her with him. He settled her against his chest and kissed her shoulder. "Thank you."

She lifted her head and looked at him with a confused expression on her face. "You're thanking me for making love to you?"

"That and other things."

She shook her head as one does at a crazy person. "Don't start getting weird on me, Jackson."

He laughed. "I won't."

She laid her nose against his neck. He hugged her to him, and lay for a long while thinking of long-ago dreams of what he wanted from his life. He'd put them all aside, but maybe . . .

He was getting ahead of himself. With Carly dozing in his arms and more content than he'd been in a while, Jackson fell asleep.

The need to relieve herself woke Carly an hour later. She lifted her head from Jackson's shoulder to look down at him. He smiled in his sleep, an expression that lent a softness to his face that was absent when he was awake. She leaned down and kissed his mouth, just a peck, but his arms tightened around her.

Now see what she started? "I have to go to the bathroom," she whispered, hoping he would ease his hold.

His grin broadened and he whispered back in a sleep-roughened voice, "Hope everything comes out all right."

Good Lord, she hadn't heard that expression since elementary school. Someone please tell her that beneath Jackson's gruff exterior there wasn't some sort of corny man waiting to get out. But he did let her go, so that was something.

She rose from the bed and padded to the bathroom in the corner. The tiny room contained a sink and a commode, and an enormous claw-foot tub instead of a shower. She used the first two, and was grateful that the hotel provided a travel kit that included a toothbrush and a tube of toothpaste. She washed the remnants of her makeup from the day before from her face and surveyed herself in the mirror. She ached in places she didn't know she had places to ache, but her skin glowed and her eyes twinkled. Maybe running for your life did that to a person. Or maybe it came from making love to the man she loved.

She preferred the second explanation, especially since he'd proved to be an amazing lover. Most of that had to do with Jackson, but part of that had to do with herself, too. She hadn't tried to hold anything back from him. She'd shown him both her love and her trust and allowed him to do with them what he wanted. And he hadn't disappointed her. He'd given her the same in return, even if he wasn't aware himself what he'd done.

Jackson's image appeared in the mirror behind her. "What are you grinning about so early in the morning?"

She shot him him a droll look in the mirror, seeing the self-satisfied expression on his face. He knew he'd pleased her and apparently wasn't above being smug. "There's no need to be cocky about it."

His arms closed around her from behind. His erection nestled between her buttocks. "No?" His lips grazed her temple, the side of her throat, her shoulder. "I wouldn't bother to lie to you and tell you that I haven't been with a lot of women. And though I'm not proud of it, none of them really meant anything to me."

His voice trailed off and she filled in the rest for him. He did care for her. She already knew that, but she hadn't suspected that he'd worried about satisfying her.

She turned in his arms to face him. "I know, Jackson, I know," she whispered, then leaned up to press her mouth to his.

His arms tightened around her, lifting her. She wrapped her legs around him. The kiss went wild, but that didn't account for the sudden sensation of movement she experienced. He was carrying her back to their bed. That knowledge excited her, as did the movements of his hands on her body. He laid her on the bed, leaving her only long enough to sheath himself. Then he was inside her, moving with such exquisite slowness that she shivered from it. "That's it, baby," he whispered against her ear.

He thrust into her again, and she moaned his name. He rolled over, pulling her on top of him. "Yes, baby."

She shook her head, setting her hair dancing, unable to say anything coherent at that moment. She looked into his eyes that had darkened to nearly black, as his hands gripped her waist, helping her move at the same slow, erotic pace. She bit her lips as one of his hands rose to cup her breast. His thumb strummed over her engorged nipple, before he leaned up and took the turgid flesh into his mouth, suckling her.

Her back arched and her head lolled back on her shoulders. She gasped in air, but with his big body around her, inside her, enveloping her, she feared she'd melt or explode or both from the heat of their coupling. He took her other nipple into his mouth as his fingers delved between their bodies to find the sensitive flesh between her thighs.

She called his name as wave after wave of pleasure rippled out through her body. She clung to him for ballast in the storm that buffeted her, and when he pulled her down to him she buried her face against his neck. His arm around her waist tightened, and the hand that rested on her hip gripped her soft flesh. A moment later, she felt him explode beneath her. It set her off all over again, arching her back and sending a wash of pure ecstasy coursing through her.

Spent, she lay sprawled on top of him, her legs wracked with a series of small tremors she couldn't control. He gathered her closer and drew the blanket over them as their bodies cooled. Trying to get her breathing back to normal, Carly inhaled, drinking in the scent of their lovemaking that still permeated the room.

His hands scrubbed down her back. "How are you doing?"

She smiled against his shoulder. "Who, me? Can I let you know when I finish floating back down to terra firma?"

He laughed and swatted her bottom. "That *was* incredible."

She lifted her head so that she could see him. "You're not going to thank me again, are you?"

"Not if you don't want me to."

She lowered her head. In truth it had been a sweet gesture from a gallant man. She brushed her fingers over his right nipple. "Thank you, Jackson."

"For what? Making love to you?"

She knew he was teasing her, echoing the same words she'd spoken to him. But she hadn't intended to make him laugh. She was thankful to him for so many things besides mind-blowing sex: his protectiveness, his care of her, and most of all for giving her someone to love.

She wasn't naive enough to believe that love was enough for them. Both of them had serious issues to resolve within themselves before they could even consider truly being together. But he'd drawn her out of that shell of isolation she'd cloaked herself in, thinking it offered her some sort of protection from pain.

No matter what, she would always be grateful to him for that.

Before she could voice any of those sentiments to him, a knock sounded on the door and Drew's voice reached them. "You guys awake in there?"

For a moment, she and Jackson exchanged a regretful look. For the time being their little idyll was over. "Just a minute," Jackson called back.

Carly glanced at the bedside clock. Eight-fifteen in the morning. Time to figure out who was trying to kill them if she expected to spend another night in the haven of Jackson's arms.

Chapter 21

After sending Carly to the bathroom, Jackson pulled on his jeans and answered the door. The first thing he said to Drew was, "I hope to God you brought us some coffee."

"I did better than that," Drew said, stepping into the room. "After I left you last night, I snuck into your hotel room, hung out awhile as if you two were there, then threw this out the window, so anyone seeing me come out into the lobby wouldn't notice." He tossed an overstuffed bag onto the bed and then pushed a paper bag containing coffee and rolls into Jackson's hands. "I see you two have been doing your part to work up an appetite."

Jackson shot him a hard look. "Don't be crass."

"I'm not. I like Carly. She'd probably skewer me for saying this, but she's a sweet kid. I just want to make sure that what's between that girl's thighs isn't the only thing on your mind this morning." He took a seat in the only chair in the room and glanced around. "By the way, where is she?"

"Hey, Drew," Carly called from the bathroom. "And you're right. I do plan on skewering you later."

Drew laughed. "How much do you want to bet she has a clearer head this morning than you do?"

"Not a penny." But he admitted Drew was probably

right. Those few hours spent in Carly's arms had him wishing for things that couldn't be, wishing that they could hole themselves up here and forget the rest of the world existed or at least that someone somewhere out there wanted them dead. That wasn't like him. He wasn't a dreamer; he was a pragmatist. But she had been the one to kiss him and slide from their bed first. So what did that say about him?

"Why don't you give her the bag of clothes I brought," Drew said in a quiet, understanding voice, "so she can come on out of there?"

He did as Drew suggested, then retrieved his coffee from where he'd left it on the nightstand. He swigged down some of the scalding liquid. "I never got an answer from her about who she might have told where she was going last night."

"Somehow, I didn't think you had."

The smug look on his cousin's face annoyed him. "Damn it, Drew, would you mind being serious for a change?"

"I am serious. Serious as the grim reaper's hand. But at the same time, I'm happy for you, Jackson. It's about time you let some woman put a hurtin' on you, and it looks like Carly hurt you real good."

He said nothing to that, as Carly stepped out of the bathroom, freshly washed and smelling wonderful. She'd put on a pair of faded jeans that threatened to unravel at the knees, low-heeled sandals, and a sleeveless beige top that clung to her curves becomingly.

"Your turn," she said to him, gesturing toward the bathroom.

"You two behave yourselves," he said. Then he went into the bathroom and closed the door. Drew had managed to pack half the contents of each of their suitcases into the one bag. Jackson smiled, realizing Carly had already laid out his toiletries and his razor on the counter by the sink. He showered, shaved, and dressed, not taking much time for any activity. When he emerged from the bathroom, Carly was sitting on the bed facing Drew, sipping from her coffee cup.

"Any earth-shattering breakthroughs while I was in the bathroom?"

"None whatsoever."

That came from Carly. Drew said, "I neglected to mention that the police are looking for you."

"A minor detail," Jackson said sarcastically.

Drew snorted. "Seems folks in this area are a little touchy about folks leaving the scene of a crime, or parking their cars where they don't belong. I already paid the fine and arranged to have the car towed. But they were more interested in speaking to Carly actually."

"Why? How did they even know she was there?"

"They found blood on the door frame and you forgot her purse in the car. My guess is they want to make sure she's all right."

Jackson shrugged and sat on the bed next to Carly. "Anything else?"

"A dead end. I'm having the plates run. I should get a call back in a couple of hours."

Jackson nodded. "And did you tell anyone where you would be last night?"

"Just Nora. And it couldn't have been her behind the wheel."

"Why not?"

"She was in a car accident a few years ago. She can barely stand getting in a car, let alone driving one."

But as much as she talked, she could have inadvertently told just about anyone where Carly would be. "When are the others scheduled to go home?"

"I don't know. The ad agency people are gone and Jarad's company, too. But I gave everyone on my staff who came up here the rest of the week off, sort of a thank-you for the inconvenience. There are only four of us anyway, not including my mother."

A horrified look came into her eyes. "Oh, my God, Jackson. I need to call her. What if the same person tries to harm her, too?"

"Taken care of," Drew said. "I spoke to John this morning. He'll be on his guard."

"You spoke to my mother's chauffeur? What good is that going to do unless he throws her in the car and drives her home?"

Jackson placed a calming hand on her thigh. "Sweetheart, John is a former police lieutenant. Your mother is in good hands."

"How do you know that?"

He didn't miss her implication: how did he know when she didn't? "One time when I was leaving Charlotte's he was waiting for me in my car. He insisted on a little exchange of information."

He didn't elaborate on how John had insisted, but by the wide-eyed shocked look that came over her face, he knew she'd figured it out. Then she threw up her hands. "I swear, nobody ever tells me anything."

He hid a smile at her indignation. He knew that whether or not anyone told her that John was a cop, that was not what bothered her. It was the whole situation. She started to pace and he let her be. He turned to Drew. "So what's the game plan?"

"I was hoping you had one. Other than making sure the local boys get a look at Carly, I don't know. Maybe Carly's mom knows something she doesn't know she knows."

Jackson shook his head. He'd already gone that route. But he had to admit, getting Carly and her mother together wouldn't be such a bad idea. He noticed she'd been calm until the talk had turned to

Charlotte. And it wouldn't hurt to get John's take on what happened. He had more experience on the job than Jackson's and Drew's put together.

"Let's get out of here," Jackson said. Carly had infected him with her restlessness and a need for something to do. After making arrangements for John and Charlotte to meet them, they set off for Sam and Adam's house.

As Jackson expected, the others fussed over Carly, who still wore a small bandage on her forehead to cover the healing stitches. Everyone but Charlotte. She hung back and off to the side, though he could sense in her the desire to go to her daughter. Jackson went to where Charlotte stood. "If it helps any, she's just angry with you. She'll get over it."

"I know that, Jackson. The same way I know she could never walk away from the company she built. But it hurts knowing I caused her such pain." Charlotte gave him a once-over. "She seems to have forgiven you."

Charlotte couldn't possibly know how he and Carly had spent the wee hours of the morning, but for the first time in his life he actually flushed in embarrassment at having been with a woman. Then again, he'd never had anyone's mother confront him as to his treatment of her daughter either.

Charlotte placed a hand on his arm. "I'm not being judgmental, Jackson. Really, I'm not. That would be a bit ridiculous considering some of the choices I've made. If you and Carly want to be together, I'm nothing but happy for the both of you."

"Thank you," he said, but neither he nor Carly had made each other any promises aside from spending that one incredible night together. What would happen when they figured out who had tried to run them off the road? Would she simply go back to her life and he to his? Would they have a brief affair only to have it fizzle out somewhere down the road? Or what if she decided that, like her singing career, her being with him was only a one-shot deal?

As Charlotte moved off to go stand beside John, he realized he couldn't imagine any scenario in which he and Carly remained together. Despite knowing she had feelings for him, when it came down to it he couldn't imagine her wanting to join her life with his in anything more than a temporary manner. Funny, that's the way he usually liked it, no strings or anything else attached, come and go, take it or leave it.

Over the years, there had been a few women who wanted more from him even though they'd known his intentions from the beginning. They'd been hurt and angry at his ability to walk away. How would he deal with being on the other end of that equation?

He watched her walk toward him, a concerned expression on her face. "What were you and my mother talking about?"

"Nothing important."

"By the expression on your face, I'd thought she was grilling you on what your intentions were toward her daughter."

"Would that bother you if she had?"

Carly shrugged. "That's the kind of thing you can expect from Charlotte. She wants to know everything you're doing while keeping her own affairs to herself. If she did, I hope you told her it was none of her business."

"Are you still that angry with your mother?"

"Not really. But I want her to understand that her days of meddling in my life are over. And that includes keeping secrets from me."

He doubted she had to worry much about that anymore. Charlotte feared losing Carly too much, and if

Charlotte hid anything else from her daughter, he couldn't imagine what it might be. He draped an arm around Carly's shoulder, leading her in the direction the others had already gone, toward the patio where the Wexler's cook had laid out breakfast for them.

Over eggs, coffee, and fresh fruit, they hashed and rehashed every detail of both past and present. "So let me get this straight," Adam said during a lull in the conversation, "here we have a woman with no known enemies who turns up strangled to death. She must have known whoever killed her, since there's no sign of forced entry, and even twenty years ago, any New Yorker would have kept her door locked. It wasn't a robbery, since nothing was touched. The only semen present matches Jackson's father's blood type, so rape isn't the motive. So what does that leave us with?"

"My money has always been on some deranged fan. Sharon had her share of them. I think she liked the idea of having men obsessed with her," Charlotte said.

John shook his head. "But a deranged fan probably wouldn't have the clout to scare Anderson into fabricating a story or disappearing once he recanted it."

"I hadn't thought of that."

"You know what bothers me?" Carly said, drawing all their attention. "Why do we assume the car running Daddy off the road had anything to do with Jackson's father's case? Whoever tried to do the same thing to Jackson and me is harkening back to that event, or why bother? There have got to be easier ways to kill people. And if it's someone close to us, as I think we all suspect, that would have made it easier, not harder, for them to get to us. But who's to say that Daddy's death and Jackson's father's trial were related?"

No one said anything to that. No one that afternoon had mentioned the killer being someone close, although Jackson believed it as did Drew. And he suspected both Adam and John did, too, but Carly had picked up on that. But still, to Jackson's mind, it would be a hell of a coincidence if his father's trial and her father's death weren't linked. Someone made threats against Carly's father, yet someone else had taken him out? Not likely.

The way Charlotte had described it, it seemed as if someone had come after Alex Thompson either as revenge for getting off the man believed to have killed Sharon Glenn or to prevent him from finding out who had. Jackson remembered overhearing Carly's father say when the trial was over, "This isn't over, Don, not by a long shot." At the time, Jackson had taken that to mean that Thompson intended to help his father find out who really killed Sharon Glenn; Jackson still believed that.

Besides, another, more pressing thought occurred to Jackson. "Charlotte, you told me that Sharon and my father fought once because some man made a pass at her. Who was that?"

"Is that important?"

"It could be. Who was it?"

"It was Paul. He had a thing for her, practically every man we knew did." Charlotte shrugged. "As I said, I think she liked the idea of having men obsessed with her, or she did until she met your father. And although Paul tries to project a cultured front, there's still a bit of Brooklyn street tough in him. He could sometimes be quite crude and cruel."

"What did he say to her?"

"She never told me, but I assumed it wasn't something pleasant. But she got him back. It was well know among the women in our circle that Paul had certain, um, problems and she used that knowledge to put him in his place."

"What sort of problems?"

"Let's just say that when they invented Viagra they had Paul in mind."

Jackson's gaze slid to Drew, who stared back at him with a speculative look. Was Drew thinking the same thing he was? That a man of Paul Samuels's vanity wouldn't take well having his masculinity called into question in a public place. But would that be enough to make him kill? Or maybe he hadn't intended to kill her. Maybe he'd gone to her apartment to talk to her and things got out of hand. Jackson had gotten a taste of the other man's hostility and his strength. It didn't require much imagination to picture this man in the type of rage it took to strangle a person to death with your bare hands. That proved nothing, but Jackson had been suspicious of him from the start.

Carly shook her head speculatively. "I've always wondered why Daddy would have a man like Paul as a law partner. They were nothing alike."

"Your father had an unfortunate tendency to see only the best in people. He admired Paul for pulling himself up by his own proverbial bootstraps. He was different as a younger man, before he'd achieved success and his ego took over. But your father figured him out eventually. They were in the process of dissolving their partnership when he died."

"Why then?" Jackson asked.

"They hadn't really worked together in a couple of years. Paul was moving on, getting more involved in the political arena. And though he never said anything to Paul, your father began to suspect him of underhanded dealing."

"In what way, Mother?"

"A client of Paul's came to your father to defend him, a quite unsavory person, if you know what I mean. When your father told him that he would probably lose the case as there was both forensic and eyewitness evidence against him, the man wanted to know why your father couldn't bribe the judge as his former lawyer had done. He assumed since they were partners, Alex knew."

"Why didn't Daddy go to the authorities with what he knew?"

"For what purpose? Such a charge requires substantiation. All Alex had was the insinuation of a criminal who never would have testified against Paul. Besides, Paul wasn't practicing anymore. He was running for office, though he never officially made it onto the ballot. I don't know what happened with that. I never asked and Paul never volunteered the information."

John said, "Maybe I can help with that." He took a sip from his coffee cup and set it down. "Back then Samuels's chief supporter was the then mayor. This guy had a seventeen-year-old hellion of a daughter who seemed determined to embarrass her father at every opportunity. Do you remember that, Charlotte?"

"I remember feeling sorry for the man, although I never liked him. She even ran away from Gracie Mansion, didn't she?"

"Umm. The official story was that she'd run off on a ski trip with some friends after her father forbade her to go. Actually, she'd run off with just one friend."

"Uncle Paul." Carly's voice held no speculation but a certainty that made Jackson wonder if she had had reason before now to suspect the man of preying on young women.

John nodded. "Apparently he has no problem getting it up if the girl is young enough."

Obviously, John missed the implication in Carly's words, but Charlotte didn't. A horrified expression came over her face. "Carly, he never—"

Carly cut her off. "Of course not, Mother. Just sometimes he would look at me in ways that made me feel uncomfortable."

Charlotte stood and began to pace the patio. "He always had an unhealthy fascination with Carly, as far as I was concerned. Carly was such a pretty little girl, but insecure, especially after her father died. That's the type they prey on, isn't it? That's why I asked him to stop coming around. I wasn't going to let anyone hurt my baby."

John rose and went to Charlotte, wrapping his arms around her. He murmured something to her that Jackson couldn't make out, which was probably for the best. His gaze slid to Carly beside him. Her face bore a determined expression he couldn't begin to comprehend. Rather than question her about it, he slipped his hand in hers. She laced her fingers with his and squeezed gently, as if for reassurance. He almost laughed. She wanted to reassure him?

Drew said, "Did you tell any of this to the police?"

Charlotte swiped at her eyes. "I told them all of it. Paul was the first person I suspected, but he was supposedly out of town when Sharon was killed and he had an airtight alibi for the night Alex was killed. He was at a fund-raiser where hundreds of people saw him. Besides, the police thought I was a kook. They treated whatever I said as the ramblings of a deranged woman."

To Jackson's mind, the police hadn't done an adequate job of investigating either murder. In the first place they assumed the guilty party got off on a technicality; in the second they didn't seem to care one way or the other. Granted, no cop was a big fan of defense attorneys who helped free the criminals they apprehended, but a shoddy investigation was a shoddy investigation. "Does anyone know where Samuels is now?" he asked.

"He owns a house out in East Chop, but I don't know if he went back to New York or not."

Jackson glanced at Drew. "Maybe it's time we find out."

Drew nodded and rose.

"You two intend to go out there?" Charlotte asked.

"That's the plan. Between the two of us, I'm sure we can rattle him enough to let something slip." He leaned over and pressed his lips to Carly's for a brief kiss. Adrenaline flowed through him, both from his contact with her and the anticipation of finally being able to know for sure what had happened twenty years ago. "Behave yourself until I get back," he whispered to her.

But when he tried to withdraw his fingers from her grasp she held fast. "Hold it right there, Jackson. You're not going anywhere without me."

Chapter 22

Carly got exactly the reception she expected from those around her: a chorus of "nos" or "you've got to be kiddings." But there was only one voice that concerned her.

Jackson said, "Absolutely not."

"Why not?" Of all people, she would have expected Jackson to understand how she felt, her need to know the truth, her need to understand. Once she'd learned her father had been killed, she needed the same type of closure he did. Didn't he see that?

Obviously not, as his expression hardened and his jaw set. "Excuse us," he said to no one in particular and led her from the patio into the interior of the house. He stopped a few feet from the front door and turned to face her. "Don't do this to me, Carly. Don't ask me to put you in harm's way, because I won't do it."

She knew what he was asking, that she not demand something he couldn't give her and allow that to cause a rift between them. She wouldn't do that. Whatever his decision, she would live with that, but she wanted to go. "Jackson, we both know you are going there because you hope to hear from the man's own mouth an admission of what he did to your father."

"I'm not denying that."

"Don't I deserve the same? Don't I deserve to hear

firsthand if Paul Samuels is the man who killed my father?"

"I'm not denying that either. But don't ask this of me."

"What makes you think he'll even talk to you?"

"There's no doubt in my mind that he'll talk to me."

The coldness that flashed in Jackson's eyes sent a shiver down her spine. "What do you intend to do?"

"Have a little discussion, that's all."

Something about the way he said that made her suspect that her idea of a discussion and his varied more than a little.

He pulled her against him with his arms around her waist. She went to him, wrapping her arms around his neck and burying her face against his throat. "Isn't there anything I can say to make you change your mind?"

He pulled back from her, enough so that they could look at each other. His fingertips traced the line of her cheek. "That's no place for you to be, Carly, and you know it."

She sighed, resigning herself to being left behind. "All right, Jackson. You win. But do me a favor? If it turns out he killed my father, hurt him just a little bit for me."

Jackson grinned. "You don't have to ask me twice." He pulled her closer, stroking her hair in a soothing manner. "It will be all right, sweetheart. I promise."

Then his mouth found hers. She clung to him as a maelstrom of emotions swept through her: fear for him, for what he was about to do, her own frustration at being left behind, and most of all her love for him, an emotion more potent than any that had ever claimed her.

She sensed an equal desperation in him, in the way his mouth moved over hers and the way his hands roamed her body. She didn't understand that sentiment coming from him. If they hadn't miscalculated, he stood on the brink of knowing what he'd spent the better part of his life trying to find out. Or maybe she misinterpreted what she felt in him. Maybe he was simply anxious to get going.

Hearing a coughing sound behind them, they drew apart.

"I hate to interrupt, folks," Drew said, coming up alongside them. "But Jackson and I have somewhere to be."

"I'm coming," Jackson said. He kissed the tip of her nose. "I'll call you as soon as I can." He headed toward the door.

Carly turned to Drew, who lingered beside her. "You better take care of him, Drew. Make sure he doesn't do anything stupid."

"The story of my life." Drew winked at her, then jogged out the door behind Jackson.

Carly stood rooted where she was as outside an engine revved and the car pulled away. The smell of roses reached her nose and she felt her mother's hands at her shoulders. "It's better this way, darling. You know that."

"I know, Mother. That doesn't mean I don't wish I were with him."

"He's a good man, Carly. You have to trust him to do the right thing."

Carly turned to face her mother. "My trust of Jackson isn't in question. I don't know what I would do if something were to happen to him."

"You love him?"

Carly snorted. "Isn't that obvious?"

"Well, now that you put it that way, I guess it is. I'm happy for you, Carly. And I'm sorry I never told you the truth about how your father died. I thought about it many times, but I couldn't see any point in telling you. I preferred to leave your memory of your father intact."

Carly shook her head. "That's just it, Mother. For a long time I hated Daddy for leaving us."

Charlotte's brow furrowed. "Why?"

"Let's face it, Daddy wasn't exactly a health nut. He drank more than he should, he smoked. If there was a piece of red meat that he didn't try to eat, I'd be surprised. He was a walking advertisement for a heart attack. I blamed him for not taking better care of himself."

"I'm so sorry, sweetie. I had no idea you felt that way."

"Do you know what the last thing he said to me was? 'Take care of your mother.' As if he were passing on his responsibility to me." The sting of tears burned her eyes, but she pressed on. "I tried. I really tried all these years to do as he asked. But I'm tired, Mother. I want something for myself now." She wasn't sure herself what that something was, except that, if she was lucky, it would involve Jackson and some sort of future for them together.

"Oh, darling. Your father never expected you to look after me. It was just a thing to say, he never intended for you to devote your life to me. Is that why you started the company? A way to take care of me?"

"Yes."

"Oh, baby." Charlotte crushed her in a bear hug. "You never had to worry about me financially. Your father left me very well off, to say nothing of the money I made as an actress. There was no need for you to worry."

Carly brushed a strand of hair from her face. "Mother, please, you spend sixty thousand a year on a spa you visit once a month, if that. I was afraid you'd run through your money and we'd be penniless."

"Come here, Carly." Charlotte took her hand and led her to one of the living room sofas. Once they were both seated, Charlotte continued. "I've never told you much about my childhood and thank goodness your grandmother died before she had a chance to have any influence on you. Let's just say it wasn't fodder for anything but a horror novel. I never knew my father and I'm certain my mother wasn't sure who he was anyway. My mother made her living on her back, if you know what I mean. She didn't consider herself a prostitute, as she wasn't on the streets; men just did her favors for her like pay our rent in exchange for her favors. That is, until a man came up to us one day and asked if he could put me in a commercial. I took to the work and the next thing I knew I was her meal ticket. Instead of selling herself, she sold her daughter.

"Don't you see, Carly? I hated it. I hated knowing someone else made their living off me. That I had no choice. I never would have done that to my own daughter. It never occurred to me that the company wasn't what you wanted. If I had known, I would have put a stop to it. I'm sorry, darling."

Carly stood, wrapping her arms around herself. She couldn't seem to keep still. "It's not your fault, Mother. I should have told you how I felt." But she'd been too angry all these years over every weakness she perceived in her mother. She didn't know why she hadn't seen that more clearly before now. She'd been dealing with her mother as if she, Carly, were still a little girl rather than a grown woman with her own mind and choices to be made. That had to end now, too.

"Where does that leave us, Carly?"

She turned to face her mother. "I don't know. My whole life is upside down right now. I don't know what I want from you or the company. All I can think about is Jackson out there with a man that might be a killer."

Charlotte stood and embraced her. "I know, darling. I know."

And Carly finally understood how Sam must have felt every time Adam walked out the door.

Paul Samuels's house rested on a plot of land guarded on three sides by a grove of maple trees and on the fourth by the waters of the Vineyard Sound. As Drew pulled to a halt in front of the house, Jackson glanced up at the A-frame structure. The entire front of the house was made of glass, the sort of house one would expect from a man with nothing to hide, not one who hoarded secrets. Or maybe the house was like the man, since both facades hid something deeper and darker inside.

Drew's meaty hand grasped Jackson's shoulder. "You sure you're up to this, man?"

"No, but let's do it anyway." Jackson got out of the car and walked up to the front door. Not surprisingly, it wasn't locked. Jackson slid the door open. Immediately the sound of Samuels's voice reached them, not speaking but moaning in pleasure. Jackson glanced at Drew. Heaven only knew what they'd find on the other side of the door, but they'd come too far to turn back.

They followed the sound of Samuels's ecstatic grunts and groans to a large wood-paneled room adorned as a hunter's den complete with several stuffed and mounted heads and bodies of slaughtered animals. For an instant Jackson drank in the surroundings before focusing on the man they'd come to see.

Samuels sat at the center of a burgundy leather sofa while a young woman knelt between his legs, doing her best to cover herself with her hands. It didn't take a brilliant mind to figure out what had been going on before they burst in the door.

Drew said, "This is way, way too disgusting for words."

Jackson said, "How old are you, sweetheart?"

"Eight-eighteen."

Revulsion roiled in Jackson's belly. Eighteen would have been bad enough but Jackson suspected she padded her age by a couple of years. "Get out of here before I call your mother."

Panic flashed in the girl's eyes before she grabbed her clothes from the floor and bolted from the room.

After she'd gone, Jackson focused on Samuels. The older man lit a cigarette as if he hadn't a care in the world. "Well, that encounter proved a lot less satisfying than I had anticipated."

"Have a little self-respect, man." Drew tossed the shirt that lay across a chair onto the sofa. "Put some clothes on."

Samuels eschewed the shirt and instead stood and pulled up the pants that lay puddled at his feet. "Now would you fellows mind telling me what you are doing in my house? I want to have something to tell the police when I call."

"Do it now. Maybe they'll be in time to track down that child you had in here."

"Too bad you didn't bring Carly with you. Maybe she'd like to take her place."

Jackson acknowledged Drew's restraining hand on his arm, but there was no need for it. He didn't intend to rise to Samuels's bait. "Isn't she a little old for you? I thought a girl had to have the word *teen* in her age to get you turned on."

Samuels's face reddened with anger. "Who told you that? Charlotte? That bitch."

"All this name-calling is entertaining," Drew interjected. "But let's get to the subject at hand. What do you know about Sharon Glenn's death?"

For the first time, Samuels's gaze strayed to Drew. "Who the devil are you?"

"Just your friendly neighborhood Spiderman. Now answer the question."

"Sharon's death was a terrible tragedy. I tried to warn her that your half-a-cop father was no good for her. She didn't listen to me, and look what happened. He killed her." Samuels dragged on his cigarette, then crushed it out. "I'd think you'd be the last person to want to dredge up the past."

"I might be, if I believed that nonsense were true. My father never killed anybody."

"That's not what the authorities believe."

"Probably because they didn't know you'd set up Duke Anderson to give false testimony against him."

"Anderson was a drunk and a liar. He wouldn't know the truth if he drank it out of a bottle."

"So then why did you bother to kill him? Old times' sake?"

"What are you talking about?"

"They found his body in the alleyway where you left it."

"You're delusional. Anderson has been missing for years."

He'd give the old guy this: he was consistent. "She saw you, you know. The night you ran them off the road, Charlotte saw you. She's kept quiet all these years because she thought you'd hurt Carly if you knew in order to get back at her and keep her silent." It was a bluff; Charlotte still claimed not to know who the man with her double was. But he knew he had Samuels when the other man's color darkened and his eyes narrowed to small slits.

"I never would have hurt Carly."

Jackson noted he hadn't denied Charlotte could have seen him, only that he wouldn't have caused Carly any harm. "Didn't you hurt her? You cost her her father and almost took away her mother. Don't you think that hurt her?"

"She was better off without him. Alex was the original sap, believing whatever people told him. He actually believed half the scum he defended were innocent. Could you imagine what she'd be like today if she'd spent a lifetime under his care? His death toughened her up, put an end to all those starry-eyed dreams of hers." Samuels shook his head in distaste. "I never regretted Alex's death."

Remembering the little girl he'd known and the woman he'd first met, Jackson understood exactly what her father's death had cost her. In the past few days, he'd seen the woman she should have been all along slowly emerging. He only hoped he played some small role in her transformation.

"You want me to tell you why I killed Alex? Why not? You'll never be able to prove anything I tell you. Anderson is dead, the woman who supplied my alibi for the morning of Sharon's death was conveniently murdered by a push-in robber, so there's no way to refute her sworn statement. No one noticed me leaving that dreadful dinner dance, or when I returned. I killed him because when we decided to dissolve our partnership, that shrew of a wife of his talked him into hiring an independent auditor to go over the books. Alex would have been content to liquidate our assets and split the profits fifty-fifty, the way we'd started. But if he'd discovered some of the ways I'd spent much of the company money, he could have ruined me. Charlotte would have seen to it."

"How would getting rid of Alex help you if his half of the business would have passed to Charlotte on his death and she was the one determined to ruin you?"

"Finally, he catches on." He grinned, a chilling, feral expression. "I had to get rid of them both, which suited me fine. Neither Alex nor Charlotte had any living relatives. Carly would have gone to Sharon. At the time, I was still listed as the executor of Alex's estate. It wouldn't be too much trouble to petition the court to become Carly's guardian in her place. After all, who would be a better caregiver? Me, an upstanding member of the legal and political communities, or some flaky actress involved in some tawdry love affair?"

And then he would have had Carly in his care. Heaven only knew what this paragon of society would have done to her, maybe not as a child but when she became old enough to be of interest to him. "Is that why you killed Sharon Glenn? To get her out of the way?"

"Yes, but not the way you mean. You see, I'd found a better plan in the form of one Sharlene Watts. I found her in the one place a woman of Charlotte's ilk truly belonged, walking the streets in Hunt's Point. She was a dead ringer for Charlotte, from her physical attributes down to her speech and mannerisms. People had told her all her life that she reminded them of the Scarlet Woman to the point she half believed she was Charlotte. I intended to give her the opportunity to be her. Not forever. I'd only need her around long enough to change the will, naming me sole beneficiary to Alex and Charlotte's estates and giving me custody of Carly."

"But your plan backfired."

"Only slightly. I arranged for Sharlene to go to a few parties, a trial run of sorts. Even her best friend, Sharon, didn't know the difference. Unfortunately, that cow Sharon spotted us at this abominable restaurant in the Bronx where we used to meet. She threatened to tell Alex that Charlotte and I had been together. I couldn't have that. Seeing the life drain from her lovely face was sweeter than I had imagined." Samuels's face took on a dreamy quality and his free hand flexed as if reliving the moment.

Jackson swallowed roughly. He'd always assumed whoever had framed his father had killed Alex Thompson to prevent him from finding out the identity of Sharon Glenn's killer, but he'd had it backward. Samuels had killed Sharon Glenn to conceal his plan to murder his business partner and claim his daughter and his money. In his mind, Jackson filled in the details Samuels left out of his story. That night on the road, he'd planned to switch Charlotte's body with Sharlene Watts, who would somehow have managed to survive intact. Or maybe he'd roughed her up enough to look as if she'd been in the accident. And when Sharlene's usefulness had ended, he would have ended her, too.

Only Charlotte hadn't died and the police came too quickly for him to make the switch. A couple of months later, the scandal with the mayor's daughter would have broken anyway, doing for his career exactly what Charlotte would have done with her investigation into the company's finances—ruining it.

"Where did my father fit into this scheme of yours?"

"He was merely a convenient scapegoat. Anderson owed me a favor and I cashed in. Who knew that weasel would grow a conscience and renege on everything he promised me? He went into hiding because he knew that if I ever found him I would kill him."

And he had.

Samuels sighed dramatically. "And now our story hour draws to a close. I want to thank you gentlemen. I haven't been able to share my exploits with anyone before, and as they say, confession is good for the soul."

"You are one twisted son of a bitch," Drew said.

Samuels shrugged, shoving his hands in his pants pockets. "Maybe, but even a lunatic has the right to defend his home. No one would blame me for shooting a couple of trespassers." He pulled a .22 revolver from his pocket and pointed it at Jackson. "Would they?"

Chapter 23

It had only been twenty minutes since Jackson and Drew walked out the door, but when Carly saw the uniformed policeman walking toward her across Sam's patio, her heartbeat trebled and her knees threatened to buckle. She inhaled sharply and pulled herself together. He couldn't be here to tell her something had happened to Jackson. He and Drew were probably just pulling up in front of Paul's house at that moment.

"Ms. Thompson, I've been looking for you."

She remembered Drew saying as much, but she figured feigned ignorance would better suit the situation. "Whatever for?"

"You were involved in a car accident last night?"

"Yes." She brushed back the hair at her temple in case he hadn't noticed her bandage. "Unfortunately my head and the window frame didn't get along."

"Are you aware it's a crime to leave the scene of an accident?"

"Even if it's to seek medical attention?"

"That's understandable, Ms. Thompson. I'm just wondering why neither you nor the car's owner, Jackson Trent, a former policeman, reported the accident, while a Mr. David Barker, average citizen from Boston, did."

"It's simple, Officer, Jackson was concerned for my

safety. We weren't seen for a while and I had a bad re-action to the pain medication I'd been given. I'm sure it just slipped his mind."

"I see."

Carly didn't like the sound of that. "What exactly are you implying?"

"Are you sure that there isn't some reason either you or Mr. Trent wouldn't have wanted to be seen by the police that night?"

"If you're suggesting either of us was under the influence, I can assure you we were both as sober as the proverbial judge. If you want to know who was drinking that night, try talking to the driver of the truck that hit us. He was flying down the road so fast he probably never saw us before he rammed into us."

"I'd love to do that, Ms. Thompson, but the truck was reported stolen by a farmer down-island and found abandoned in the parking lot of the Harbor Inn."

Carly lifted one shoulder in a shrug. "Sounds like kids joyriding to me."

Officer Gonzales shook his head. "Kids joyriding generally leave evidence: empty beer bottles, food wrappers, used condoms. At the very least, they leave fingerprints. The cab of the truck had been wiped clean. Not a fingerprint anywhere, not even the owner's. And then there's the question of why you and Mr. Trent didn't return to your hotel."

"It's simple. I had a fight with my mother earlier in the day. I don't know about your mother, Officer Gonzales, but mine can be very trying. Jackson knew I didn't want to return to the hotel to face my mother for round two, and considering my condition, I wasn't up for it anyway. He simply took me somewhere else."

"At two in the morning?"

She nodded.

Officer Gonzales cast her a skeptical look, which he

extended to every member of the group. Clearly, he didn't believe a word she'd said, and who could blame him? But at the moment her endurance was wearing a little thin.

Luckily, Charlotte rose from her chair and came to stand beside her chair. "Officer, can't you see my daughter hasn't completely recovered from her ordeal? Couldn't any further questions wait until later?"

Ariel said, "Perhaps you'd like to take the matter up with my grandmother, Isabel Ludlow? I can give you her address."

Carly pressed her lips together to stifle a grin. The Ludlows were one of the oldest and wealthiest black families on the island and one of the few that lived there year-round. Gran, as just about everyone referred to Ariel's grandmother, knew everyone on the island and was known to be a personal friend of the mayor, this man's boss. Ariel had called out the big guns, but considering that Gran was in Florida with the rest of the family, having her tell this man anything would be a very expensive call.

Officer Gonzales frowned and his eyes narrowed as he scanned the group again. "I don't know what you people are up to, and I don't want to know. Keep out of trouble or I won't care who your grandmother is." He focused on her again. "Ms. Thompson, if you'll sign for it, I have your purse in my car."

"Of course." She followed him through the house to the drive out front where his patrol car was parked. She waited at the curb by the passenger door while he walked around to the driver's-side door. He pulled out a clipboard and a plastic bag with her purse in it. He came back around and handed her the clipboard. She took the pen under the clip, signed her name on the appropriate line, and handed it back to him.

He took the clipboard and tossed it in the open car window. "By the way, where is Mr. Trent?"

"He went to see about his car."

He cast her another one of those skeptical looks as he handed over the bag containing her purse. "Are you sure there isn't something you want to tell me, Ms. Thompson?"

"Of course not." But the desire to throw herself in his arms and beg him to take her to Paul's house to make sure Jackson was all right nearly choked her with its intensity. But she'd promised Jackson to stay where he'd left her and she would honor that, even if it drove her nearly out of her mind with worry. She smiled sweetly at the officer. "Have a nice day."

Reluctantly, the man got in his car and drove away.

Drew snorted in derision seeing the size of the gun in Samuels's hand. "Put the peashooter down, before you put someone's eye out."

"What's the matter, Officer? Not used to having a gun drawn on you? That's right. I know who you are, Andrew Grissom from the Forty-seventh Precinct in the Bronx. You have quite a reputation, I understand."

Drew laughed, a sound that sent a chill through Jackson and caused Samuels's hand to tremble. "That's not a gun. This is a gun." In a second he had the magnum he carried trained on Samuels. "Now why don't you put the weapon down before you find out why no one really needs another hole in the head?"

Jackson looked from Samuels to Drew. The two of them faced off in a way that didn't include him. If Samuels intended to shoot either of them, he'd have done so before Drew got the chance to draw on him. Instead he seemed intent on baiting Drew and had so far succeeded. Drew didn't take out that canon of his unless he intended to use it. But Jackson didn't intend to let Samuels take the easy way out, if that's what he was after. Jackson wanted him rotting out the rest of his natural days in the smallest, dankest cell the U.S. prison system could provide.

"Don't even think about it, Drew. This bastard's mine."

Samuels laughed derisively. "What do you plan to do, He Who Can't Hold a Gun?"

Jackson grinned, knowing Carly's little .22 was nestled at the small of his back. He was half tempted to use it to give Samuels that hole in the head Drew mentioned. But Drew would probably split a gut seeing the little woman's-style revolver in his hand. Some things you just didn't live down. "The day I need one to deal with a punk-ass like you, I'll check myself out."

"I wonder if you'd say that without your burly friend here as backup."

Samuels turned to Drew and Jackson read his intentions in his eyes. He was on Samuels in a second, before Samuels had a chance to fire or Drew had a chance to answer. He slammed Samuels into the far wall with such force that the trophies mounted on a shelf above threatened to come down on them. One of Jackson's hands grasped the wrist of Samuels's gun hand, the other clenched around the man's throat.

He smashed Samuels's hand against the exposed brick. "Drop it," he snarled, already hearing the snap of bone breaking. The gun dropped from his fingers to crash to the floor. Samuels didn't even wince. Instead he tilted his head and spat in Jackson's face.

Jackson's grip tightened on Samuels's throat. This lunatic wanted him to kill him. Jackson shifted to brush his sleeve across his face. "Nice try, Samuels. But you're going away for what you did to my father and Carly's. I'll see to that."

"You'll never have her. She might let you warm her bed for a while, but you'll never have any more of her than you have right now. Carly's too smart to fall for a washed-up excuse for a cop."

Fury flashed in Jackson, white-hot and uncontrollable. His ears buzzed and his eyes burned. He slammed Samuels against the wall again, snapping his head back against the brick. "Don't you ever say her name to me again. Do you hear me? Don't even let her traipse by in one of those sick fantasies of yours or I will kill you."

Samuels looked him right in the eye, a defiant hardness in his gray eyes. He rasped out one word. "Car-ly."

Jackson's other hand joined his first at Samuels's throat, cutting off his breath, turning his face a mottled red, then a deeper purple. Samuels rasped for air, the fingers of his one useful hand clawing at Jackson's grasp, his arms, his shoulders, anywhere, struggling vainly to free himself.

Then Jackson felt Drew's hands on his, trying to break his hold. Jackson held on tighter. A few more seconds and the world would be rid of Paul Samuels and the world would be a lot better off.

"Stop it, Jackson. Let him go. He's not worth it."

Drew's softly spoken words, the same ones Sharon Glenn once told his father, reached him through the haze of his emotions. Abruptly he let Samuels go and backed away, repulsed by what he'd almost done. He didn't stop until he couldn't go any farther. He slumped down against the wall until he hit the floor. His rage spent, his eyes burning, he propped his elbows on his knees and rubbed his eyes with the heels of his hands.

It was over. It was finally over. He knew who'd tried to frame his father, but that was all he had. All the anger, all the shame, the outrage, the loneliness, every emotion that had haunted him most of his life seemed to have evaporated to be replaced by an emptiness so profound it was as if someone had reached in and scooped out everything inside him.

He realized the buzzing he'd been hearing must have been police sirens, because they stopped now and there were sounds of activity outside. Now he knew what Samuels had wanted, at least in part: to delay them enough for the police to arrive. They must have tripped some sort of house alarm when they'd come in here and Samuels must have known it was only a matter of time before the cavalry rushed in. Any officer coming in finding his hands on Samuels's throat might have shot first and asked questions later. Or at the very least he'd have one hell of an assault case against him.

Too weary to further decipher the workings of Paul Samuels's mind, he rested his forehead on his forearms and waited for the police to come. All he could think about was getting back to Carly. Maybe she could fill him up again.

Chapter 24

It was nearly nightfall when Jackson and Drew walked through Sam and Adam's front door. Jackson left Drew to explain to the others what had happened at Paul Samuels's house. He went to find Carly, who had spent most of the time he'd been gone in one of the upstairs rooms alone.

He pushed open the door to the bedroom without knocking. She stood at the window, wearing a robe much too big for her, looking out at whatever view the room provided. Her head snapped around to face him. "Jackson," she whispered.

Her gaze traveled over him to settle on his face. She looked at him with a mixture of relief, concern, and questions. He wanted to answer all of them, but not just yet. First he needed to hold her, to feel connected to the one person in this world on whom his whole life rested.

He went to her, gathering her to him, inhaling her scent, and absorbing the warmth her body offered him. He made the mistake of pressing his mouth to hers, because then his need for her took over, obliterating everything else. His mouth ground down on hers and his grasp on her tightened. Desire, as fierce and wild as his rage had been, consumed him, robbing him of any semblance of rationality or control.

He backed her against the wall as his fingers sought and found the sash to her robe and untied it. He pushed apart the fabric as he pulled away from her to look at her. For one electric minute, his gaze wandered over her, her breasts, her small waist, the gentle curving of her hips, those long shapely legs, while she stood braced against the wall, breathing heavily, the expression in her eyes either wary or anticipatory, he wasn't sure.

"I need you, Carly," he whispered.

Her eyes drifted shut and she murmured one breathless word. "Yes."

And then his hands were on her soft, soft flesh, stroking, kneading, caressing, as she gasped out her pleasure at his touch. He pushed the robe from her shoulders, and with his hands on her hips, he lifted her and buried his face against her throat. Her legs wrapped around his waist as her fingers tugged on his shirt, trying to free him. He leaned her against the wall and obliged her, pulling the shirt over his head and tossing it across the room.

He groaned as her soft flesh met his. His breathing hitched and his groin throbbed with the ache to be inside her. Somehow he managed to divest himself of the rest of his clothes and sheath himself. He plunged into her and she cried out. Her nails scored his back as he thrust into her again and again.

With a hand at her nape, he pulled her mouth down to his. The kiss was wild, as wild as the fire that raged in him, the need for her fulfillment and his own. He broke the kiss and gazed up into her passion-filled eyes. He brushed a lock of damp hair from her face. "Come for me, baby, please."

He thrust into her again and her back arched and her legs contracted around him. She cried out his name as her body shivered and trembled with her release. His own orgasm rushed up on him with such force he had to brace his forearms against the wall to withstand it. He buried his face against her throat as his own tremors subsided.

When he trusted his legs to hold him, he carried her to the bed and settled them under the covers. She lay on her back while he lay on his side with his head propped up on his hand looking down at her. Her chest heaved with the exertion of her breathing and her hair was damp with perspiration. Her eyes were closed, but when she opened them she looked at him with an expression of concern. "Jackson?"

He sighed. When he imagined coming back to her, he hadn't pictured taking her against the damn bedroom wall. It was only their second night together. She deserved better than that from him. "I'm sorry, baby."

"For what?"

"That's not how I wanted to make love to you. Why didn't you stop me?"

"If I'd wanted you to stop, I would have told you." She stroked her hand over his chest, pausing to massage his nipple with her thumb. "What's a little wild animal sex between friends?"

Jackson threw back his head and laughed. Way back, when Carly believed he'd been sleeping with her mother, he'd claimed to be sharing the same with Charlotte. She laughed too. He loved the tinkling quality of her voice, the mischievous glint in her eye. He loved her, period. He wished he could voice that sentiment, but he couldn't find the words. Instead, he kissed her mouth, a brief caress that left him wanting so much more. He let his fingers trail down the side of her face. "There is so much I want to say to you."

"Just tell me it's over, Jackson. Tell me Paul Samuels killed my father."

He sighed, in a way grateful she'd misunderstood his

meaning. In light of what he planned to do in the morning, it wasn't fair of him to tell her now anyway. "I'm so sorry, sweetheart."

He watched as her eyes brimmed with tears that didn't spill. "Why?"

"To keep him from finding out he'd been cooking the company's books." He would never tell her the depth of Samuels's obsession with her. Maybe one of these days he'd tell her he'd almost killed him because of it.

"That's what all this was about? Money? Then why did he kill Sharon Glenn?"

He elaborated on the story Samuels told, ending with his belief that Samuels had killed Duke Anderson out of revenge and had tried to kill them to keep them from finding out the truth, though Samuels still hadn't admitted to being in the truck that night.

Carly shook her head. "So my mother wasn't hallucinating? There really was a woman who looked like her."

He nodded.

"What happened to her?"

"I don't know." It hadn't occurred to him to ask, but in all likelihood she was dead, too.

"You know, it's funny, both Charlotte and I knew something was off with him, albeit for different reasons, but neither of us suspected he harbored such brutality and greed. I put up with him because I thought he and Charlotte had become friendly again, and she put up with him to keep an eye on him. Imagine the grief we might have saved ourselves if we ever actually talked with each other than at each other."

"Then you've forgiven her?"

"Of course. She's my mother. I've realized lately that I haven't been such a model daughter that I can afford to cast a lot of stones. We've got a lot of work to do on our relationship, but we'll get there."

She smiled up at him, her eyes twinkling in the dim light. This time when he took her mouth, he could feel the restlessness in her, the longing, because they stirred him, too. His hands moved over her deliberately, as he intended to pleasure her slowly. His mouth followed the same path, sampling every inch of her, from the delicate column of her throat to the sweet juices that flowed between her thighs.

She moaned his name, an urgent call he couldn't ignore. He sheathed himself and joined with her, thrusting deeply. She arched against him, matching his rhythm. Her legs wrapped around him, holding him to her, and her fingers gripped his back.

"Jackson," she cried, as her body spasmed beneath his, lost in a maelstrom of ecstasy. He followed her, letting his own release overtake him, making his body tremble, leaving him exhausted and sated and contented to have Carly fall asleep in his arms.

Carly woke in the middle of the night. The light on the desk in the corner illuminated Jackson hunched over a chair at the foot of the bed. She rose to a sitting position, drew her knees up, and wrapped her arms around them. "What are you doing?"

He turned toward her slightly. "Packing. I'm going back to New York."

The angle of his body revealed the suitcase that rested in the chair. He was either taking her things out or putting his things in, she wasn't sure. "You were just going to sneak out on me in the middle of the night?"

"No, I would have woken you in the morning."

But he wanted to be ready to slip out of the door as smoothly as possible. She donned his discarded T-shirt and got out of bed. She leaned her back against the wall so that she could face him, but he wouldn't look at her. "What if I want to go with you?"

He shook his head. "I have some things to take care of."

"Without me?"

He darted a glance her way. "You'll be fine, Carly. Samuels is behind bars. Drew talked his captain into giving him a few more days off. He'll be around if you want him."

In other words, she didn't need him anymore. Was that all he thought he was to her, someone to protect her and nothing more? "I've fallen in love with you, Jackson. Doesn't that count for anything?"

His head snapped up and he straightened. "It's all that does matter." His hand lifted to cup her cheek in his palm. His thumb traced the path of her lower lip. "I wish I had something to offer you."

All she wanted was his love. That would be enough. But she understood what he meant. He'd defined his whole life in terms of avenging his father. Now that he'd accomplished that, who was he? What did he have left? Ariel had warned her this might happen. She'd said, "Don't be surprised if finding out who set up his father pushes him over the edge in a way that not knowing never did." Still, it hurt her to know he'd rather seek out his answers without her rather than with her.

He rezipped the bag. "I'll pick up the rest of my things at the hotel in the morning. I'll pay the bill, but you can check out whenever you want."

She nodded, not knowing what to say. Didn't he see he was ripping her heart out? She could tell by the anguished expression on his face that he did, but it also didn't change his mind about what he thought he had to do. Despite what she wanted, she knew she'd let him go without a fuss. She'd take the chance that their love was strong enough to bring him back. But not yet.

She took his hand and pulled him toward the bed. "Be with me one more time before you have to go."

The next morning, Carly woke to the sound of gentle tapping on the bedroom door. "Jackson," Drew called in a stage whisper. "Get your lazy ass out here."

Carly didn't have to check to know he wasn't beside her, but his pillow still bore the imprint of his use and the spot where he'd lain was still warm. Drew hadn't missed him by much.

She found the robe she'd worn the night before and finger-brushed her hair into some semblance of order. She opened the door to Drew, who seemed to be surprised she, not Jackson, answered. "He's gone, Drew," she said.

"Where to and when's he getting back? I need to talk to him."

"He's gone, gone. He went back to New York."

Drew's eyes narrowed suspiciously. "You sent him away?"

She opened her mouth to defend herself, but Drew rushed on before she got a word out."

"Damn it, Carly, that man loves you. He would have given his life for you. He almost killed for you. And—"

"Hold it." She held up a hand to forestall any further ranting on his part. "I didn't ask him to leave. *He* left."

For a moment he stared back at her with an almost comical look of confusion. Then he swore, a word she wasn't sure he intended for her to hear. "What the hell was he thinking?"

Since that conversation was likely to take more than a few minutes, it was best one of them wasn't standing in the hall. "Why don't you come in?" Carly stepped aside and motioned for him to take the one chair in the room.

He ignored it and turned to face her. "He asked me to see if I could get another couple of days off, but he never mentioned it was because he planned to leave."

She leaned her back against the door to close it. Jackson probably hadn't told him because he knew Drew would at least try to stop him. She supposed she owed Drew some sort of explanation since Jackson hadn't bothered to give him one himself. "He has some things to resolve. Personal issues."

"And that couldn't have waited?"

Carly shook her head. "I don't think so."

Drew swore again, this time unapologetically. "So he left you here alone."

"You make it sound as if he abandoned some child in the supermarket. I'm a grown woman. Besides, you're here, John's here, Adam's here, and my dear godfather is in police custody. Nothing's going to happen to me."

He regarded her for a long moment, his eyes intense. In a quiet voice he said, "How can you let him go so easily? I thought . . ."

"I do love him, Drew," she said, completing his sentence. "And if you think this is easy for me, you're wrong. Knowing he could walk out on me when I practically begged him to stay has just about torn my heart out." Emotion clogged her throat, making it difficult to continue. She inhaled, trying to settle the torment inside her. "But don't be angry with him. Not on my account. It's like that old saying, if you love something set it free, if it doesn't come back—"

"Hunt it down and kill it?"

"No, it was never yours to begin with. Jackson has to decide what he wants."

"And you're willing to let him make that decision by himself?"

She sighed. "He didn't give me much choice in the matter, but yes. Make no mistake, he'll have some serious groveling to do if he wants to come back to me, but I understand why he felt he had to leave."

Sighing, Drew shook his head. "I'm willing to let calmer heads prevail. Me, personally, I'd just like to beat the spit out of him. But we'll do it your way."

Carly smiled. She appreciated Drew's protectiveness and his outrage on her behalf. "I bet that woman you married is kicking herself now for letting you go."

Drew rolled his eyes. "I gotta go. If you need me, I'll be in my room."

As he passed her on the way out the door, she hugged him impulsively. "Thank you."

He shrugged off her embrace as well as the sentiment behind it with a few gruffly mumbled words and left.

Looking around the room, Carly sighed. The room still held Jackson's presence, his scent, and the thrill of his lovemaking still resonated in her body. She'd told Drew the truth of her intentions. She wanted to be with Jackson, but she wasn't going to wallow in self-pity without him. She needed to get dressed, needed to get some food in her stomach to settle it. After that she didn't know. She'd planned to stay on the island another few days, but that prospect held little appeal now. Maybe she'd just go home and get back to real life as best she knew how.

With no decision made about what she wanted to do, Carly showered and dressed, combed her hair, and put on her makeup. She strove for some semblance of normalcy, but the only thought that she seemed able to focus on as she made her way down the stairs was that she was about to begin day number one without Jackson.

Chapter 25

Five hours later, Jackson dragged himself into his apartment to the sound of a ringing phone. He'd already decided to let his machine get it when Drew's voice crackled over the speakers. "Where the hell are you? If you're there, pick up the d—"

Jackson cut him off by picking up the receiver. "I'm here. What's the matter? Is Carly all right?"

"Are you sure you give a damn?"

Jackson sighed, noting the anger in Drew's voice. He supposed he should have told Drew that he planned to go home, but he'd known his cousin would neither understand nor approve. "Is Carly all right?"

"She's fine. But you might want to consider getting your narrow butt back up here?"

"Why?"

"You remember your little encounter with a farmer's truck two nights ago? It wasn't wearing its proper tags when you met. The plates belong to a certain Porsche owned by guess who?"

"Gary Vespers?"

"Bingo."

Jackson sank down on the sofa next to the phone. That didn't make any sense. Why would Vespers stick his own plates on a car he intended to use as a weapon? Or had Samuels done it, hoping to implicate Vespers in the attempt to run them off the road, thereby casting suspicion on someone other than himself? As far as he knew, the two men didn't know each other. Or had Vespers's car simply been a random choice among the cars parked in the lot behind the hotel? Either way, it confirmed that the accident had been no accident, and for all he knew Samuels and Vespers were somehow in this together.

"When did you find this out?"

"Last night. I called my guy back when we got to the house. After you and Carly closeted yourselves in the room, I decided it could wait until morning. I had no idea you'd go running off at the crack of dawn."

Jackson ground his teeth together. And he regretted leaving her the way he did. He'd told her he'd wake her in the morning, but once he'd awakened again he hadn't done it, knowing he never would have left if she'd asked him not to. He had some things to settle before he could even hope to make things right with her. He still did, but they would have to wait because Carly's safety came first before any other considerations.

"Is Vespers still there?"

"He hasn't checked out."

Jackson checked his watch. "I'll be back before nightfall."

"What do you want me to tell Carly?"

"Nothing. I'll talk to her when I get there."

Carly was grateful that no one save her mother seemed interested in eating breakfast that morning. Carly found Charlotte in the little breakfast nook off the kitchen. She poured herself a cup of coffee and sat next to her mother.

Charlotte put down her copy of the *Vineyard Gazette*

she'd been reading and patted her daughter's hand. "I saw Jackson drive off in a taxi this morning."

Carly nodded, glad she didn't have to explain Jackson's actions to anyone else.

"How are you holding up?"

Carly shrugged. "I don't know. I never expected to fall in love with him, Mother. Part of me still finds the whole experience a bit surreal, considering all we found out about Uncle Paul. I'm sorry I wasn't there with you when you found out he killed Daddy."

Charlotte waved a hand dismissively. "It's what I suspected all along and couldn't prove. I'm just glad it's over."

"Me too." She leaned her temple against her mother's shoulder. "But what am I supposed to do now?"

Charlotte's arm closed around her shoulders. "You do what women have always done. Hope for the best, but do what you have to do."

Carly nodded, realizing she knew what she wanted in one area of her life, at least. She lifted her head and gazed at her mother. "I want my company back. I want to run it and to own the lion's share of it. I want your two percent, Mother. I've earned that."

"Yes, you have, darling. We'll arrange things however you want. You know the only reason why I brought up my owning more of the company than you did was that I knew you'd toss Jackson out when you needed him."

Carly smiled. "I kinda figured that out for myself."

Charlotte brushed a lock of hair behind her shoulder, regarding her with an expression she didn't understand. "You're a stronger woman than I ever was, Carly. If your father had ever left me, even if I suspected he'd be back, it would have devastated me. When he died, I felt so lost for so long. If it weren't for you, I don't know how I would have survived it."

"What did I do?"

"You existed. You gave me a reason to pull myself together. And I realized that in my grief I had done you a disservice. I'd put more responsibility on your shoulders than needed to be there. You felt you had to take care of me when the obligation should have worked the other way around. I've always been sorry for that."

"I know, Mom, but at least you improved with age. I got worse. In the last few years, I shut everyone out, even you. You know, one of my sorors called me out of the blue a couple of weeks ago and I blew her off. Maybe I should call Allison back and apologize."

Charlotte smiled. "It would be a start."

"And no more secrets between us, please, unless it's a birthday party."

Charlotte lifted a hand as if being sworn in. "I promise, but there's one more thing you should know. Why don't you come back to New York with John and me? It's not something I can tell you; I have to show you."

"All right." Well, that took care of her decision as to whether to stay on the island or leave it. But she didn't want to go back to the hotel, not with her emotions as raw as they were now. That was where she'd come to know Jackson, to fall in love with him. They'd shared their first real kiss by the window in that room. "Do you think John would mind picking up the rest of my things from the Wesley?"

"I don't see why he should."

Carly stood. "I'm going to get the things I have here together and let Drew know I'm going."

When she told him of her plans he did not look pleased. "You can't leave now. Jackson is on his way back."

Carly planted her hands on her hips and glared at Drew. "What did you say to him? I thought you agreed to do this my way."

"I didn't make any threats of physical violence, if that's what you're thinking. But he is on his way back."

Carly shook her head. Drew had to have told him something to get him back here. And she didn't want to see him if he'd been bullied into returning by Drew. The next time she saw him, she wanted to know he was back to stay—or to tell her that he couldn't. She doubted even a five-hour drive could have sealed his decision so quickly.

"I'm going back to New York with my mother. John will be with us. We'll be fine." She zipped her suitcase and lifted it from the stand. "Tell Jackson I'm sorry he made the trip for nothing."

She avoided Drew's attempts to take the suitcase from her and went down the stairs and out to the car where John and her mother waited for her. While John stowed her bag in the trunk, she climbed into the backseat. She turned to look at Drew, who stood at the front door, an expression of disapproval hardening his features. She didn't care for the idea of leaving either, but there really was no point in staying.

John slid in behind the wheel and shut the door. He looked from Charlotte to her. "Are we ready to go?"

"As ready as I'll ever be," Carly said and fastened her seat belt around her.

When Jackson pulled up in front of the hotel it was to find three police cars and an ambulance in front of the building. His heartbeat trebled as he scanned the crowd on the porch to find Drew but no sign of Carly. He raced from the car to where Drew stood. With a hand on his cousin's arm, he pulled him aside. "Where's Carly?"

"Relax, man. She's not here. She left for New York with her mother a few hours ago."

Jackson inhaled, willing his heartbeat to settle down. "Then who's the meat wagon for?"

"Turns out Vespers did check out but not the way I meant. He had the do-not-disturb sign on, but the maids had to clean the room. One of them went in and found him dead. A neat little shot to the forehead with a .22. Not self-inflicted. Maybe it's a good thing you weren't here after all."

Jackson nodded. More than a hundred people could have witnessed him manhandling Vespers at the shoot. And after last night, he wouldn't be surprised if the local cops wouldn't have considered him a suspect.

But how did Vespers's death tie in with everything else? Just that afternoon he'd speculated that he and Samuels could have been in this together somehow. Had Samuels killed him when his usefulness ended? That might make sense if Samuels was on the loose, but he was still in jail. "At least we know Samuels didn't have anything to do with it."

Drew shook his head. "The local boys let Samuels go two hours ago. They're looking for him now."

Chapter 26

John drew to a halt in front of a large white building with forest-green accents around the windows and door frame. Lush green lawn surrounded the building on three sides and smaller buildings dotted the landscape, which, from what she could see, also boasted tennis courts and a swimming pool. The canopy above the door read RAVENWOOD SPA.

Carly's gaze flew to her mother. "The place you pay a fortune for. I'm not in the mood for a facial."

"Neither am I. There's someone here I want you to meet."

Charlotte led her to a corner room on the second floor and rapped softly. A woman's voice called, "Come in."

Carly reached for the knob, anxious to find out who might be on the other side. Charlotte held her back with a hand on her arm. "Sometimes she recognizes me and sometimes she doesn't. I hope today is one of her clear days." Charlotte pushed open the door.

The room was larger than Carly had expected, painted a pristine white. Sunlight streamed in through the window where a woman sat in a wheelchair, her hands folded in her lap. "Hey, sis," the woman said. "Come on in."

The woman's nut-brown complexion and black hair

matched Carly's mother's in tone, but otherwise the two women looked nothing alike. The face of the woman in the chair looked smashed; that was the only way Carly could describe it to herself, as if someone had destroyed it and tried to rebuild it with what was left.

Charlotte took her hand. "Come meet your aunt Sharlene."

Carly's head reeled with the impact of what Charlotte said. All these years she'd had an aunt she'd never known about. She wondered why her mother had never told her about her before now. She stepped forward, approaching the woman cautiously. She stopped a couple of feet in front of the woman. "Hello, Aunt Sharlene."

The woman's eyes, the same chocolate brown as Charlotte's, brimmed with tears. "Carly?" the woman asked. "This is Carly? Come down here, girl, and let me get a good look at you."

Carly knelt beside her aunt, her curiosity piqued as well. She smiled as her aunt brushed her hair from her face, then touched her fingertips to her cheeks, tilting her head one way and the other. She beamed at Charlotte. "She's lovely, Charlotte."

Charlotte beamed back. "Isn't she?"

Carly rose from her uncomfortable position on the floor. "Go ahead, discuss her like she isn't here."

Charlotte laughed, but Sharlene's expression grew grim. "Why did you bring her here, Charlotte? You know the danger better than I do."

Charlotte took her sister's hand. "It's over, Sharlene. It's finally over. We finally got that bastard who did this to you. You're free."

Tears brimmed in Sharlene's eyes and cascaded down her cheeks. Sobs racked her body. Charlotte went to her, stooping to embrace and comfort her. After a moment, Sharlene sat back, gratitude shining in her eyes. "Thank you."

"I promised you I would get him. On occasion I manage to keep my word."

"What is going on here?" an imperious female voice demanded, making all three women jump.

Sharlene wiped at her eyes. "Olga, you know my sister, Charlotte. This is my niece, Carly. This is the first time she's visited."

Olga regarded her and Charlotte skeptically. Carly recognized in her a protectiveness of her charge and a resentment of anyone who disturbed her peace. "As long as you're all right," Olga said.

"I'm fine."

"Visiting hours are over and it's time for your aquatherapy."

Sharlene rolled her eyes. "Do you think the world really needs to see this old body in a swimsuit? Damn, I used to have great legs." She looked down at her lap to the withered ones she possessed now. "Oh, well." She glanced up at Carly. "You come back and see me, okay?"

Carly smiled. "That's a promise. And I always keep mine."

Her aunt winked at her as Olga wheeled her out the door, leaving it open.

Carly turned to Charlotte. Though she suspected she knew the answer, she asked, "Why didn't you ever tell me you had a sister?"

"Not just a sister, a twin. Believe it or not, we were once identical twins. That's before Paul got to her." Charlotte sat on the bed and folded her hands in her lap. "For most of my life I didn't know. My mother only bargained for one child, though she probably shouldn't have had any. She kept one of us, me, and gave Sharlene up for adoption. I can't say I never suspected Sharlene existed. When your grandmother got angry with me she'd mutter about wishing she'd kept the other one. But I didn't really believe until Sharon came to me that time thinking I was cheating on your father. I dismissed other people's claims that they'd seen me in one place or another, but Sharon would have known the difference. Or so I thought."

"But the night Daddy died, you knew for sure."

Charlotte nodded. "I was so stunned to see her that I didn't pay attention to the man with her. He had his back to me, trying to drag her toward the car, but she resisted. That's what foiled Paul's plan. And he took out his rage on her later. He beat her so badly he left her unconscious and crippled her. Her face was so broken that the police had to identify her by fingerprints. The doctors put her together as best they could. Over the years, I've offered to pay for a plastic surgeon, but she refused, saying that she'd earned her scars and she intended to keep them."

Charlotte exhaled. "I would never have found her again except for a woman who showed up at your father's funeral, a nurse who I heard telling someone about some poor comatose patient wearing a red dress who'd come into the hospital where she worked. When Sharlene finally came to, she didn't remember anything, not that night, not the man she'd been with, not her past. The only thing she recalled was that she had a daughter, Eleanor. I brought her here to keep her safe. Paul left her for dead and I wanted to make sure he thought he succeeded. I searched for the girl, but never found her. She should be a grown woman by now."

"Right you are, Charlotte. Or should I make that Auntie Charlotte?"

Carly had been so absorbed in her mother's story, she hadn't noticed anyone else standing in the doorway. "Nora," Carly said, her voice registering both surprise and disbelief.

Nora tapped the door closed behind her with her foot. She raised her arm to reveal the .22-caliber gun in her hand. A malevolent grin spread across her face. "Hey, cuz."

Chapter 27

As sure as he knew his own name, Jackson knew Samuels was not still on the island if Carly was not. He asked Drew, "Where were they headed? Home?"

"To New York, yes. But I heard Charlotte mention something about making a stop somewhere. I don't know if that's on the way or once they get there."

"Damn." He needed to warn Carly, but when he dialed her cell phone number he got her voice mail. He left a message that Samuels was out and to please call him, but unease gripped him as the minutes ticked by and Carly hadn't called him back. He vacillated between heading back to New York and staying where he was. Not only did he not relish the idea of setting out for the third time that day, he feared Carly and her mother might be as close as Boston or somewhere in Connecticut and going to New York would only delay him finding them.

Unable to do nothing at all until he heard from Carly, he took the ferry into Wood's Hole with Drew and sat down in a restaurant to wait.

"You're Sharlene's daughter?" Charlotte asked, the expression on her face as incredulous as her voice. "Why didn't you tell us?"

"That's a laugh. I intended to tell you. That's why I took the job, to be near my family. Now I'm glad I didn't. Why should I have shared my identity with the woman who's kept my mother hidden from me all these years? Until a month ago, I thought she was dead."

"I wasn't hiding her from you, I was hiding her from Paul Samuels or whoever had put her here. If I'd known—"

"You'd what? Arrange a tearful little family reunion? Too late. I've got my own little family reunion planned. A gathering of all those people who took my mother away from me." She waved the gun in a way that indicated they should stand. "Let's go."

Charlotte started to rise, but Carly put a restraining hand on her arm. "We're not going anywhere with you."

"You think not? Why don't I just shoot Mommy Dearest now? Then you'll get to know what it's like for someone to take your mother away from you. Would you like that, *cousin*?"

Carly said nothing to that, only glared at the woman who held them captive. She didn't doubt that Nora would do what she said she would. There was an intensity to her and a resoluteness in her expression that said she was all business. Carly stepped in front of her mother. "Why don't you put the gun down so that we can talk?"

"Nice try. Did you learn that technique from your little shrink friend? And don't think of doing something stupid like both of you rushing up on me. I'm bound to shoot at least one of you, and guess who I'll be aiming for?"

Carly swallowed, trying to figure out what to do. At least if they got out of the room, there was a chance to alert someone else of their predicament, and Nora couldn't hold the gun out in the open without someone noticing. Besides, John was waiting for them in the car. She turned to Charlotte. "Let's go, Mother."

Charlotte nodded and stood. Nora pulled the door open and stood aside for them to precede her. "Don't try anything cute, and you might get out of here alive."

Carly took her mother's arm and walked cautiously down the hall. They might get out of the building alive, but how much longer? Clearly, she was over the edge, though Carly still wasn't sure what had pushed her there. For the first time she wished Jackson hadn't taken her gun from her, because at the moment she could blow Nora away and not regret it for a moment.

They neared the elevator where a security guard waited for a car to come. He nodded to them, then looked up at the light panel above the door. "Sometimes these things take forever."

Carly smiled at him, hoping to catch his gaze. When he looked at her again, she glanced downward toward the gun at his hip and then cut her eyes in a way that she hoped indicated Nora standing behind her.

The guard stared back at her, a cocky grin on his face. For heaven's sake! He thought she was flirting with him. Annoyed and desperate, she looked down at the gun again, this time forming her hand into the shape of a gun at her side. Immediately, she felt the barrel of Nora's gun in her back. Carly had no idea how this idiot guard couldn't have noticed that, but he took a step back from them. "Maybe I ought to take the stairs."

Once he'd gone, the gun dug deeper into Carly's back. "I told you not to get cute with me. Now I'm going to show you something I was going to spare Mommy Dearest from seeing."

The elevator came, an empty car that offered no chance of alert or escape. The three of them got on and rode to the first floor, but rather than go through the main door, Nora forced them out a back way that led directly to the parking lot. There were only a few cars left in the visitors' parking lot, John's included, and absolutely no one in sight. She hoped John noticed their appearance and was ready to take Nora down.

"Don't expect any help from your police lieutenant friend," Nora said, as if reading her mind. She pushed Carly toward the passenger-side door. "He looked a little hungry so I fed him some lead."

Carly looked inside the open window and saw John slumped against the driver's-side door frame. The engine and air-conditioning were still running. Blood oozed from a wound in his belly. Carly squeezed her eyes shut. She could imagine what had happened. John wouldn't have suspected Nora of any wrongdoing any more than she or Charlotte had. He must have rolled down the window to speak to her when she shot him.

"Don't worry, I wasn't trying to kill him. He's not in this."

A chill ran down Carly's spine at Nora's words. She'd known from the minute Nora pulled out the gun that she meant to kill them, but hearing her intentions stated so boldly was unnerving.

"John?" Charlotte pushed between her and Nora to look inside the car. "Oh, my God! John!" Charlotte started to shriek.

"Shut up, you cow," Nora barked and struck her across the temple with the butt of the gun. Charlotte crumpled to the ground. Nora picked her up as if she weighed nothing and started toward a white car parked a little farther down. She turned the gun on Carly. "Move it," she said.

For a brief moment, Carly contemplated making a run for it, as a moving target was harder to hit than one

standing still. But she had no idea how good a shot
Nora might be, and she'd never leave her mother at
this crazy woman's mercy. She had no choice but to follow.

   After a half hour of sitting, Jackson had decided to
take the chance that Carly and Charlotte had gone to
New York, or at least would end up there, and had
started on the way home. With Drew at the wheel, they
made the majority of the trip in three hours instead of
five. At the New York/Connecticut border they
stopped for gas, something to drink, and to finalize
whatever they planned to do once they got back to the
city.
   They sat at one of the picnic tables outside the rest
stop. "I'm going to head to Carly's," Jackson said. "I figure Charlotte and John would have dropped her off on
their way into the city."
   "Makes sense," Drew conceded in a tired monotone.
   Jackson sighed. Neither one of them mentioned the
one fear that drove them both: that Carly and Charlotte hadn't made it back to New York. He tried her cell
phone number again and got the same voice mail message he was beginning to hate. He was about to try
Carly at home when his cell phone rang.
   A tentative relief swept over him seeing Carly's home
number on the display. "Sweetheart, are you all right?"
he asked without preamble.
   "Thanks for asking," Nora said. "But I think there's
someone else here you'd like to talk to."
   "Don't come, Jackson. Don't come." Carly's rapidly
spoken words were followed by the sound of flesh
meeting flesh, then a crashing sound.
   "Carly," he shouted into the phone, but it was Nora
who answered him.

"I've got your girlfriend and her mother here. If you'd like to see them again, I suggest you meet us at Carly's place. Just you, not that behemoth that hangs around with you, and no cops. If I so much as see a police cruiser I might lose my patience. And hurry. We'll be waiting."

The line went dead. He looked to Drew, who was watching him avidly. "Nora has Carly and Charlotte."

"Nora? What do you mean she has them?"

"She's holding them hostage."

"What the hell has Chatty Cathy got to do with anything?"

"You think I know? I've got to get to them."

"Where?"

"Give me the keys." When Drew complied, he headed to where Drew's car was parked. He unlocked the driver's-side door but didn't get in. "She wants me to come alone."

"Oh, no, you don't. That's not how the drill goes and you know it. I'm not letting you walk into that alone."

Jackson got in and revved the engine. He admitted that if it were anyone else he would have played it differently, done what Drew wanted. But he couldn't take that chance. Not with Carly. He was grateful Drew didn't put up too much of a fight to stop him, merely stood to the side silently disapproving. Jackson pulled out of the spot and into traffic. Out on the highway, Jackson pushed the accelerator to ninety. With any luck, Nora thought he was still up on the Vineyard. She wouldn't be expecting him so soon. That might give him the leverage he needed to make sure Carly and Charlotte got out of this thing alive.

Chapter 28

"That wasn't very smart of you, was it?"

Carly dabbed her tongue at the corner of her mouth and tasted blood. She must have been cut when Nora backhanded her, sending her crashing to the floor. Nora grasped her upper arm in a viselike grip and hauled her up, only to push her backward onto the sofa next to Charlotte.

No, it hadn't been smart to defy Nora and warn Jackson, but truth be told, she hadn't done one smart thing since Nora showed up gun in hand and told them to march themselves out into her car. They should have made a stand where they were. Everyone who'd ever watched a crime drama knew not to let some psycho transport you somewhere she could kill or maim you at her leisure.

But Carly hadn't been thinking of her own safety when Nora carried Charlotte off. At the time she'd wondered why Nora seemed to suddenly be in such a rush. Carly found out a few seconds later, after she'd gotten into the car. A cadre of spa security guards were pursuing them. Obviously the one by the elevator wasn't as dull-witted as she'd thought, merely a bit slow in rounding up his fellow guards. Nora had torn out of the parking lot before they were able to stop her.

And now Nora intended to bring Jackson into this

mess, too. Carly had to take the chance to try to stop that. But he'd come. She knew he'd come anyway and so did Nora. Carly only hoped he would ignore Nora's warning and bring Drew with him anyway. Something in Nora had snapped and there was no telling what she would do if she got them all here the way she wanted them.

Carly tested the bonds around her wrists one more time, but the rope held firm. She glanced at her mother, who hadn't yet regained consciousness. Carly wished her mother hadn't freaked out so completely, giving Nora an excuse to hurt her, but she supposed seeing the man you loved slowly bleeding to death might do that to a woman. Carly only hoped the security guards at the spa had found John and given him whatever medical treatment they could.

With no hope of freeing herself or getting any assistance from Charlotte, Carly decided to try another tack. It would be hours before Jackson made it back from the Vineyard and Carly couldn't chance that Nora would get tired of waiting and decide to act. She'd seen a news report once where a woman talked a serial killer into releasing her by convincing him she was more than what she appeared to be to him—a woman who fit the profile of the type of woman he liked to kill. At one time, Nora had seen her and Charlotte as more than the women who deprived her of her mother's affection. Maybe she could be made to see that again. Carly struggled to sit up as best she could.

Immediately Nora scowled and lifted the gun to train it on Carly. "What do you think you're doing?"

"Just trying to get comfortable. It will be a long time before Jackson gets here."

"If that fool hadn't gone back to that godforsaken island to be with you, this could be over by now."

Carly asked the one question that had troubled her

since Nora demanded she get him on the phone. "What does Jackson have to do with any of this? Twenty years ago, he was barely a teenager."

"But his father wasn't. His father is the reason Duke Anderson, that spineless wimp, turned on my father."

Carly shook her head. "Your father?" Her mouth dropped open as realization dawned. "Paul?"

"Who says you're as dumb as you look?" Nora laughed bitterly. "Not that he ever acknowledged me. It wouldn't do for a man with political aspirations to admit to siring a child by a twenty-five-dollar-a-trick hooker, would it?"

"I guess not."

"I was there in the house when your boyfriend and that mammoth he travels with came in. None of them knew I was there. I had come to confront him one last time, to give him a chance to change his mind about me. But he lied to them, he hadn't just met my mother. He'd known her quite some time. You know it wasn't just jail bait that turned him on. It was anything he wasn't supposed to have, anything forbidden. Believe me, I know."

Carly squeezed her eyes shut as nausea roiled in her belly. The more she learned about all of them the sicker this situation became. She didn't want to hear any more about Paul, especially not what he might have done to his own daughter. "So once Duke Anderson resurfaced, Paul killed him to keep him from talking?"

"My father didn't kill Anderson. I did. As a show of my loyalty to him. To show that I would do anything to keep him safe. You know what he did when I told him what I'd done?" Nora's voice rose in volume and pitch. "He laughed at me. He told me that Anderson was no more of a threat to him now than he had been twenty years ago. If anything, I had put him in more danger since the police were already looking into the case again. That's why he resurfaced. Some report aired saying the police were looking for him and some buddy of his ratted him out to the police looking for a reward. My father said Anderson's death gave credence to the idea that someone wanted him silent."

Nora paused, breathing deeply, maybe trying to get herself under control. "He threw me out of his house. He said he didn't care what I did, as long as I didn't touch you. Always you, Carly. You're the only one he ever cared about. He denied me, his own flesh and blood, but you . . ."

Nora wiped her eyes with her sleeve. "Given my father's predilections, you'd think his obsession with you would have been sexual, but it wasn't, not really. He actually thought he would make a better father to you than Alex did. In truth, my father wanted everything your father had, the privileged background, his ease of dealing with other people, even her." She nodded toward Charlotte. "Instead he had to settle for second best."

Carly noticed Nora spoke of Paul only in the past tense, not the present. Although she almost dreaded the answer, she asked, "Where is Paul?"

"Where he can't do anyone else any more harm." A now-familiar malevolent smile spread across her face. "Don't worry. You'll be joining him soon enough."

Chapter 29

Jackson parked around the corner from Carly's house, crossed the neighbors' lawn, and headed around the side of the house to where the startled neighbors were barbecuing in the backyard. They sat or stood gaping at him like a frozen tableau as he crossed to the other side. Two seconds after he'd gone they'd probably be on the phone to the police, but with a little luck he'd take Nora down before they got there.

A low fence and dense foliage separated the two properties. He quickly crossed it and ran in a crouch to the side of the house. In all likelihood, Nora held her two captives in the living room. At least that's what Jackson hoped. If that was true, Jackson could slip in through the back door, the lock of which had never, to his knowledge, been fixed, around the guest bedroom, and into the side entrance of Carly's study. At no point would Nora be able to see him if she remained in the living room with her charges.

But first he needed to know if the women were where he expected to find them. Keeping low, he crept to the one living room window on that side of the house and peered in. Luck was with him. All three women were in the living room, Carly and Charlotte on the sofa with their hands behind their backs, undoubtedly tied that way. Nora paced in front of them, a small-caliber revolver clutched in her hand.

If she'd stood still for two seconds, he might have risked a shot from there, but if he missed, she would know he was there. She could shoot both Carly and Charlotte before he could get to them. He needed to get inside.

Careful not to be seen, he backed away from the window and headed around to the back door. It slid open effortlessly when he tried it. He propelled himself inside and closed the door behind him just as quietly. He retrieved Carly's gun from his waistband and peeked around the alcove that hid a small mudroom. He edged his way out of the alcove, careful not to make a sound, though he could hear Nora ranting in the other room about Samuels being her father. With him as a parent, no wonder the chick was nuts, but he didn't waste any sympathy on her. He didn't necessarily want to hurt her, but he would if it came down to it.

He passed through the side door of Carly's study. Only a few more feet and he'd be there. But all of a sudden, the buzz in his ear that was Nora's voice quieted. What the hell was she up to now? As he neared the door to the study he saw her reflected in the glass panes of the door. She had her arm around Carly, her hand clamped over her mouth. The gun in her other hand was pointed at Carly's temple. And if he could see them . . .

"Come on out here, Jackson. I've got your girlfriend here and I'm not afraid to shoot her. In fact, I'm looking forward to it."

Carly's reflection shook her head, but he stepped out anyway, his gun trained on Nora. "Put the gun down, Nora. You don't have to do this."

"Don't I? Don't you think someone should avenge what was done to my mother? That bastard that fathered me left her little more than a vegetable and Charlotte locked her away in that home to keep her away from me."

Jackson took a step toward her, hoping to better his aim. He'd shoot Nora if he had to, but in so many ways he dreaded that prospect. If he slipped up and hit Carly he'd never be able to live with that. He had to hope he could talk her into giving up. Firing would be a last resort.

"I know what it's like to lose your mother, Nora. Mine died when I was five years old."

"That's not the same at all. You still had your father. They didn't put you in a home, one after the other, with people who were supposed to care for you. People who didn't want a child, they just wanted the check. They couldn't have cared if I lived or died except the money would be cut off."

"What has that got to do with Carly or me?"

"You took her away from me, all of you. And I would never have known if she hadn't asked me to track down Charlotte one day. The stupid woman told me Charlotte was in her sister's room. But I found her too late. She doesn't even know who I am. I snuck in to see her and she didn't recognize me, her own daughter. After all these years I find out she's alive and I still don't have her back."

Nora's voice had risen and tears ran from her eyes. She was close to really losing it and Jackson didn't want her hands on Carly when she did. "Do you really think this is how your mother would want you to avenge her?"

"What does she know? She's not my mother anymore, not the mother I knew." Nora shook her head, gravely. "The one thing I knew as a child was that my mother loved me. I didn't care what she was to the rest of the world, how people used her. She was good to me.

And now she doesn't know who I am. My father and Charlotte took her away from me."

"Then why did you kill Gary Vespers? He didn't have anything to do with your mother."

"That little weasel was on to me. He overheard part of a conversation I had with my father and questioned me about it. I think he intended to go to Charlotte with what he'd heard. That's why I put his license plates on the truck that night. I thought you might go after him instead, but you didn't. So I took care of the problem myself."

His gaze slid to Carly. She looked scared, but not panicked. In fact she seemed to be looking to him for some sort of direction. But he'd run out of chitchat to keep Nora occupied and in the distance he heard the whirr of police sirens. There was no telling what chaos might ensue once the cops got here. He needed to resolve this thing now.

"Put the gun down, Nora," he reiterated in a softer voice. "If you hurt her, you'll be dead a second later."

Nora shook her head. "I'm dead already."

Jackson's finger curled around the trigger, but before he had a chance to fire, Nora shrieked and released Carly. Carly dove for the floor and Jackson fired, hitting exactly where he'd aimed for. Nora staggered backward, looking down at the wound in her shoulder, a stunned expression on her face. Then she lifted her arm clumsily, trying to aim at him. Before he had a chance to fire, a bullet ripped through the window, shattering the glass and catching her right at the center of her forehead. She staggered backward again, but this time her legs gave out under her. She fell backward to the floor, her dead eyes staring up at the ceiling.

Jackson dropped the gun and went to Carly. He sat on the floor with his back against the sofa and pulled her onto his lap. At first all he could manage to do was hold her. After a moment, he untied her wrists. Trembling, she flung her arms around him, holding him close, and he realized he was trembling too.

And suddenly the house was swarming with cops and emergency personnel. The last two to come in were Drew and another, older man Jackson didn't recognize. Drew stopped beside them and hunkered down as best he could. "Glad to see you two are still in one piece."

Carly lifted her head. "Hey, Drew."

"Hey yourself." He chucked her under the chin with his fist. "You are some trouper. What did you do to make her let you go?"

Carly glanced at him and he wondered how she could manage to find a smile at this particular moment. "I licked her hand."

Drew blinked. "You what."

"I licked her hand." She stuck out her tongue to demonstrate. "I tried it on someone else once who was trying to keep me from telling my father he'd made fun of my hair. When I licked his hand, he let go, then I kicked him in the leg."

Jackson laughed. He hadn't remembered that part of their first meeting, but he was damn glad she had.

Charlotte groaned, drawing all their attention. "Carly," she called in a hoarse whisper.

Carly bolted from Jackson's lap and went to her mother. "I'm here, Mom."

For a long moment the two women embraced. Charlotte was the first to pull back. "John?"

Drew said, "They found him and rushed him to the hospital. He lost a lot of blood, but he should be fine."

Charlotte nodded and finally let the EMTs close enough to examine the swollen bloody wound at her temple. While Carly attended to her mother, Jackson turned to Drew.

"How'd you get here so fast?"

Drew shot him a droll look. "If you're going to strand a man somewhere and don't intend for him to follow you, you shouldn't leave him ten minutes from his own house."

Jackson snorted. "I suppose not. I have to admit I'm glad to see you, man. Was that your handiwork?" he asked, nodding in Nora's direction.

Drew shrugged. "I know that's your spot, but I wasn't taking any chances."

He wasn't making any complaints about whether or where Drew hit. He was just glad it was over. Once Charlotte, who claimed to want nothing more than a couple of Darvons and a glass of wine, had been loaded into an ambulance, he led them into Carly's study, careful to make sure Carly didn't get a good look at Nora or the composition of what now stained her off-white carpet.

Drew introduced his companion as the Detective Dutton who had reopened the case on Sharon Glenn's murder. Unbeknownst to Jackson, Drew had called him when they'd stopped, putting him on the alert to Samuels's disappearance and Nora's kidnapping of Carly and Charlotte. Dutton didn't seem too pleased to have someone else doing his work for him, but he planned to close the case again, naming Paul Samuels as Sharon's murderer.

Once Samuels had gone missing, the Vineyard police had searched his home up there and found a videotape of Paul confessing to both Sharon's murder and that of Carly's father hidden behind one of the bricks in the fireplace wall that had cracked. Apparently Samuels was such an egotist he couldn't resist reporting his exploits, even if it was to himself.

After a few minutes, Drew and Dutton left them. Jackson sat beside Carly on the sofa. "You know we will have to go down to the station house to give statements. There's no doubt it was self-defense, but we'll have to make it official."

She nodded, looking absolutely spent. He didn't feel much better himself.

She leaned into him, burrowing closer. "I can't stay here, Jackson."

"I know, baby. You should think about packing a few things and staying somewhere else until this mess can be cleaned up."

"Somewhere else like where?"

She speared him with such an intense look that it dawned on him what she was really asking, if he intended to offer her a place with him.

He shook his head. "I can't, Carly. Not yet, for all the reasons that made me leave the island in the first place. Nothing has been resolved yet."

She nodded and pulled away from him. "I guess I'd better pack those things and head over to the hospital to check on my mother." She stood and before he could pull her back to him, she headed out of the room.

He rested his elbows on his knees and put his head in his hands, wondering if after all they'd been through with each other and for each other, he hadn't lost her just then.

Chapter 30

For all Jackson knew, Carly didn't want to see him. In the three weeks he'd been away from her, she could have found a new man better suited to her, one that didn't come with the baggage he brought. She could have realized she'd never been in love with him or maybe he'd given her enough time for whatever feelings she did have to cool. A million scenarios played out in his mind as he showered and dressed, but still he had to chance it. He put on his jacket, grabbed his keys, and headed out the door.

On the drive from his apartment in the Bronx to the Palace Hotel in Manhattan, he debated what he would say to her, how he would explain what he'd done, why he'd done it, and ask for her forgiveness for staying away so long. He only hoped it would be enough.

Scarlet Woman's anniversary party was being held in the second-floor ballroom. He found the room easily enough, as a table had been set up outside the entrance where a trio of young lovelies checked tickets under the watchful eyes of a like number of security guards dressed in matching tuxes.

He approached the woman closest to the door. She glanced up at him with an eager expression on her face. "Can I help you?" She extended her hand, he presumed for him to give her his nonexistent invitation.

He flashed her his best smile, hoping it was disarming. "I'm sorry, I don't have an invitation, but I am a friend of Carly Thompson's."

He saw immediately by her change of expression that she was about to tell him to get lost. But one of the security guards motioned him over. "He's cool."

Jackson hadn't really paid any attention to the man before, but he recognized him now: the guard he'd lit into on the beach. Jackson would have thought the man would rather pulverize him than grant him a favor, but he appreciated his largesse. "Thanks."

The big man shrugged. "Water under the bridge."

Jackson could only hope Carly would be in an equally forgiving mood tonight, but he doubted it. He entered the large L-shaped room and surveyed his surroundings. Clusters of circular tables decorated with shades of red and black dominated one side of the L. The other side was a large dance floor where a live band did its best to keep the room jumping. At the juncture between the two, a giant mock-up of a Scarlet Woman lipstick took the place of the obligatory ice sculpture. Two more, not quite as large, adorned either end of the small dais in the front of the room. He expected to find Carly seated there, but at this late hour the dais had been deserted.

He'd purposely come late, hoping no one would pay too much attention to a latecomer slipping in, and since the party was winding down, there wouldn't be too much time to wait before he and Carly could be alone. The first part of his plan would have been a bust if it weren't for the guard recognizing him. He'd have to wait to see how well the second part went.

But first he had to find Carly. He walked the length of the side of the room that housed the tables but didn't see her. He finally spotted her at the edge of the dance floor, speaking with a tall, striking woman in a burnt-orange dress.

Despite her companion's attractiveness, Carly took up his whole attention. She wore a low-cut red dress that molded to her body like a second shimmering skin. Her hair was pulled back at her nape, but tendrils framed her face becomingly.

As he made his way through the crowd toward her, she turned to look directly at him. She watched his approach with an expression he couldn't begin to fathom. But Lord, she took his breath away. By the time he reached her, he simply stared at her, unable to think of a single intelligent thing to say.

A sardonic smile tilted her lips at his quandary. "Is that for me?" she said and plucked the single red rose he carried from his fingers.

He blinked, kicking his brain into low gear. "I think Charlotte's going to have to find herself another color."

She smiled, in earnest this time. "Jackson, this is my Alpha Delta X soror Allison Wakefield. Allison, this is Jackson Trent, the man I was telling you about."

Allison's shrewd gaze studied him before settling on his face in a way that suggested she found him wanting. If she did, she'd have to get in line behind Charlotte, John, the folks up on the Vineyard, and most vocally Drew, who'd told him he'd better hurry up and quit contemplating his navel and make things right with Carly. Otherwise, he might find his big ugly carcass nailed to the wall. Things were bad when your own relations turned against you.

He extended his hand to Allison. "It's a pleasure to meet you."

She had a firm, confident handshake that seemed to fit in with the rest of her personality. "Thank you."

He almost laughed. No pretense with this one. He

liked that. "I hope you won't mind if I borrow Carly for a few minutes."

"That's up to Carly."

Both of them turned to her, but he'd bet he was the only one holding his breath for her decision. She turned to Allison first, thanking her for coming to the event. The two women exchanged good-byes with kisses on the cheek and promises to call the next day.

When they separated, Carly ignored the hand he offered her. With a gesture of her hand she beckoned to him in the opposite direction. "This way."

He followed her through the crowd to the exit leading to the elevators. She stopped at the elevator bank and pushed the up button.

"Where are we going?"

"I have a suite rented here. I thought whatever you had to say was best said in private."

True, but she gave him the impression she wasn't sure of what he wanted to say. Could she honestly believe he'd shown up here tonight, after putting each of them through three weeks of torture, only to tell her he didn't intend to stay? He planned to disabuse her of that notion as soon as possible.

The elevator arrived and they squeezed on to ride in silence to the fifteenth floor. She offered him her key to open the door. Once he opened it for her and let her pass, he followed her inside, shut the door by leaning his back against it, and pulled her to him. She didn't exactly resist, but she didn't run to him either. For a moment, their gazes locked, his hot and intense, hers mutinous. He tried to think of something to say to soothe her. He settled on the one true sentiment in his arsenal. "I've missed you so much, Carly."

Her expression softened and her teeth clamped on her bottom lip. "I've missed you, too."

He sensed a "but" at the end of that statement, but

before she could voice it he claimed her mouth with his own. At first, she kissed him back with all the passion he had come to know in her, but abruptly she pulled back, pushing against his chest for him to let her go. He did as she wanted, releasing his hold on her by slow degrees.

She stepped back from him, shaking her head. "No fair, Jackson. Don't make the mistake of thinking we can simply pick up where we left off."

"I know that, baby." He knew she needed more from him than a few kisses and a few sweet words. He'd hurt her by staying away and he knew he had to make up for that if she'd let him. But he'd needed something, too, some indication that the love she'd claimed to feel for him wasn't merely a mirage. The passion in her kiss had given him his answer.

For a moment, he thought she might say something more, but she pivoted and walked farther into the room.

He followed her to the small sitting area off the suite's single bedroom. Carly busied herself turning on the lamps. He watched her with his hands shoved in his trouser pockets, waiting. When she turned to him, the pained expression in her eyes got to him.

"All right, Jackson. What do you want to say to me?"

"Carly," he began. Every sensible thing he'd planned to say fled his brain. He said the only words he could think of to tell her. "I love you, Carly. I'm sorry if my leaving you hurt you, but I had to settle some things within myself first. I thought you understood that."

"I did. I do. Have you settled them?"

"Yes." He'd spent countless solitary hours in his apartment contemplating his life, what he'd done with it and what he had yet to do. And he'd known that if he couldn't release the past he'd never have any kind of future with Carly. He'd finally dealt with the contents of the boxes in his living room, looked around and realized he owned nothing else of any value whatsoever, not one damn thing he couldn't walk away from without missing. What a sad commentary on who he'd let himself become.

"Do you want to be with me, Jackson?"

"How can you ask me that? It's what I've wanted almost from the very beginning. Even when you offered me what I couldn't take, I wanted you, and not only sexually. I wanted your love, too. What took me so long was deciding if I had a right to ask that of you."

She shook her head. "What are you talking about?"

"I devoted my life to two things, being a cop and finding out who framed my father. Until recently, I'd failed at both of them. Is that the sort of man you want to saddle yourself with?"

She offered him a sad smile. "I don't have any choice. I'm in love with you, Jackson."

"Of course you have a choice. You could walk away."

"Is that what you want me to do?"

His answer was a fervent "no."

"Then what's the problem?"

He laughed, not with humor, but at himself. For so long, he'd thought of himself in terms of what he hadn't accomplished, instead of what he had. Perhaps that was the hardest thing to let go. "Come here," he said.

She shook her head. "I need you to promise me something first."

"What's that?"

"Promise me it's really over. That neither your past or mine still stands between us. That the next time the road gets rough, we stand and face it together. I love you, Jackson, but if you're not in this for the long haul, tell me now and I *will* walk away. For so long I was content to just survive, to not expect much of anything for myself. I can't live like that anymore."

It occurred to him how similar their lives had been, albeit for different reasons. Both of them had sacrificed what they wanted for what they felt obligated to do. Both of them had come to a place where they could finally rest. Still he knew she possessed the strength to do what she said, to walk away and not look back. He acknowledged that, remarkably, so did he. But what would their lives be without each other and the love they'd discovered together? He honestly didn't want to contemplate that.

He closed the gap between them and took her hand. He led her to the sofa, sat, and pulled her onto his lap. He didn't know what words to say to convince her of his devotion to her and his commitment to a life with her. He figured he'd start with the moment he'd first started wanting one. "Charlotte told me you moved back into your house."

She looked at him as if he had suddenly sprouted a new nose. "When did you talk to Charlotte?"

"A week ago. How do you think I found out about this soiree you were having tonight?'

"I hadn't thought about it. I was too shocked that you'd shown up in the first place."

He could understand that, considering that he hadn't tried to call her once in the time they'd been apart, or rather he'd never actually let a call go through. He'd known that only a face-to-face meeting would suffice. "Do you remember that first morning?"

"You mean when I treated you to the orange juice facial?"

He laughed at her assessment. "That's the one. Then you let me into your house, a space so incompatible with the woman I'd known so far. I realized your home was your sanctuary, the one place you could be your-self."

He stroked his hand along her thigh. "I haven't had that for a long time, Carly. Not since my father was alive. I envied you then, because I knew I could never allow myself that luxury while I hadn't accomplished what I set out to do. How could I rest when my father couldn't?"

"I doubt your father would have wanted you to put your life on hold to avenge his."

"Any more than your father truly expected you to take care of your mother?"

"Touché. It didn't stop me from feeling obligated."

"Me either. But I realized two things while I was away from you. I never should have left the force the way I did. The shooting took place right after I'd decided I had to give up on finding out who'd killed Sharon Glenn. I felt like I'd failed my father in one area and failed myself in another. It wasn't the best time to be making grand decisions, but that didn't stop me from royally screwing up my life."

"Does that mean you've changed your mind about quitting?"

"If that's all right with you."

She smiled in a way that told him she could cheer-fully smack him at the moment. "I meant it when I said I would never expect a man to change what he wanted for me. If that's what you want, I'm behind you, as long as you don't go looking for trouble, you let it find you."

He hugged her to him. "And you promise not to run after me trying to press a gun into my hand?"

Laughter rumbled in her chest. "I don't have any doubts about you being able to do your job, Jackson. I was only worried because what went on with Paul Samuels was personal, not professional. I was concerned you had so much invested in finding out who framed your father you might do something rash."

And he had. If it weren't for Drew, he'd probably be in a jail cell rather than holding her in his arms.

"What's the other thing you realized?"

"That I'd never really put my life on hold for my father. I was simply waiting."

"Waiting for what?"

"Waiting for something to matter to me more than he did. I could have walked away from it, Carly. I could have gone the rest of my life not knowing, except leaving the real killer unknown left you in danger. That I couldn't bear."

He cupped her face in his palms, forcing her to look at him. "I can't promise you that I'll never again do anything that will hurt you. That would be unrealistic. But I can promise you that I want to spend my life with you and that I'll do my best to make you happy. I love you, Carly. Tell me that's enough."

Her answer was to cover his mouth with her own. Her arms folded around him in that loving way she had. But it had been too long for either of them. The kiss soon turned wild, sending a shock wave of desire coursing through him. He wanted her, and he could tell by the restlessness in her that she wanted him, too.

When his fingers found the zipper at the back of her dress, her hand snaked around to stop him. She pulled away from him and looked at him with an amused, sensual gaze. "Let's go home," she suggested.

That sounded like a plan to him.

Epilogue

Labor Day weekend the couples gathered again at Sam and Adam's house on the beach for one last hurrah before the end of the season. Jackson, who lounged in one of the beach chairs arranged around the patio, gazed about and felt contented. John had recovered from the shooting, but that didn't prevent Charlotte from doting on him as if he were still a convalescent. As they had driven up this time, Charlotte brought Mr. Jingles with her, who snarled at anyone who came near either of his two humans.

Sam had finally started showing. Adam fussed over her, but she wasn't complaining. Still, Jackson hoped he wasn't that much of a worrywart when he and Carly got around to having children. He supposed he ought to worry about her marrying him first. Although she'd been adamant about securing his verbal agreement that he intended to build a life with her, she exhibited no haste in proclaiming the same in front of God, witnesses, or the county clerk's office.

Their marital status, or lack thereof, might not concern her, but it bothered him to merely live with the woman he wanted to make his wife. Besides, he still harbored the suspicion that she hadn't pressed him for marriage because she still didn't trust him enough to say yes.

For now he'd settle for basking in the sun while she and Ariel did God only knew what inside the house. He could wait, but not for long. Tonight was going to be their night.

The back door opened and Ariel came out followed by the assorted children of the family. Ariel and Jarad had two sets of twins. Sam and Adam had a little girl and an eighteen-month-old son named for Adam's father. Carly brought up the rear of the group. She wore a tiny red bikini and a mischievous grin on her face. Her right hand was behind her back, making him wonder what devilment she had planned.

He gazed up at her when she stopped beside his chair. "Can I help you?"

"Your presence is requested down by the water. We're going to make a sand castle."

"And if I refuse?"

She produced a pistol from behind her back and squirted him with ice-cold water.

He sputtered and jumped up from the chair as water dripped from his face down his chest. The children found his predicament hilarious, laughing and dancing around him. The adults were no better. Adam's booming laugh resounded louder than the others.

With feigned annoyance, he focused a narrow-eyed gaze on Carly. "What is wrong with you?"

She shrugged. "You were expecting orange juice?"

That did it. He lunged for her, but she shrieked and darted away from him. He chased her down to the beach before he caught her and swung her into his arms. Both of them were laughing and out of breath. He hugged her to him, nuzzling her neck. In the last two months, he'd laughed more than he had in years, felt freer than he had his whole life. She brought that to him. Or rather they gave that to each other. They were rediscovering themselves in their own way and there was joy in the discovery.

Not one to waste a perfectly good opportunity, he pressed his mouth to hers. Her arms tightened around his neck and a soft moan escaped her lips. But now wasn't the time to take it any further, especially not with an audience. The children had followed them down to the beach, still laughing and dancing and entreating Carly to squirt Uncle Jack again.

He set Carly on her feet. When she looked up at him with a bemused expression, he mouthed one word. "Later."

That night, after the children were asleep, the adults reassembled on the patio for a few minutes of quiet conversation before going to bed themselves. Jackson sat in the same chair he'd occupied earlier, this time with Carly on his lap. The evening was cool, and although she wore a sweater over her sundress, he still felt her shiver. He scrubbed his hands up and down her back to warm her, as conversation turned to those not present.

Charlotte informed them that Sharlene had moved out of the spa into another facility closer to the city. None of them had told her about Nora and no one intended to, figuring it was better to let her think her daughter was forever lost to her, which, in fact, she was.

Sam told of her sister Lupe, who along with her husband, Joe, had wanted to join them for the holiday but couldn't fly as she was seven months pregnant with the couple's first child.

And Jackson relayed Drew's regards and his distress at having been assigned a new female partner.

Later, as he and Carly strolled on the beach, she

asked him, "What has Drew got against having a female partner?"

Jackson shrugged. "I don't think it has to do with her being a woman. She probably doesn't put up with much of his nonsense." He squeezed her hand. "Did you hear Adam accepted an assignment in L.A. Robbery Homicide?"

"Sam told me, and I'm glad. She said I inspired her since I didn't pitch a fit when you wanted to go back on the force. I think they'll both be happier."

He thought so, too, but he wasn't concerned with his friend's happiness right now. He drew to a halt and swung her around to face him. Illuminated by the full moon, her eyes were luminous and questioning. He brushed back wisps of her hair that floated around her face. "So when are you going to marry me, Carly?"

Those weren't the words he intended to say, but they served nonetheless. A smile spread across her lips. "If that's what you want, I'll marry you whenever you want."

"You don't want to get married?"

"I didn't say that, but I don't need to. You made *me* a promise, Jackson. That's the one that counts. But I suppose our children will want to be able to claim your last name legally."

For a moment the world around him spun. "Our children?"

She laughed. "No, I'm not pregnant, but being around all the kids I realize I want to be. I want to fill our house with children, love, and laughter. I don't want to leave any room for secrets or lies or pain."

In the darkness, he smiled. He couldn't guarantee that their lives would never be touched by pain or loss or unhappiness, but he knew he'd do his best to make sure they weren't. "How about if I promise to pick up after myself, to put out the trash, and to not forget our anniversary more than once a decade?"

She made an exaggerated sigh. "I see I'm going to have to keep my sledgehammer handy."

"Your what?"

Laughing, she threw her arms around his neck and pressed her soft body to his. "Every now and then, Jackson, there are some things a woman's just got to keep to herself."

He pressed his lips to hers for a lingering kiss, full of love, hope, and the passion they shared. He supposed he could live with that.

Dear Readers,

I hope you have enjoyed reading *Lady in Red*. I didn't really conceive this story until I was asked to write this book as part of the 2004 Summer Series, but Jackson and Carly quickly became characters near and dear to my heart. It has also been an immense pleasure and honor to kick off a series that also features Sandra Kitt, Gwynne Forster and Donna Hill—three of my literary "sheroes." I was reading these ladies' works long before I ever got serious about my own writing.

As many of you know, my love affair with Martha's Vineyard goes way back to my own childhood. It is there I first started writing romance, it is where my first romance, *Spellbound,* is set, and it is a place I return to time and time again. I hope all of you have that special place—a spot rife with magic just for you, or if you haven't found it yet, that you make one for yourself and those you love.

I would love to hear what you think about *Lady in Red* or any of my other books. Please feel free to e-mail me at dsbooks@aol.com or write me at PO Box 233, Baychester Station, Bronx, NY 10469.

All the best,
Deirdre Savoy

ABOUT THE AUTHOR

Native New Yorker Deirdre Savoy spent her summers on the shores of Martha's Vineyard, soaking up the sun and scribbling in one of her many notebooks. It was there that she first started writing romance as a teenager. The island proved to be the perfect setting for her first novel, SPELLBOUND, published by BET/Arabesque Books in 1999.

SPELLBOUND received rave reviews and earned her the distinction of the first Rising Star author of Romance in Color and their Best New Author of 1999. Deirdre also won the first annual Emma award for Favorite New Author, presented at the 2001 Romance Slam Jam in Orlando, Florida.

In her other life, Deirdre is a kindergarten teacher for the New York City Board of Education. She started her career as a secretary in the school art department of Macmillan Publishing Company in New York, rising to Advertising/Promotion Supervisor of the International Division in three years. She has also worked as a freelance copy writer, legal proofreader, and news editor for CLASS magazine.

Deirdre graduated from Bernard M. Baruch College of the City University of New York. She is president of Authors Supporting Authors Positively (ASAP), the founder of the Writer's Co-op and lectures on subjects related to the craft of writing. She is listed in the American and International Authors and Writers Who's Who, as well as the Dictionary of International Biography.

Deirdre lives in Bronx, New York, with her husband of 10-plus years and their two children. In her spare time she enjoys reading, dancing, calligraphy and "wicked" crossword puzzles.

BOOK YOUR PLACE ON OUR WEBSITE AND MAKE THE ARABESQUE ROMANCE CONNECTION!

We've created a customized website just for our very special Arabesque readers, where you can get the inside scoop on everything that's going on with Arabesque romance novels.

When you come online, you'll have the exciting opportunity to:

- View covers of upcoming books

- Learn about our future publishing schedule (listed by publication month and author)

- Find out when your favorite authors will be visiting a city near you

- Search for and order backlist books

- Check out author bios and background information

- Send e-mail to your favorite authors

- Join us in weekly chats with authors, readers and other guests

- Get writing guidelines

- AND MUCH MORE!

Visit our website at
http://www.arabesquebooks.com